Make You Mine

Honeybrook Hollow

Nora Everly

For all the animal lovers!
Pets make life better!

Also by Nora Everly

The Sweetbriar Mountain Series:

In My Heart

Heart Words

From the Heart

Heart to Heart

Change of Heart

Honeybrook Hollow:

Next to You

Make You Mine

By Your Side

Sweetbriar Short Stories:

Holiday Hearts

Conversation Hearts

Let It Snow

The Cozy Creek Collection:

Fall at Once

From Smartypants Romance:

Oh Brother!

Crime and Periodicals

Carpentry and Cocktails

Hotshot and Hospitality

Architecture and Artistry

Teachers' Lounge

Passing Notes

Star Crossed Lovers:

(*As Piper Everly, co-written with Piper Sheldon*):

<u>Midnight Clear</u>

Get exclusive sneak peeks of upcoming releases through Nora's newsletter and Facebook group, The Everly Afters.

Chapter 1
Ren

"Before I sign the check, I want you to meet my granddaughter."

Damn it.

To be clear, I was never against meeting anyone's granddaughter. But I *was* against being set up with one, especially when the introduction subtly hinted that her donation hinged upon it.

"Ah, nothing like romance born out of mild obligation." I tried to keep my expression neutral as she patted her purse and winked at me.

"Pardon me?"

"Your granddaughter sounds like a wild temptation, Mrs. Ross."

Think of the center, think of the center.

"She's a good girl. You're going to love her."

I didn't bother returning her smile. She never noticed anyway. This was the worst part of this job, and I'd rather be anywhere else right now. I could feel my frustration mounting with every interaction. The furrow of my brow was going to give me away if it got any deeper. God, my head pounded. I needed to get out of here.

Twinkling lights and shimmering candles filled my vision as my gaze drifted around the room, adorned with flower-bedecked tables, bouquets resting on pedestals, and elegantly dressed guests. These dinners aimed to bring donors and charities together. Two hundred fifty guests filled the grand ballroom of this upscale hotel in Portland, Oregon, tonight. But damn it, I'd forgotten the name of the place. These events were beginning to blur in my mind.

I was *so* incredibly fortunate to meet every daughter, granddaughter, sister, niece, cousin, and best friend of marriageable age—all sarcasm intended—tonight. Somehow, instead of attending a charity dinner, I found myself trapped in an alternate reality version of *The Bachelor*, encountering woman after woman, yet I had no desire to get married again. All I wanted was to go home, crack open a beer, and relax in front of the TV rather than endure whatever version of hell this might be.

I couldn't even get drunk. The glass of champagne in my hand was for toasting, not drinking. My reputation had to remain untarnished. As the face of a growing charity, image was everything. With a yank, I pulled my chair out and sat back down, shoving a tiny quiche into my mouth while I went through my mental list of excuses I could use to get out of here.

My younger brother and I established Lyla's Place, a women's center to honor our mother. We provided self-defense classes, a GED program, referrals for mental health care, and legal services.

Apparently, I failed to realize that to raise funds, I needed to include *myself* on the list of things we offered. But I was not charming. Banter and casual flirting were not my strengths, and I was uninterested in playing games, especially since I'd never known the rules.

"Fuck," I muttered beneath my breath.

"Go on. Get out of here." Lost in thought, I jumped as a hand gripped my shoulder. "You can go home." My brother, Jake, had returned to our table after his trip to the bathroom. He grinned and took his seat across from me. "I've got this. You've done enough tonight."

I glanced around the ballroom again as memories of our old apartment flooded back. The stark contrast between my current life and the run-down apartment we had once shared with our mother and sister was undeniable.

I worked hard to get to this point. I joined the Marines to help pay for my education, which I followed with college and law school. Afterward, I entered family law, specifically helping women secure everything they deserved from their worthless husbands—something my mother could never afford.

I wanted to help people, to step in in all the ways no one had stepped in for my family. I didn't want any part of this spectacle tonight. I wanted to do my job. I wanted to talk about how many women and children Lyla's Place could help rather than put on an expensive suit and become the preening asshole everyone seemed to expect me to be.

So, yeah, the thought of cutting out early to go home was almost irresistible.

"Are you sure? How did tonight turn into a match-making thing again? I don't understand how this keeps happening. I'm done with this." I said with a low growl of frustration. "Do you know how hard it is to keep fucking smiling and being pleasant to strangers? I want to help people without having to—"

"Speak to people?" My brother supplied helpfully, grinning at me over the rim of his glass of champagne. 'I understand, and once Violet is ready to socialize again, we can take over doing this if you want." They had a new baby at home. His wife was still recovering. "Look, you're a good guy—successful, not bad to look at. You're also single, and everyone knows it. That's why they keep trying."

I looked away, frowning. "Yeah, but it's not fair to you when Violet isn't here to keep you company."

"Don't worry about me. Now that I'm happily married and off the market, they'll bounce right off my deflector shield." He pulled his phone from his pocket and showed me yet another picture of my adorable baby niece. "Just look at her, man. All I have to do is pull this out and soak in the compliments."

"She is the cutest." I huffed a cynical laugh. "Though you being married with a baby won't stop some of them from trying, you know that, right?"

He set his jaw and raised an eyebrow. "It will. I'm not worried about it."

"I love that for you."

Shit.

I never thought of that. Jake settling down and marrying the love of his life just put an even bigger target on my back for the matchmaking grandmothers. My brother was genuinely happy, completely in love with his beautiful wife, his stepsons, and their baby, and I was truly thrilled for him. But that ship had sailed for me. Considering how we grew up, it had never even been docked in the first place.

He hesitated. "Are you sure you should be alone?" he asked again, and the question was absolutely loaded. "You seem a bit down tonight. Are you okay?"

He'd fixed his life. Clearly, he thought mine should change for the better as well.

I steeled my gaze and met his eyes directly. "Yeah, man. I'm sure."

"Okay, but—it's been almost three years since Tabby, and, uh, I'm not trying to pressure you into talking if you're not ready. I really don't want to do that, but—" He dragged a hand down his face. "I'm not great at this. I'm here for you, Ren. You know that, right?"

My wife passed away almost three years ago. Jake supported me as he always had, and I appreciated it, but found it difficult to discuss. In fact, I refused to talk about it anymore—to anyone.

Tabby had been the best friend I'd ever had. She grew up in the apartment next to ours, and we went all through school together. I would always miss her. But I didn't want to think about her now, so I shoved the memories out of my mind.

"I know, and it's okay. This really isn't the place for a heart-to-heart, Jake." I gestured around the ballroom. "I mean, come on." I let out a chuckle.

He had good intentions, but I was not about to delve into my tragic past at a charity dinner, for fuck's sake.

"This is bad timing. I'm sorry. I shouldn't have brought it up." He glanced over my shoulder. "They're coming. Go out the back. I'll tell them you have a headache or you ate some bad seafood and shit your pants. That ought to keep them at bay for a beat." He winked. "Don't worry. We can talk about this later."

Or not.

"Thanks." My hand pressed against my sternum in an almost unconscious gesture. One that did not go unnoticed by Jake.

Sympathy filled his eyes as his smile softened, and I didn't know how much longer I could avoid having an honest conversation with him, especially since Lyla's Place was now up and running, and I was moving from Portland to be closer.

Fucking great.

I stood up to go.

"Later, man." He eyed me speculatively. "We'll have dinner soon. I'll text you. I think it might help to talk about it. Don't you think it's time?"

"I won't say no to dinner, but I'm fine. I'm always fine."

Contrary to what he obviously thought, I didn't want what he had. Love was beautiful yet precarious. It was dangerous and fleeting and far too easily lost. It wasn't worth the risk. I knew that better than anybody.

He slid his chair back, standing to embrace me with a back-slapping hug. "You will be. I'll make sure of it."

I pulled away, shaking my head at his well-meaning but unintentionally foreboding words. Then, I made my way to the exit, winding through the crowd and not stopping until I reached my car.

With each mile away from the city, I felt more relaxed. Letting out a sigh, I removed my tie and tossed it over my shoulder, exhaling sharply in relief as I undid the top two buttons of my dress shirt and leaned back against the seat.

Streetlights and skyscrapers blurred into my rearview, and starlight flickered through the trees as I entered the mountains. Lowering the windows, I inhaled deeply as the combined scent of pine and petrichor filled the car. There was something magical about mountain air. I could feel it, misty and clean against my skin, and I let it wash away the stress of the evening.

I had just bought a house in Honeybrook Hollow, one of the small villages along the highway to Mt. Hood, and tonight would be my first night there. I had sold my apartment in Portland and was almost finished clearing the place out. I'd also resigned from my law firm and would join Jake to work at his small law office in Sweetbriar, the next town over. This arrangement would give me more time at Lyla's Place and allow for a slower pace.

It was time for a change. Past time, if I was being honest.

I'd been busting my ass for years, and I needed time to—I had no idea what I wanted, but I knew I needed to take the time to figure it out.

Honeybrook Hollow was a mere dot on the landscape, easily missed if you weren't looking for it. The highway twisted and turned as I ascended into the mountains, each curve revealing a new vista of tall pines and dots of light from the homes scattered here and there.

Welcome to Honeybrook Hollow. The sign marked the turnoff from the highway onto Sycamore Street, which ran the length of the town. As I approached, I could see the small town lights twinkling like so many scattered stars in the distance. The road narrowed, forcing me to slow down as I navigated the way to my new home.

I turned on Loganberry Lane to go home. I needed a good night of sleep and a fucking sandwich. I was starving. Caviar and toast points were not my thing. My stomach growled in approval.

Jake probably thought I was just lonely. But I wasn't lonely, I was just bad with people—talking, relating, trusting. Plus, he had no idea about me and Tabby. We had kept the truth about our relationship just between us. I would always love her, but we were never *in love.*

She had leukemia when we were kids. A few years ago, it returned, so I stepped in after her husband left. We got married, and I ensured she was well cared for. When she died, I lost my best friend, and it has been tearing me apart ever since. I missed her.

Maybe I should talk to Jake. If anyone would understand how I felt, he would. He had loved Tabby, too. But the thought of talking about my feelings was exhausting.

I turned into my driveway and cut the engine. My house was a simple one-story on a street lined with more of the same. Painted beige with blue trim, it was L-shaped and basic. With three bedrooms, two bathrooms, and a big backyard, it was more space than I needed, but the idea of owning a house appealed to me. Maybe I'd get a dog or two to keep me company after I'd settled in.

The only thing wrong with this street was the Victorian eyesore at the end. It wasn't run down, but it loomed over the street like it was watching it. The stark white paint job and spiky turrets did nothing to hide that it was likely riddled with the ghosts of residents past.

Past me would already be home in bed, getting enough sleep so he could win in court the next day. This version was something I was still figuring out.

Honeybrook Hollow was not known for its nightlife, and the options were limited to one bar. With a turn of the wheel, I drove around the Victorian and was back on the main drag. Businesses lined each side, a couple of restaurants, and a general store. There was a bookstore down at the end that I wanted to check out, but I hadn't yet found the time. Maybe tomorrow.

I just survived another night of being flirted with and fussed over, I think I fucking deserved a damn beer.

At the end of the road sat the Honeybrook Inn,

which is what put this town on the map. It was a tourist favorite amid one of the country's premier ski destinations. I was not a skier—yet—but the idea of it had promise. Everyone should have a hobby, and I'd spent too many years doing nothing but work.

Slightly outside of town, down a gravel road, was where I was headed. Bubba's Bar belonged to one of my clients. In fact, I had helped her secure the place during her divorce. Perhaps it was time to check in on her—it was as good an excuse as any, and Paige was always good for a laugh.

My tires crunched through the parking lot. I pulled to a stop beneath the lone light and got out. Shrugging out of my jacket, I tossed it inside the car and slammed the door. I wiped my hands on my slacks, suddenly nervous. When was the last time I had a drink in a bar solely just for fun?

Had I ever?

I realized I hadn't and almost turned around to get back in my car.

I was almost forty-three years old and had never had a drink in a fucking bar that didn't involve a business meeting of some kind. Jesus Christ—Jake was right about me—I was a workaholic.

Steeling myself against the nerves threatening to send me into a cold sweat, I looked up and frowned in uncertainty when I caught sight of the bright purple neon glow coming from above the door that spelled out the words Twilight Tavern in swirling script. With a shrug, I pushed open the door and entered.

"It's my hero!" A cheerful voice called to me from behind the bar. "Come over here. Let me get you a beer." She patted the bar in front of her. "On the house forever for you, Ren."

Paige didn't take no for an answer when it came to being her friend. She was relentless in her pursuit of finding out even the most mundane facts about me. She baked cookies and brought them to all our meetings. She told me all about her kids and her family. But for some reason, it had been easy to talk to her, so I allowed it.

"Twilight Tavern?" I grinned as I greeted Paige, the bar's now official sole owner and my former client. "I thought this place was called Bubba's Bar."

No matter what she chose to call it, it resembled a classic country western bar, with wooden floors and booths in the corners. High-top tables were scattered throughout the space, and an alcove led to a room that housed a pool table. A jukebox blasting old eighties rock stood next to a small stage in the far corner. Neon flashed in the windows, and strands of lights threaded through the beams overhead provided illumination, along with moonlight streaming through the windows and a few strategically placed ceiling fans with dimly glowing bulbs hanging beneath.

"I changed the name." She glared toward the central part of the bar, where her patrons were studiously avoiding looking directly at her. "And I don't want to hear another word about it," she loudly announced to the room. "I love it. It's what I always wanted to call it. I mean, did you see the sky when you drove up? The mist?

The freaking stars? It's the perfect name." She crossed her arms over her chest, practically daring me to say something negative. She was a pretty blonde, tall and curvy with sparkling brown eyes and a smile that could get anyone talking—me being a perfect example of that.

"I like it." I approached and slid onto a barstool. The place was busy, but the vibe felt off.

"What were you up to tonight? You look tense." Pot, meet kettle. Tension radiated off her in waves. I decided to ignore it and let her make small talk. I could find out what was going on later.

"I just came from a charity dinner in Portland, hoping to raise funds for Lyla's Place."

"Ahh, hobnobbing with the rich and snooty." She scoffed with a sardonic grin. "My ex was real good at that, as you know."

"Yeah, I did not grow up that way. And I'm sick of hobnobbing. Why can't people just do good things without having their asses kissed first?"

"Isn't that the eternal question?" She asked, turning to grab a glass from the shelf behind her. "Why can't people just lead with kindness? It's not that fucking hard."

"I wish I knew," I muttered as she filled the glass and slid me a beer.

"Thanks." I took a sip and tried to stop worrying about fitting in. Paige owned the place, and it seemed like she didn't fit in either.

"Hey! It's the mysterious Ren." I squinted into the

dim light of the bar, watching as a tall, curvy blonde approached from the restrooms.

It was Piper, Jake's wife's best friend and Paige's younger sister. I'd met her a few times over the years but had never found the time to get to know her.

Each time I saw her, her hair looked different. Tonight, it was a pale shade of honey blonde. The long waves shimmered under the lights as she moved. God, she was gorgeous. I'd always thought so.

She wore a simple white T-shirt and jeans. But the way they hugged her curves made it hard not to stare. Her brown eyes were warm, inviting, shimmering with a light that drew me in every time I saw her. It wasn't just her appearance; it was her entire presence that captivated me. There was something undeniably magnetic about Piper, something that made it hard to look away. I had always been attracted to her, but tonight that feeling was more intense than ever. Shaking my head, I dismissed the thoughts. I hardly knew her.

"Is anyone else giving you shit?" She asked Paige as she sat next to me.

"Everything okay?" I asked.

"No to both questions," Paige answered. "But I'll be fine—eventually. The townsfolk appear to be a little bit peeved that I got the bar in the divorce. Who cares that we opened it together, right? Who cares that I'm the one who kept it open when Eli wanted to sell it a few years back?"

"Ugh, they're only talking about you because no one

cares when they talk about themselves, okay?" Piper's hand hit the bar to emphasize her point. "And apparently, it doesn't matter that he is a lousy, abandoning, cheating pig-man, right?" she scoffed. "Leaving you alone with the kids while he goes gallivanting all around town with his new piece of ass. If he ever shows his face around here, I'll—"

"I'll be okay," Paige cut her off. "No use getting upset over him—again."

Paige's husband was a real dirtbag. The kind of man I loved raking over the coals. However, this was not the setting I was accustomed to when a woman was ranting about her ex.

I cleared my throat with a nervous cough. Should I apologize for men everywhere? Or should I go find a table? My eyes darted back and forth between them as I tried to decide what to do.

"The patriarchy is alive and well, and I'm over it. That's all I'm saying. I'm done with men. After what happened with Richard, I mean it this time. For good. The end. Just me, the cats, and Cody."

"Oh god, girl. You're grim as all hell tonight. Have a shot." Paige grabbed the tequila from the shelf behind her and filled a shot glass for Piper. "Richard is her ex, and Cody is her dog. They're trying to share him, but it's not quite working out." Paige informed me before turning her attention back to Piper. "One shot, Piper. You need to chill out. Let's toast. One shot will make it all better, or at least ten percent less shitty. I don't know. Whatever. I'll pour."

Deciding to leave them to their moment, I stood to go.

"No, you too, Ren. Please stay." She filled a second shot glass and pushed it toward me.

"To sisters." She clinked her shot glass to Piper's. "And to mean ass divorce attorneys." She turned to me with a grin. "I owe it all to you."

I curved my lips in a sardonic smile and raised my glass to hers. "I wish I could have gotten you more. But the state of Oregon doesn't allow me to go after his soul. Not yet, anyway."

"He turned out to be a soulless jerk anyway. Trying would have been a waste of time. You two go find a table," Paige encouraged. "I'm going to zone out and start taking inventory, and there's no point in drinking alone."

"I—" Piper started to protest.

"I insist. I'll have Noah bring out some wings, okay? Someone around here should have a little bit of fun. Entertain my sister, Ren. She could use it. She's had a bad couple of weeks."

"Make it cheese fries, and I'll leave you alone to work," she grudgingly agreed.

"You got it. Noah!" Paige yelled. "Grab some cheese fries for your Auntie Piper."

"Will do." Her eighteen-year-old son shouted back. I knew he wanted to be a chef someday. He was a good kid.

I stood up to find a table, not realizing how close Piper would be when she stood up too. She had a faint spray of freckles across her nose. I'd never noticed—god, they were cute.

Her eyes riveted on my collar, it was undone, tie now

gone, before flicking her gaze up to mine with an awkward laugh. A flush covered her cheeks, rosy and warm.

"Shall we?" I asked, surprised by the gravel in my voice as I offered her my arm.

My heart thumped in my chest in reaction when she took it. "Why not, right?" I sucked in a startled breath when she aimed a radiant smile up at me. "Drinking alone *is* kind of sad. However, I did not intend to drink tonight in the first place. I just dropped by to check on Paige."

"Funny. So did I."

"She has a way of bringing that out in people, doesn't she?"

"She does," I agreed. "I have to confess that making small talk is not one of my strengths. Awkward might be my middle name."

"It's not his middle name," Paige snickered behind the bar.

Laughing, Piper leaned into my side as we walked toward a booth in the corner. "Should I ignore her?"

"God, please do." I watched, intrigued, as she laughed without restraint; her eyes alight with humor and held tilted back like she put her whole body into the feeling.

While Paige was full of brash humor and dry as dirt jokes, Piper seemed... *different.*

I wasn't sure what to make of her, but I had the oddest feeling that maybe I was glad I had decided not to go home.

I eyed an empty booth in the corner and guided her through the crowd toward it, my hand hovering at the small of her back, so careful not to actually touch her.

Chapter 2
Piper

Ren was my best friend's brother-in-law, but I had only met him a few times over the years. He lived in Portland and was always busy with work. Even Violet, my lifelong bestie, hardly knew him until recently. He was the toughest divorce attorney in Oregon. He'd managed to get Violet's douchebag ex out of her life and had done the same for Paige.

I'd always found him fascinating, in an abstract way, with his extreme good looks, successful career, and seemingly relentless drive. He'd always struck me as stand-offish and broody. He was intimidating but never in an asshole way.

He seemed different tonight—gone was the usual suit and tie perfection. His collar was undone, his shirt slightly wrinkled, and he seemed approachable.

Paige seemed to adore him. I knew he had gotten her everything she wanted and then some from her divorce, but obviously, she'd worked her magic and turned him into a friend, too.

This version of Ren was *hot*.

He looked down at me, and I shivered. Yeah, he was hot for sure. He'd always been the epitome of tall, dark, and handsome, and that hadn't changed. But tonight he was magnetic with his towering height and broad shoulders. His hair had always been perfectly styled, with a sophisticated look. Now, he was a bit windblown and tousled, and it was sexy as hell.

Those eyes, though—his eyes were the bluest I had ever seen, piercing and intense, as if they could see right through anyone.

As we walked towards the booth, I couldn't help but shiver when he looked down at me. He was hot, and not just in the physical sense. There was a depth to him, a complexity that made him all the more intriguing.

"Is your name Lorenzo?" I asked to get the conversation rolling as we approached one of the circular booths.

"Uh, no. Just Ren."

"Come on. Ask him what his middle name is," Paige shouted.

I stopped at the booth and sat down, looking up at him with my eyebrows raised in expectation and a grin lifting the corner of my mouth.

"Thanks a lot, Paige. It's McCormack," he informed me with a shake of his head as he sat across from me. "I managed to keep my middle name a secret for nearly my entire life. But that sister of yours is nosy as hell and very persuasive; she got it out of me during our second meeting."

"Oh yeah, there's no keeping anything from her. So you're Ren McCormack Moretti. And I know from Violet that your brother is Jake Ryan Moretti. Could the two of you be more adorable? Your mom was clearly an eighties movie fan."

"She was."

"Mom, were you a fan of the Ark, or animals traveling in pairs?" My nephew, Noah, shouted over his shoulder as he approached our table with a plate piled high with cheese fries for Ren and me to share, along with my favorite peach iced tea.

"Thanks." I took the tea and sucked back a huge sip.

"Oh, you're so funny. You can thank your dad for that," Paige shouted back. "Maybe I should start calling you J.C., or what about Justin? I could never choose between the two of them."

"No thanks." He huffed a laugh. "Noah is fine."

"How are you doing tonight, Noah?" I stood up to hug him. Paige's kids were having a tough time after the divorce, and I had vowed to support them in any way I could.

Noah was a handsome boy, er, man. He had just turned eighteen and worked as a cook here. He had always dreamed of becoming a chef; he would start culinary school the following year, and I couldn't be prouder.

"My therapist says I'm grieving the man I thought Dad was versus the man he actually turned out to be." He pulled away and shrugged. "I mean, I guess I'll be okay."

"You will be. And he can still be that dad to you again someday."

"You mean, how Grandpa is *that* dad to you?"

"Fair, but ouch."

"I'm sorry. I'm supposed to dial back the sarcasm. And also stop deflecting." He rolled his eyes. "It doesn't replace my feelings."

"Okay, Chandler Bing."

"Funny, but also accurate."

"Sarcasm is how we Darlingtons survive the horrors," I explained to Ren. "Sometimes it can get a bit dark."

"Right? What would we do without it?" Noah grinned. "So, I'll be back with your extra ranch."

"My relationship with ranch is arguably my longest-lasting relationship outside of the family. I love how you always remember."

"Unfortunately, it's my superpower. I never forget anything."

"Oh, honey—"

"I'm alright." He waved off my sympathy and returned to the kitchen.

"Poor kid." Ren turned his eyes back to mine. "I'll hold off on expressing my opinion of his dad."

"He's a prick." I waited until Noah was out of earshot. I was never one to hold back, except in front of the kids. "I hate him. If I could kick him in the junk every morning to start my day, I'd do it. Who needs coffee? Am I right?"

Noah had been the one to catch his dad in the act with their next-door neighbor. He'd also been the one to catch my ex when he'd come over to my place to drop off some sourdough bread he had baked. Paige had taken him directly to their therapist for an emergency appointment, worried about the double whammy trauma of busting both of our exes *in flagrante delicto*.

He burst out laughing. "No one better dare cheat on you."

I looked away without answering. But I'm sure my expression said it all. It still stung that I'd missed all the signs.

Maybe my mother was right, and I was too trusting. One thing about Paige and me is that our taste in men was terrible. I, along with my mother, blamed our father for this. Dad had daughters all over Honeybrook Hollow —Paige and I had three half-sisters from the women he was with after our mother. And yes, he'd cheated on all of them.

"I'm sorry, did I strike a nerve? I didn't mean—"

"Let's just say I'm disgruntled, disillusioned, and disgusted with the entirety of mankind and leave it at that."

"I didn't mean to bring up something painful."

"Not your fault. You're not the one who cheated on me—with my business partner, I might add. You're not the one I wasted almost two years of my life on. And he wants to share the dog we got together, which I have to decide what to do about. All of this keeps him in my life when I would much rather forget he exists. Damn it." I picked up a fry and stuffed it into my mouth to stop the rant. "It's best not to get me started," I mumbled with my hand in front of my face to hide my chewing.

"Hey, no worries." His eyes were understanding. "If there's anything I can do, let me know."

"There's nothing to do. We weren't married. I'm never getting married. I knew better than that, at least. I let him sort of move in with me, but he's gone now, thank god."

"You don't have to need a divorce to ask for my help." His eyes went dark. "I know what it's like to feel powerless or trapped in a situation you can't control—" He cleared his throat. "Now I'm the one who shouldn't get started."

"Looks like we have something in common." I held my glass up for a toast.

He clinked his beer to my iced tea with a sardonic grin. "Like recognizes like. Apparently, the saying is true."

"It absolutely is." The bar's entrance door opened, the motion catching my eye. I spat out the small sip of iced tea I had just taken, the sticky liquid soaking the table in front of me as I sputtered out a cough, and my stomach bottomed out. Grabbing the napkins with shaking hands to wipe up my spill, I slunk down in my chair, praying that I had somehow turned invisible in the last five seconds. "Fucking hell."

He turned to look. "What's happening?"

"Speak of the devil, and he shall appear." I stared into my glass, watching the ice cubes bob on the surface and wishing I had another shot of tequila to drink instead.

"Your ex?"

I nodded, slipping into a mental abyss while the sounds of the bar drowned out my thoughts. I was too pissed to speak as the lying, cheating, dog-stealing scumbag noticed me and smiled as he waved a hand over his head to get my attention.

He cheated on me. We broke up, and he moved on. He wants to make peace with me, so I'll start talking to my partner again. Apparently, she's taking her betrayal hard—she's all broken up about the fact that I won't forgive her. He keeps insisting that we can all be friends again. Um, no thank you.

"You're not welcome here, Dick!" Paige shouted. "I have the right to refuse service to lying, cheating, weasel-faced buttholes. Get the hell out!"

"Nice to see you as always, Paige." Was it bad that I was glad when he turned to go to the bar instead? "And it's Richard. Did you forget about me already? You seem to have an issue with names lately, so I'll forgive you. Twilight Tavern? Cute."

He took a seat on a stool right in front of Paige. She glared at him without answering.

Did he want to die tonight?

"I'll have a beer, please," he said with a smirk. "This is your bar now, isn't it?" Oh yeah, he was a friend of Paige's ex-husband, they'd all gone to high school together, I was a couple of years behind. Paige was the one who set us up. Isn't that ironic?

How I'd ever fallen for his act, I would never know. But to be fair to myself, he was very attractive and had started off being charming and sweet. I would have never gone out with him if he'd shown this side of his personality on day one. I had to quit beating myself up over this.

"Just get out of my bar, please."

"I need to talk to Piper first."

"Want me to get rid of him for you?" Ren asked, concern etched all over his face.

Paige started shouting before I could answer him.

"She doesn't want to talk to you, *Dick*. She dumped your ass. Did that not paint a clear enough picture for you?"

I let my eyes drift shut. This would be bad. Paige had been on edge ever since the divorce, and my breakup with Richard only made it worse. She felt guilty; I'd finally gotten her to stop apologizing to me a few days ago. But, as usual, it looked like I would have to maintain the peace.

Turning on his barstool, he faced me. "Piper, can you tell your sister to stop acting crazy? I just want to talk to you. No big deal."

I inhaled a huge sigh and pinched the bridge of my nose. "She's not acting. You should know that by now. But yeah, Paige, you can let it go. I'm fine," I opened my eyes to say. "It's fine. Everything is fine."

"We need to talk about Cody—among other things." Cody is the gorgeous and sweet golden retriever we adopted from the animal shelter outside of town. "I figured you'd be here."

He cheated on me, practically stole my damn dog, and now he was here to taunt me?

So right, that's typical Richard—he had made a scene to provoke my sister and force me to talk to him to diffuse the situation. If we didn't have Cody to talk about, he'd be dead to me, and I was pretty sure he knew it. Never let a man move in with you and get a dog together. Bad ideas all around. It was too bad for me; he was a lousy cheater, but at least I fell in love with Cody more than him.

The energy in the room changed as everyone's gaze moved from Paige to me. I felt the heaviness of anticipation as a rush of adrenaline coursed through my body.

Without thinking, I slid around the booth, plastering myself against Ren's side until our thighs pressed together.

Sliding my hand up his neck to his cheek, I whispered. "Just go along with it. *Please.*"

I kissed him. A quick peck on the lips. I pulled back to find him blinking in confusion before he seemed to catch on to what I was asking of him.

"I got this," he whispered, grabbing my hand to kiss the back.

A huge smile spread across my face, along with a well-timed blush.

This was perfect. "Thank you," I mouthed.

He nodded, rolling his shirtsleeves up his perfectly tanned, muscular forearms like he was getting ready for—something. I watched his bright blue eyes light up, and a swift jolt of relief shot through my body.

Focus, Piper.

But good lord, how was I supposed to focus when he was making arm porn right in front of me?

"Would you like another drink, sweetheart?" he asked with a subtle wink, ensuring Richard could hear him.

"Uh," I snapped back to reality with a jolt. "Yes, please."

"Oh crap." The slap of the swinging kitchen door against Noah's butt startled me. He stood there frozen, holding a bowl of ranch dressing. His eyes widened as he watched the unfolding scene.

"Shit. Mom," he called out to Paige. "No fighting. Remember what Chief Barrett said last time? Call him. Please."

"I'm not going to fight anyone," she grumbled, placing the beer bottle she had been brandishing behind Richard's back on the bar before raising her hands. "See? Don't worry, honey. I'm good. I promise."

"You, too, Aunt Piper. Watch her, Ren. These two—I don't even know what to say. I mean, it was justified, but still."

I rolled my lips guiltily, eyes darting away from Ren. "Don't worry. I'm good too, Noah."

Ren's eyes zeroed in on Richard. "If *Dick* keeps it civil, can't see why there would be any fighting necessary tonight." His dark scowl swung to me, the dip of his eyebrows and furrow in his brow more prominent. "I'll take care of you," he promised under his breath.

I nodded, fighting the temptation to take his hand and bring him home so he could *take care of me* there instead. We were not thinking along the same lines, but I didn't care. He was hot. I was pissed. It was all too much, so I allowed myself the temporary thrill to distract me from the temptation to let loose and punch Richard's lights out. I had a long fuse, but he was rapidly pushing me to the end of it.

"Piper, it's about Cody and his appointment with the vet on Monday."

Of course, it was...

"Okay. What's the problem?" I asked without looking at him.

"Well, you weren't answering your phone, and his health is important, don't you think?" Richard spoke my name as if he owned me. As if he were about to scold me. I was incensed.

"She's busy tonight," Ren answered for me as he draped an arm around my shoulders. Damn, he smelled good.

Should I lean in?

Screw it. I leaned, resting my head against his clavicle. His skin was so warm, his shirt soft. I inhaled deeply, turning my nose into his throat. God, I wanted to lick him. Yum.

"Are you dating this guy?"

"We're seeing where things go," Ren answered before letting his arm fall to my shoulders to pull me closer. "Aren't we, baby?" His breath tickled my ear as he whispered right into it, then kissed me lightly on my temple.

Oh god.

I shivered. "Yeah," my voice sounded slightly like a moan, and I wasn't even embarrassed.

"Maybe this is a bad time." Richard's smile didn't

reach his eyes. "I'll call you tomorrow. You want to be involved in Cody's life, right? At least that's what you said. If that hasn't changed, answer the phone so we can make plans. Yeah?"

"Okay. Bye." I didn't even look as he got up to leave. I was too caught up in my rapidly developing attraction to Ren. He was sexy, and even though he looked like he could take on Richard and every other guy in this bar at once, he still seemed non-threatening. The dichotomy intrigued me.

I sat here confused. Here I was, all sworn off of men, and now in the middle of a hormone rush over the hot hunk of beefcake sitting next to me.

"Here's your ranch." Noah plopped the dish on the table and high-tailed it back to the kitchen.

"Thanks." Ren's voice jolted me out of my stupor.

"Just so you know, we don't get into fights willy-nilly. I mean Paige and me." I blurted. "Some guy was getting handsy with one of the waitresses a few weeks back and wouldn't stop. He grabbed her ass and pulled her onto his lap. It was basically a full-on assault. So we got her away from him and slapped him around a little bit while the police were called. It was mostly self-defense. Oh, that, and Noah's dad told him a few things about Paige and me from back in high school, but that was so long ago it doesn't count anymore, right?"

His lips twitched. "Totally doesn't count. And it sounds to me that the guy with the waitress needed to be taught a lesson."

"Right?" I grabbed my glass and took a sip, suddenly

parched. "It freaked Noah out, though. Then the guy had to go and try to press charges on us. It was a whole thing. Anyway, it's all good now. There was an entire bar full of witnesses who saw what he did. He backed off, and now he is banned."

"Good. Was he arrested? Charges pressed?"

"Yes to all of it. It's all pending. And thank you."

"You're welcome." He slid back to his side of the table and picked up his beer. "Unfortunately, some men don't respect boundaries unless they come from another man. Dick seemed like the type. I wasn't questioning your ability to take care of yourself."

My jaw dropped because, wow. He was respectful and protective without being chauvinistic. I melted a little bit inside as I started to like him even more.

I jumped in my seat when Paige showed up at the edge of our table, bursting with energy.

"I have the best idea," she declared as she set a glass of water in front of Ren. "Lots of lemon, just how you like it."

"Thank you." His eyes shifted to mine, with his eyebrows raised in amusement.

"Great," I muttered. Paige's ideas were *not* always the best.

"You know your thing, Ren?" She slid into the booth beside me, nudging me over with her hip. "The match-making? Neither one of you is interested in dating right now. You should start taking Piper as your date when you have to go out hobnobbing for charity. It'd be perfect. And look at what happened with Dick tonight. He's gone; got one look at the two of you together, and bye-bye, bitch-boy. You can fake date each other. Piper can keep the eligible bachelorettes away from you, and you can protect her from Dick and whatever plans he's cooking up in that stupid head of his. You can go with her to her bakery grand opening hoopla—" She shot me a look. "—what? You know you don't want to go by yourself. Then you can both stay lonely and sad just the way you want, and no one will bother you. Moving on? Finding happiness with someone? Who? Not the two of you."

Ren burst out laughing, and I perked up. This idea was neither harebrained nor dangerous. I was impressed. I was also a little bit offended, but I shrugged it off.

"This is really not a bad idea." I smiled at her. "Who's trying to set you up, Ren? Is it Violet? She's determined to matchmake everyone from Sweetbriar to Honeybrook Hollow and all the way up to Mt. Hood. That woman doesn't know when to give up."

"No, she hasn't tried anything yet. Probably too busy with the baby." He grabbed a fry and popped it into his mouth.

"It doesn't matter. If you're into this, then I am, too. I like how Richard turned tail and ran off. I'm tired of dealing with him. But I can't keep Cody away from him. He loves us both too much, damn it."

"Isn't doggy custody drop-off coming up? Do you want me to be there when he shows up?" Paige had three kids: Noah, her oldest, and two daughters: Lark, who was sixteen, and Briar, who was thirteen.

I hesitated because I wanted her to drop by, but

didn't want to put her out. I hated asking for help. "No, I'll be okay." He had finally agreed to let me see Cody, and I couldn't wait. I didn't want to do anything to ruin it.

"I'm coming." She side-eyed me and grabbed a fry. "I shouldn't have asked."

"Best sister ever." I dipped one in ranch and held it up for a cheers. "But also, be cool. Please?"

"*Pfft*, I know, and I'll be cold as ice, I promise. Now, make plans with Ren. I have to get back to work." She touched her fry to mine and then stuffed it into her mouth.

Ren and I stared at each other. His mouth opened to speak, but he didn't say anything.

With inward cringe, I imagined what he thought of me.

Between Richard showing up, Paige blabbing that I wasn't interested in dating anymore, and me forcing him to play along with my attempt to save face, he must think I was a desperate weirdo.

And freaking Paige. Was she trying to set me up with him? Hopefully, she knew better than that. Too exhausted to protest and kind of not really wanting to fight it, I kept quiet.

Ugh, I was not a mess. Emotionally exhausted, is what I was. Not to mention perpetually pissed off, and sick of dealing with Richard's shit. Could a girl get a freaking moment to breathe? To get her shit together in peace? Apparently not. Damn.

"He has another dinner for Lyla's Place coming up soon," Paige interrupted my thoughts with an amused eye roll. "And I know you don't have any plans. He schmoozes with the bored and wealthy to raise funds. Free food, free drinks, and an evening in a swanky hotel—your job would be to keep the ladies off him so he can do his job. Right, Ren?"

"Yeah, something like that." He cleared his throat. "I'd love it if you came with me. I think it's a great idea. It could even be fun."

"Sounds intriguing." I held my hand out to shake. "I'd love it too. You have yourself a date." He took my hand, and I tried not to stare as his broad palm enveloped mine. His thumb brushed over the pulse point on my wrist, but his gaze was unreadable.

Paige clapped her hands together and then stood. "Yay! Look at me being helpful, and no one had to get arrested!"

Ren's expression softened, and he leaned forward slightly. "I guess we're all set then," he murmured, his eyes holding mine for a moment longer.

Paige shot me a wink and a mischievous grin before returning to the bar.

"I'll take this as my cue to go home." Struck with a sudden wave of nervous energy, I slid out of the booth to leave. "I'm pooped, and my bed is calling me. Goodnight, Ren."

"I'll get your number from Paige and text you some-time next week. But I'm walking you to your car."

"Oh, thank you."

Ren walked closely beside me, hands tucked casually in his pockets, as we made our way to my car. The warmth of his presence was both comforting and nerve-wracking, and I did my best to appear nonchalant. We stopped by my car, and he waited patiently as I unlocked the door and got in.

"Make sure to lock the doors," he said, his voice gentle but firm.

"Will do. Thank you, Ren," I replied, glancing up at him. My eyes were drawn to the slightly open collar of his shirt again, and I felt a flutter of attraction mixed with a twinge of nervousness.

"Goodnight," he added, stepping back and giving me a small wave.

"Goodnight," I echoed, locking the doors as he had instructed.

He stood there watching as I backed out of the parking space, then drove away.

As I drove home, I couldn't stop replaying the evening over in my head. The unexpected fake date and the way he'd looked at me—it all felt like the premise of a romantic comedy. But my life had never been like the movies, and I knew better than to get my hopes up again.

Chapter 3
Piper

It was early morning; the sun had just risen in the sky, but I was already up, feeding my two cats in the kitchen. Nimbus and Smog were meowing desperately for food as they wound themselves through my legs. I swear they acted like I was starving them to death every morning.

The aroma of fresh coffee lingered in the air, and bright sunlight filtered through the sheer curtains. It was gorgeous, cheery as hell, and I wished I didn't have to see Richard today. But the one person I really didn't want to see was Dana. If he brought her here, I'd lose my damn mind on both of them and find a way to dognap Cody.

They stared up at me, rubbing against my calves as I scooped food into their bowls. I knew they were happy he was gone. They'd started using their litter boxes again now that his shoes were no longer here to poop in. The amount of hissing and kitty cat jump scares had also lowered to zero. It was nothing but purring, sweet little head butts, and cuddles now that Richard was out of here and back at his place.

"Don't worry. He is not coming back to stay. Ever." I reiterated before padding through my dining room and into the parlor to wait for Paige, glancing at the grandfather clock along the way. She should be here any minute.

I was dressed to *un*impress. When we broke up, Richard seemed shocked that I let him go without a fight. I guess he'd expected me to beg him to stay or something else ridiculous and pathetic. I needed to make myself as unappealing as possible so that he knew I absolutely did not give one solitary shit about him or anything he had to say to me. So it was all about the caftan, fluffy slippers, and ratty bathrobe combo. I added a pea-green face mask and a non-attractive ponytail for good measure. Ponytails could be cute, but the look I was going for was Founding Father—think George Washington on the dollar bill. A quick glance in the foyer's mirror told me I'd succeeded.

The doorbell rang, and I continued shuffling to the door, slippers scuffing against the freshly refinished wooden floors as I walked.

Paige stood on the porch with a face full of determination laced with sympathy—no thanks to the pity, I was fine. Totally freakin' fine.

"How are the kids?" I asked, hoping to avoid a conversation about my recent life choices.

She breezed past me, taking in my appearance with a knowing smirk. "They're good. Any more coffee?"

"In the kitchen, help yourself. I'll be on the porch.

Wait," I called to her. "I'm sorry to drag you out here. You can't stand Richard, and I know you're busy—"

She held up a hand to quiet me. "I knew the risk before I accepted the mission—it's all good. I can handle him. In fact, I *want* to handle him. I don't understand why you have such a hard time accepting my help. Okay, I'm lying. I totally get it. But it's *me*. I'm always here for anything, whether you think it's ridiculous or not."

"I love you."

"Love you back. But first, I need some coffee, and then we can discuss your outfit. I like it. You're in your self-care era. Or are you in your old-lady era? Who are you today? Blanche or Rose?" She studied my face. "No, you look grumpy. Today is a Dorothy day for sure, or possibly Sophia. It's too early to tell. Did you steal that caftan from Grandma?"

Despite my grouchy mood, I burst out laughing. "Nah, we went shopping together. I have a bunch more upstairs."

"Nice." She held her hand out for a high five, then went to the kitchen to fix herself a mug of coffee.

I went to the porch, battling the impulse to hiss and rush back inside, when I was suddenly enveloped in early morning sunlight. Oregon's reputation for being overcast and rainy was legit, but today, for once, the sky was clear. Could this be a sign of good things ahead? Doubtful. I frowned at the street before settling onto the porch swing.

Paige joined me and got straight to the point. She wore jeans and a deep purple Twilight Tavern branded

T-shirt. Renaming the bar felt personal to her, almost like restarting her life. It was inspiring. The way she bounced back, albeit fueled by plenty of anger, was what I wanted to do. I was tired of moping around and feeling sorry for myself. I wanted to be like her. Being perpetually pissed off and trigger-happy with rage always simmering beneath the surface was way better than being sad and pathetic any day.

"So, Dick still wants to be happy happy friends with you, huh? How convenient after all the shit he started between you and Dana. I'm not happy with her either, by the way." She rolled her eyes over the rim of her mug and blew on the hot coffee.

I sighed deeply, feeling the weight of his recent attempts to 'make it up to me' and forgive Dana. "Yeah, he hasn't given up. But I won't go down that road. Both of them are cut off. No communication aside from what is necessary for the bakery." I set my cup on the table next to me and then pointed to myself with both thumbs. "All my roads are closed for reconstruction. I need a do-over like you."

Paige nodded, her understanding clear. "Yes, you do. Both of us will never put up with any more shit from any man ever again. Cheating is a deal breaker, especially after what Dad put Mom through for all those years. You've come so far. We both have. We deserve better, and we're going to get it."

"You're so right, and I'm so done. But, um, about Ren? Are you sure *you* don't want to be the one to go with him to his charity dinners or whatever? You *should* be interested in him. I mean, he's really nice. Honestly, he seems too good to be true. Wait, is he? Is that why you aren't going for it?" I felt an odd pinch in my chest at the thought of Paige and Ren together, but I shook it off.

She laughed, shaking her head. "I will never set you up again after being completely wrong about Richard; do not worry about that. Plus, I'm not interested in dating anyone now or maybe even ever again, fake or not. He was my divorce attorney, Piper, and you, more than anybody, know how nuts I've been since Eli took off. Let's just say Ren knows way too much about my marriage." She closed her eyes, shaking her head from side to side. "God, he's seen me at my absolute worst. There was ranting, quite a bit of raving, and so many tears—just way too many freakin' tears. There was snot involved, running mascara, and a couple of mental breakdowns. I ruined at least two of his shirts. It was ugly, Piper. We can only ever be friends. I can't even think of going there with him. Plus, he's hot, but I'm just not attracted to him. He's in my permanent friend zone."

"That makes sense." I fumbled in the basket next to my chair and unearthed my knitting, which so far was nothing but a ball of yarn, two needles, zero skills, and some wishful thinking. "I get it. Okay."

"Now, what's with all this old lady shit?" She pointed to the porch's overhang. "Is that a hummingbird feeder? And are you knitting?"

"Maybe I want to find things that bring me joy. Relationships have never brought me anything but trouble.

And what do hummingbirds do but be cute and drink sugar water? Total joy."

She grinned. "Well, more power to you. It's actually adorable. Remember when Grandma tried teaching us to knit all those years ago? I could never quite get the hang of it."

Recalling the memory, I laughed. "Yeah, she always said you were too impatient, which totally makes sense, by the way. I'm trying to slow down and pay attention to what I truly need. And to be honest, I don't think it's a man. I have this house—and once I can figure out how to get rid of Dana, my bakery, the hummingbirds, good coffee, and my pets. Last night, I saw raccoons, Piper. Over there by the apple tree. They were so cute, like weird little fucked up cats. I love it here. I love it even more now that Richard moved out." I sighed, tossing the knitting aside. "I'm not sure if the knitting will stick, though. I might need an easier hobby. Maybe I'll finally start writing that cookbook I always talk about. What do you think about that?"

"Do it. Your baked goods kick ass. But knitting or not, I think you're onto something. And you never should have let him stay here in the first place. You didn't even want him to."

"I know. I caved. But at least I made him keep his old place and say it was a trial run. Give me that, please."

"You got it. We've both been doing the best we can."

"It's like we went from being girls to girlfriends without anything in between." She set her coffee down and stretched, tipping her head back so the sun could shine on her face. "This is a gorgeous morning, and this porch is amazing. I'm so glad you bought this place."

"Thanks. Yeah, I'm beginning to think my life was ruined when men started finding me attractive. I've never *not* had a boyfriend. What is up with that?"

"It's time for a man break." She dropped her head down and focused on me. "But let's talk about something else for now. It's too early to be having this many feelings. Deep thoughts are for bedtime, to keep you up at night. Or maybe I can come back later for lunch, and we can get into it. My brain is not fully online yet."

I laughed. Paige was not a morning person. "Well, I'm taking time for myself. I want to dilly-dally. I want to reflect on nonsense. I'm going to romanticize my life now, Paige, and I think you should, too. Like, touch grass, become one with nature, the moon and the stars, or whatever—all that woo woo stuff Grandma and Mom always talk about. I come first from now on because I can't keep pouring from an empty cup."

"I totally agree with all of that. I'm in. Let's romanticize having coffee together whenever we can. I like this."

"Deal. And I think we should start going for walks again like we used to do with Mom."

"You've got yourself a walking buddy."

"And yes, to front porch coffee mornings, too."

"Agree. You make the best coffee. I'll bring breakfast next time."

We continued chatting as the scent of blooming roses blended with the coffee, creating a comforting atmosphere that eased my mind. I relaxed into the morning with Paige in my new favorite place to be.

Owning this house was a dream, just like opening my bakery. When we were kids, my mother would take me and Paige for walks every evening after dinner, and this old Victorian at the end of Loganberry Lane had always fascinated me. It was beautiful, grand, and regal, and it had captured my imagination ever since I first saw it.

Unfortunately, the street now had two rows of dull tract houses on either side instead of the vineyard that originally belonged to the previous owners. Still, I could overlook the bland beige eyesores as long as I finally got to live in my dream house.

As we sipped our coffee and the conversation shifted to gossip and chit-chat, my worries faded as they always did whenever I was with her.

Just then, a text notification interrupted our moment. I glanced at my phone to see it was from Richard.

He had a work emergency and couldn't drop off Cody as planned. All the worries came crashing back along with a surge of anxious adrenaline. My stomach sank, and I once more worried that *this* was my life now. I couldn't give Cody up; I loved him too much to do that. But I couldn't keep Richard in my life this way either.

And hello? He was a CPA. What kind of emergency could he possibly have?

"Well, Richard isn't coming today," I announced.

"What an ass. I should get going then. As usual, I have a bunch of shit to do and not enough time to do it."

"I'm glad you stopped by."

"Of course." She set her mug on the table next to my rocking chair. "Thanks for the coffee. It's going to be okay, Piper. We haven't even delved into all the ways we can get Cody back, okay? Like I've been saying, the only way to deal with Dick is nefariously. I can't believe I was so wrong about him."

She made it halfway to her car before turning around with a tilt of her head. "If you want to plan a dognapping, I'm down. I'm always available for shenanigans and other assorted petty crimes. You know that." Every family had that one member who was always willing to throw hands and start some shit. In mine, it was Paige.

"I know you are, but I'm still kind of hoping things will miraculously work out. I don't want to be nefarious. I don't have the mental fortitude for that. I'm a lover, not a fighter." I wasn't worried about Cody. Richard took good care of him. I just wanted us to stick to our agreement. It was for the best.

"Ahh, you still have hope, that's cute. I give it a week." She flicked two fingers out in a mock salute. "Later. Call me when you're ready to step it up."

Watching her leave, my thoughts turned back to Ren. Last night had been interesting. He seemed to be an anomaly in the world of men. Paige adored him. And ever since he got her through her divorce, Violet sang his praises whenever his name came up, and *I* now thought he was the sexiest thing since sliced bread. He was fun to talk to and even more fun to look at. And I had a fake date with him coming up, too. Was it a wise choice to agree to that? Probably not, but I couldn't resist.

My face mask itched as it baked onto my skin in the sunlight. I should have gone inside and washed it off, but sadly, I lacked the motivation to move. I hadn't been sleeping well lately. Too many changes, both good and bad, were keeping me up at night.

I kicked my feet up on the porch railing and watched the neighborhood while sipping the last of my now-cold coffee. I didn't remember a single one of my neighbors, yet I could greet all the dogs by name. The house closest to mine had finally sold, and the moving truck that had been there for the past few days was gone. Hopefully, the new neighbors had a cute dog. Otherwise, I would forget they existed as soon as we met.

I closed my eyes and let the rare sunny day ambiance wash over me. If I allowed myself, I could go to sleep right here. Maybe I should.

Footsteps pounded on the sidewalk coming from the side of my house, startling me out of my daydreaming, and I sat up to look.

Loganberry Lane curved around my house and joined Sycamore Street, the main drag of Honeybrook Hollow. Most of the town's businesses lined it on either side, including my bakery. I could walk to work through my backyard if I wanted to.

"Hey, Piper." Ren's low, gravelly voice carried down the street as he jogged towards me.

His athletic frame created a striking silhouette as he approached. His dark hair was tousled from the run, and sunlight glinted off the beads of sweat on his forehead, accentuating his strong brow and beautiful blue eyes. A playful grin adorned his face, radiating charm and warmth, and that sexy aura of kindness I knew was just waiting to come out. He raised a hand to wave at me. Why did he have to be so damn hot?

"Fancy seeing you here," I called out, trying to mask the excitement I shouldn't be feeling.

"I couldn't resist a run. I can't believe the sun is out." He slowed down as he approached, tipping his head back to let it shine on his face just as Paige had done before.

"It's shaping up to be a gorgeous day. But seriously, what are you doing here? Do you have a meeting with Paige or something?"

"No." He gestured to the house next door. "That's my place." He squinted, taking me in as he headed up my walkway. "Aren't you a vision of relaxation."

Crap. I slapped my hands against my cheeks and cringed. The face mask! Dressing to *un*impress had backfired on me.

Or maybe it was a good thing.

Now wasn't the time to feel attracted to Ren or any other guy. I was better off being alone, taking time for myself exactly like I'd just told Paige.

And what the hecking heck? Ren was my new neighbor? Was he giving up his big city life of work and whatever else he did there? To live here? Next to me? In tiny little Honeybrook Hollow? Why? Gah!

Men were not hobbies, and sex was not love. I wanted the real thing or nothing at all. This was my new motto, and I would not throw it away just because Ren and his hotness were taking up way too much space in my brain.

"Comfort above all else, right?" I joked, feeling a bit self-conscious but still mostly happy to see him, damn it. "So that Jeep that replaced the moving van in the driveway is yours?"

"Yep."

"Well, howdy neighbor." I grinned at him. "Welcome to Loganberry Lane. Come sit down. Would you like a cup of coffee?"

"Okay, sure. Thank you. I was going to text when I got home, but here you are. We should talk about our date, make some plans, stuff like that."

He hopped onto the porch and sat across from me on the cute wicker couch I'd bought shortly after moving in. "But no thanks to the coffee." He took a sip from the water bottle he was holding. "I'm good. So this is your house, huh?"

"Yep, I moved in a couple of months ago. I've always loved it, so I bought it when it went up for sale." I picked up my yarn to distract myself from his gorgeous face and body—god, he was too sexy for his own good.

"Are the neighbors nice?" he asked. "I haven't met anyone yet."

"I haven't gotten to know any of them. I love all their dogs, though."

He chuckled, as if he thought I was cute. Then he smiled and gestured to the house next door to mine. "I live in such a boring beige box compared to your place. This is something else."

"I love it here. I needed this. Peace, solitude—"

"Creaky wooden floors, ghosts..." he teased.

"Well, my cats stare off into the distance in this place way more than at my old apartment. But nothing has gone bump in the night. Not yet, anyway."

"You're a brave woman, Piper."

"I try to be." I peeked at him over my knitting. "Having the cats helps. They're good company, even though one of them has developed the new hobby of staring at my bedroom ceiling and whining at me."

He chuckled softly. "I've heard that cats can be pretty perceptive. How about your dog? Is he here? Is everything okay with that situation?"

"No, he's not here," I heaved a beleaguered sigh. "Richard had a work thing, but Cody is the worst guard dog ever. He's a golden retriever and falls in love with everyone he meets. He'd probably love it if there were ghosts here. The more beings available to give him attention, the merrier."

"I can't wait to meet him. I've always wanted a golden retriever like Lassie."

"That's a collie, silly."

"Oh, Benji?"

"He's a mixed breed."

"Shit, Beethoven?"

"St. Bernard. You're really bad at this."

"What, making conversation?" I looked up from my knitting to see him trying to smile at me. His mouth was quirked higher on one side.

"Haha, you're cute."

"Ahhh, *cute*. Just what every forty-two-year-old man wants to be," he joked.

"There's nothing wrong with being cute," I insisted. "In fact, you should *want* to be cute. It's better than being an arrogant asshole like most of you are."

"Attorneys?" He leaned in closer. "Some of us do try to maintain a small sense of charm." His voice lowered to a conspiratorial whisper. "Or is it men in general?"

"Men in general," I confessed while inwardly excluding him from the running list of arrogant assholes I'd met in my life.

"I won't even begin to argue with your opinion of men. In my line of work, I see the worst."

"I bet you do," I mumbled. "I can't believe I'm having an entire conversation with you in my ratty bathrobe and a face mask. Whatever must you think of me?"

"Your nightgown underneath reminds me of something from the Golden Girls." Was he trying to make me feel better?

"Oh god." I was mortified. "Thank you, it's a caftan." The face mask served me well and hid my flaming cheeks. "I dressed like this to show Richard I don't give a crap about him or what he thinks of me. Don't tell anyone."

"No worries. I can keep a secret."

"You're an attorney. You must have loads of secrets."

"That I do. Here's one, pass me your knitting." I handed it to him and watched in awe as he finished the row I was working on.

"Wow, your skills are impressive."

"My mom taught me. It's relaxing."

"Not for me. I'm considering another hobby."

He set the knitting aside and leaned back on the couch, crossing his long legs at the ankle. I allowed myself a quick peek at him. The muscles in his torso were accentuated by the fitted T-shirt that clung tightly around his pecs and biceps. It took all I had to keep my eyes from wandering over his body to look my fill. I managed one discreet up and down, but it was hard not to keep staring. "Want to hear another one?"

"Huh?" I muttered, distracted, as I felt an urge to know everything about him. "Oh, I mean, sure. I love secrets."

"I like talking to you, Piper."

I let out a nervous laugh as I reeled in my desire to flirt my ass off. "Thanks, they used to put my desk in the hallway back in school." Cracking jokes was my preferred way of handling unexpected compliments, so I went with that. "Fair warning—I can definitely talk, and sometimes I just can't stop."

"That's not the drawback you seem to think it is."

For a moment, neither one of us spoke. Silence stretched between us, not quite awkward, but not *not* awkward either. I was intrigued.

He leaned back and pulled his phone from his pocket. I jumped when my text notification went off.

"Now you have my number. I'll text you tonight, to make plans and go over the ground rules. I've got to get going now."

"Oh, okay." A soft laugh escaped me. "Well, not if I

text you first." I was such a goober, *not if I text you first*. Like I would ever have the nerve to text a man first. Fake or not, I was not one to make the first move.

"Until next time," he said, standing up and looking at me like he liked what he saw, even though I was more than an entire mess right now.

"Yeah, next time." I echoed softly as I watched him walk to his house, my heart still racing.

I snatched my phone from the table next to my rocking chair to save his number.

Hot Neighbor, I entered before hugging it to my chest.

Chapter 4
Ren

My mind was a tangle of thoughts, and all of them were, *what the fuck?*

Had I flirted with her? There was no doubt about it; I had.

I couldn't recall the last time I'd been so charmed by a woman. Unlocking my door, I went inside, kicking it closed behind me as I fought the urge to take out my phone and immediately text her.

I couldn't shake her image from my mind. She was adorable in that pretty caftan and worn-out robe, with a hint of green face mask lingering on her skin. She was enchanting.

I liked her already, and that was unlike me.

I moved to the kitchen and refilled my water bottle, sipping slowly to steady my nerves.

But was it?

I had been alone for so long that I felt I barely knew

myself anymore. Even in my marriage, toward the end, I had been alone. Tabby had been so ill—

The memories of our past crept in, uninvited and persistent. I'd lost myself in the routines of caregiving and the isolation that came with it. For so long, all I had was work and Tabby. Now, I was free, and the concept of a new beginning was both exhilarating and terrifying at the same time.

I went to the living room and collapsed onto my couch, attempting to rationalize my feelings. I glanced at my phone, the temptation to send a text growing stronger with every passing second.

My thumb hovered over the screen, but I knew better than to rush into anything—the entirety of my work was comprised of extricating people from marriages they'd rushed into, for fuck's sake.

I put the phone down and picked up my book, hoping to distract myself, but the words blurred, replaced by the memory of Piper's lovely smile and green-tinged cheeks. The blush beneath the mask was undeniable, and I wanted to figure out all the ways I could make her do it again.

"Get your shit together," I muttered to myself, slamming the book shut with a curse. It was absurd to feel this attracted to her when we had barely spent any time together. I needed to ground myself in the present, in the new reality that I was beginning to build, not get wrapped up in a woman.

The minutes ticked by, but the restless energy persisted. Maybe a change of scenery would help. After a quick shower, I got into my car and drove off to find some-where to clear my head.

Figuring it was as good a time as any, I decided to head to my old apartment to grab the last of my things. I'd been putting it off. I had some clothes left in my closet to collect, and I was still contemplating getting rid of a few odds and ends.

The drive was exactly what I needed. Being on the road gave me space to think and reflect on everything that had happened over the past few years. Portland had always been a place of memories, good and bad. And now, it was going to be my place of transition.

Arriving at my old apartment, I was instantly hit by a wave of nostalgia. I moved through the rooms methodi-cally, gathering the last of my things, each a relic of a life I was determined to leave behind—or at least not allow to hold me back anymore.

I let the exhaustion I had been feeling lately wash over me as I sat mindlessly on my old couch, not realizing how tired I was until my head hit the cushion. My thoughts flowed between Tabby and Piper as I drifted off to sleep, finding it strange that each had become a symbol of my past and present. So far, Piper was like a tiny spark of hope, and maybe it wouldn't amount to anything, but it felt good to think about her, so I let my mind wander.

I awakened to the early morning light and the sound of my stomach growling like crazy. The steady hum of traffic outside and the occasional chirping of birds were quite a change from the peaceful sounds of Loganberry Lane the night before. I rubbed my eyes and glanced around the room, feeling the weight of the past pressing down on me. Yet there was comfort in knowing I was closing this chapter, that I was finally ready for it.

My eyes landed on Tabby's old desk, the one piece of furniture I had long avoided confronting. It held the echoes of her presence, the hours she'd spent there, working, living, and ultimately dying. The weight of grief settled on my shoulders as I picked up one of her journals. How could I bear to part with it?

I found a box in the corner and began filling it with her belongings—her favorite pen, which I had given her after we graduated from college, and a framed snapshot, taken by my mother, of the two of us as children. On the brink of tears, I steeled myself. These items were essential; they were part of the past I didn't want to forget.

Recognizing this as another step toward closure, I taped the box shut. I had to honor my past to move forward into the future; I understood that now.

I would leave the couch and the empty desk for the movers to take away. Shouldering the duffle with my clothes and clutching Tabby's box to my chest, I took one last look around before leaving and locking the door behind me.

The drive home was quieter than the trip to my old apartment, likely because my thoughts weren't racing around in my head anymore. I pulled into the garage and went inside. I set the box containing Tabby's belongings on the kitchen table, feeling the weight of what it signified along with a newfound sense of clarity.

Gazing out the window, I saw Piper step onto her

porch wearing that same ratty robe as yesterday but with a different caftan beneath it, black, with multi-colored flowers in a random pattern. God, she was gorgeous, even when actively trying not to be.

Seeing her there, I felt a strange mix of anticipation and comfort, odd but welcome. I decided to get some breakfast and make coffee. As the aroma of coffee and toast filled my kitchen, I couldn't help but glance out the window again, watching Piper as she seemed to be absorbed in her own world as she worked on her knitting, what she was working on, I couldn't tell. Maybe someday, it would turn into a scarf.

I sat on my couch to eat, convincing myself I wouldn't watch her from the window like a creep, even though I knew it was a lie. I shouldn't observe her this way, but she was wearing her ratty robe, so her ex must be on the way with her dog, which worried me. Telling myself it was a valid reason, I kept the curtains open to keep an eye on her despite my better judgment.

After my first sip of coffee, I saw him pull into her driveway and frowned when I noticed he didn't have Cody with him.

What the hell was he up to?

I watched as she walked over to him with a forced smile that she couldn't quite make sincere.

They exchanged a few words, and her body language made it clear that the conversation wasn't going well.

I set my coffee on the end table and walked toward the window, ready to intervene if necessary. I strained to catch snippets of their conversation, wishing I could open the window. She waved her arms to the sides in frustration while he remained smug-faced as he watched her lose her temper. The tension was palpable, even from here.

My heart sank as I watched him thrust a piece of paper into her hands before turning on his heel and walking back to his car. She stood there, staring at the paper, her face a mask of confusion and hurt. She was frozen in place, and I felt an almost overwhelming urge to rush over and offer comfort, advice, or anything to make her okay.

But I hesitated.

Instead, I moved away from the window.

This was not my business. He was gone now, and she was in no danger. Which meant if I kept watching her, I'd be nothing more than a nosy neighbor and possibly a creep.

A soft knock echoed from the entryway as I returned to my coffee, trying to forget what I'd seen.

I froze, heart pounding in my chest, before cautiously moving toward the door. Slowly, I opened it to find her standing there, clutching the crumpled piece of paper. Brimming with tears, her eyes met mine, and for a moment, words failed me.

"I'm freaking out. I didn't know where else to go," she whispered, her voice cracking with the weight of her emotions. "Violet has a new baby, and Paige would not be rational about this. I can't talk to her right now. And you're just so—never mind. I'm sorry to barge in on—"

"Shh, no apologies." I stepped aside. "Come in." I

invited her in without hesitation. She rushed through the living room and slumped onto the couch, the paper falling to her side as I moved to join her. "What happened? What can I do?"

She took a shuddering breath before answering. "Richard said he's considering suing me for custody of Cody if I don't talk to him about Dana and everything that happened." Fresh tears spilled down her cheeks as I reached out and gently squeezed her hand.

"Ownership," I blurted as I defaulted to what I knew best rather than pull her in for a hug like I wanted. "In Oregon, it's ownership and not custody. Pets are considered property. Do you have any receipts, vaccination records, vet bills, anything that you paid for?"

She nodded. "I have a few things. But he's saying that since he was the one who signed all the papers at the shelter, he has the primary claim."

I frowned, thinking through the legal implications. "It could be complicated. But having any records at all could help you," I reassured her. "Let me help you find a good attorney who specializes in these cases."

She looked at me, her eyes filling with hope. I would not let her down. I'd get her that damn dog back if I had to fucking steal him myself.

"Thank you," she breathed. "I'm sorry to intrude like this. You barely know me. I just—"

"Hey, it's okay. I'm glad you came to me."

"Okay. Uh, yeah. This isn't awkward at all." She wiped beneath her eyes with the sleeve of her robe. "I'm a mess again."

"It's understandable. God, I'm sorry—" I came to my senses and offered her a tissue box from the coffee table. "Here, take one. Where are my manners?"

"Manners? No, where are mine? It's not like you were expecting guests, let alone a freaked out, crying one. I'm sorry for barging in on you like this."

I smiled gently. "Don't worry about it."

She took a deep, trembling breath and looked around. "It's really nice in here. You have good taste."

I chuckled, not sure of what to say. "Thanks. I was going for cozy and comfortable."

She nodded. "Yeah... I just wish Richard would show some compassion. Cody loves both of us, but I've always been the one to take care of him. He's going to be so confused. I know he's a dog, but he needs a routine. He needs *me*. I don't understand why he's doing this. Why now?"

I rubbed a hand down my face. "Probably because of me. Of us. At the bar. He thinks we're dating."

"But that can't be it, we broke up, and he's with Dana now. I have been completely clear with him. He still wanted me to be friends with Dana, but I told him I needed time. He told me he understood that."

"Yeah, but having another man around made it sink in. You're moving on. And you don't need their friendship or whatever he's trying to get out of you. Plus, if he's friends with Paige's ex, he knows I won't let you take his shit."

"Crap. That makes sense. So, he's punishing me," she deduced. "And Cody, too, by extension."

"It seems that way."

"I was pissed at him before. He hurt me, but I could have moved past that and gotten along with him for Cody's sake. But now I hate him."

"I don't blame you. This is a shit thing to do."

"He's a selfish prick, just like Paige said. And don't even let me get started about Dana and what a manipulative little witch she turned out to be."

I didn't answer. It seemed like she needed to get this off her chest. Listening was the best choice. I nodded at her to continue.

"She was right. I told her I hoped things would miraculously work out, and she said she'd give it a week. She's always right. He is such a dick."

"I'm so sorry." I could see the frustration written all over her face.

"I just don't get why he has to make everything so hard. It's like he wants to control me or at least control the situation—the one he caused by the way. The sad part is, I would probably still be with him if he hadn't cheated on me. I knew he was wrong for me, and I let him move in. I let him move into my childhood dream house! What is wrong with me?"

I reached out to touch her arm. "There's nothing wrong with you," I said softly. "You wanted to believe in him. That's not a weakness."

"But look where it got me. I'm stuck picking up the pieces while he's just out there using Cody as leverage and being an asshole. He told me I have to be available to talk at all times, and I have to be reasonable about Dana, or he'll sue me and—"

"Wait, has he sued you? Or is he threatening to? Can I see the paper? You'll get through this, no matter what. I'll help you get Cody back."

"I can't believe this is happening. He wants me to *listen to reason.*" She waved her hands around, making air quotes. "Basically, he is going to hold Cody hostage unless I do what he wants and be nice to Dana because she feels bad—" Her face flushed with emotion as she vented, every word dripping with hurt and betrayal. Then suddenly, she stopped. Her eyes widened in realization, and an awkward silence fell between us.

"What an ass," I finally said. "You don't deserve this. I promise I'll do whatever I can to help."

"Oh god. I talk too much." Her eyes slammed shut as if by closing them, she would disappear. "I warned you. Oh my god. I am completely mortified." She snatched the paper from Richard, stood, and bolted toward the door. "I am so sorry. I have to go."

I got up to follow her, but the door slammed shut before I could say anything more. The weight of her presence hung in the air. She needed time and she needed help, and I hoped she would let me be the one to give it to her.

I sighed heavily, feeling helpless. Not knowing what else to do, I reached into my pocket and pulled out my phone.

Quickly, I typed out a message to her.

Me: Hey, I hope you're okay. Can we talk later?

I hesitated for a moment before pressing send. I wanted her to know she wasn't alone. But I didn't think I had the right to chase after her.

The three dots appeared instantaneously, but a return text never came. I knew she must be feeling vulnerable; how could I make her understand that she had nothing to worry about from me? I would never judge her.

I grabbed my keys, deciding to head to Coffee Cabin. I needed more coffee and didn't want to just sit here doing nothing.

She texted back while I was still driving. I pulled into the parking lot and answered her, telling her she had nothing to be embarrassed about.

Who hasn't lost their shit from time to time? I'd be a liar if I said I always kept my cool.

Chapter 5
Piper

I ran into my house in time to hear my text notification go off.

I glanced at it, anxiety churning within me. It was from Ren. He was checking on me. I picked it up to text back, but I couldn't—not now. I was too humiliated and embarrassed even to face a message on my phone.

I had let my emotions take over, revealing too much too soon. Actually, I'd revealed things I should never reveal to anyone. I was an open book. I was too trusting, talked too much, and never knew who I should believe in. I sank onto my couch, overwhelmed, wishing the earth would swallow me whole.

How could I ever face him again?

I couldn't, not ever. I'd have to find another fake boyfriend to fake out Ren, who had just faked out Richard for me. What the hell had I been thinking?

I was thirty-eight years old and acting like I'd been transported back to high school. No, that wasn't it. I'd been a lifelong doormat whose weak ways were now catching up to her, and it had to stop. I could stand up for someone else with no problem. But when it came to myself? Forget it.

I had been too much of a wimp to tell Richard off for good and insist that he let me have Cody because we both knew he belonged with me. Richard liked Cody just fine, but Cody loved me, and I loved him. I was the one who had wanted to get a dog. Richard was simply along for the ride. I should have never let him be the one to sign the damn papers.

Burying my face in my hands, I felt the weight of every wrong decision I'd made lately piling up on me. But I didn't want to cry anymore. I'd done enough of that for today and the past couple of months, too, if I were being honest with myself.

Nimbus and Smog, as if on cue, darted into the parlor and hopped onto the couch on either side of me. Each headbutted one of my arms as they purred their brains out. They hated Richard. From the first cat turd we found in his shoe, I should have known. Animals could sense evil. They tried to tell me. Why didn't I listen to them?

My phone buzzed on the table with another message.

I hesitated for a moment, then reached for it, fingers trembling as I swiped up to see the message. His words glowed on the screen like tiny little beacons of hope. Stupid, freaking dumbass hope.

Hot Neighbor: Not stalking you, just wanted to add an addendum to the last text. I'm a good listener if you want to talk, and you never have to feel embarrassed about a damn thing. Not with me.

I stared at the words, my mind racing through a myriad of possibilities about what I should text back. I wanted to explain myself. But, damn it, if wanting to be understood wasn't the root of a lot of my problems. It made me too open, too free with my heart. I couldn't do it anymore.

The fear of further humiliation held me back. Nimbus and Smog must have sensed my inner turmoil as they nestled closer.

I took a deep breath. Ignoring him would accomplish nothing. Slowly, I typed a response, trying to strike a balance between honesty and self-preservation.

Me: Thank you for letting me vent. You are very kind. I'm sorry for running off.

I hit send and placed the phone down on the table. That sounded like something a well-adjusted, normal, human woman would text back, right?

Focusing on my future was what I should be doing.

My bakery was almost ready to open, and man-stealing, lying Dana or not, I was still happy about it. I had this house to finish decorating. I had two awesome cats and a great family. And I'd get my freaking dog back, too. Richard couldn't keep him forever. He was just trying to control the situation, and he would get over it once he realized I could not be controlled—not anymore and never again. The point was I had a lot to be grateful for, and screw Richard and Dana for trying to ruin it.

"*Argh!*" Frustrated with myself, I let out a mini scream, which sent Smog running up the stairs. Nimbus, a fan of drama, hopped onto my lap and curled up.

Just as I began to take another deep breath, my phone buzzed again. It was Ren. Reluctantly, I picked it up and read his message:

Hot Neighbor: Don't apologize. Heading to Coffee Cabin. I've haven't tried it yet. Can I grab you something? To cheer you up?

Oh shit.

I blinked. "I think he's going to come over here, Nimbus. What do I do?"

Without thinking, I texted him back.

Me: My family owns the Coffee Cabin.
You'll love it.

Ambiguous answers were always a great tactic when you didn't want to make a choice.

I held my breath, waiting for a reply. I should have been relieved when I didn't get one, but because I was a hopeless romantic, I was disappointed instead. Damn it.

My grandparents owned the Coffee Cabin, a cute little drive-through coffee hut designed to resemble a mini log cabin. It was located in the corner of the massive parking lot of the Honeybrook Inn, which they also owned. Once it became clear that locals would walk or jog by to grab their morning coffee, they'd put in a few covered outdoor sitting areas. Hopefully, he'd sit there and drink his coffee. But if he didn't, The Coffee Cabin was real close, so he'd be here soon.

My baby sister, Eliza, ran the place for my grandparents. Maybe I should call her and ask her to keep an eye out. *Or not.* She was nosy, just like the rest of my family, and I didn't want anyone to know about Ren.

"Time for me to get a move on, Nimbus." I gently shifted him onto the knitted throw in the corner of the couch and stood, smiling as he stretched and then went back to sleep. Nimbus, a floppy gray and white ragdoll cat, acted like a baby when tired. He'd be out for a few hours. I covered him with the corner of the blanket and patted his fluffy little head.

Whether or not Ren stopped by, I was going to get my ass up and do something. Sitting around and feeling sorry for myself was pointless. I'd start by washing my face. He had seen enough of me with green cheeks, for the love of god.

Feeling more like my usual upbeat self, I grinned, my wide smile cracking the dried, green face mask around my cheeks, the flakes falling to the floor.

I was supposed to put the finishing touches on the bakery's grand opening day. Something Sweet's grand opening was coming up soon. It was a childhood dream come true to create beautiful wedding cakes, cupcakes, and a variety of other sweet treats for a living. We were throwing a big party, and I was in charge of the planning, but Richard had killed my mood. Damn him.

I stomped into the bathroom and splashed warm water on my face, taking a washcloth from the shelf to wipe away the remnants of my face mask. I decided being mad was better than being sad as I glanced around my downstairs bathroom. I took in the cozy, old-fashioned, floral décor. I had enjoyed choosing it when I moved in.

It was important to focus on the positive aspects of my life, like my house, the bakery's grand opening, my cats, and finally getting Cody back.

If Ren didn't show up today, it didn't matter. My happiness didn't depend on him or any man. And screw Richard. I was done with letting him ruin my life. I had plans to make: to throw an epic opening day bakery party and get my dog back.

I finished drying my face, feeling better and ready to

start my day, even if it meant facing the unknown with Ren. I had embarrassed myself, but he seemed kind enough to let it go. He would make a good friend, I decided as I took one last look in the mirror.

With a renewed sense of determination, I headed upstairs to my bedroom. It was done up in soft pastels. It was serene and all things girly, exactly as I'd always wanted.

At my vanity, I slicked on some pink lip gloss, took down my messy bun, and ran a brush through my hair. Then I slipped on a pair of my best jeans, dark blue, faded at the knees, and they did great things for my ass. I added my favorite chunky white cable knit sweater, over-sized and soft. I needed to feel good about myself again.

I glanced in the mirror as I slipped into a pair of Converse. Dressing like this might have been a subtle attempt to impress Ren if he showed up, but it was also about reclaiming my confidence and taking control of my day. No more moping around in my pajamas and ratty old robe.

I took a deep breath, feeling the soft fabric of my sweater brush against my skin, and smiled. Ready to tackle my to-do list for Something Sweet's opening, I grabbed my notebook and pen, determined to stay busy. Then, a knock at the door sent my mind whirling all over again.

I flew down the stairs, my heart pounding with antici-pation and curiosity. After taking a moment at the bottom, I steadied my breath and opened the door to reveal Ren leaning casually against the porch rail, his eyes twinkling in the sunlight. My racing heart skipped a foolish beat, but luckily, I quickly regained my composure.

"Hey, I had a feeling it was you," I blurted a bit too excitedly.

He straightened and offered me a cup of take-out coffee. "Well, I couldn't leave you to face this all alone, could I? Eliza said to tell you hi, and she told me your favorite drink is a hazelnut latte." He eyed me carefully. Concern for me was etched all over his face.

"Thank you." I took the drink and stepped aside to let him in, feeling nervous and relieved at the same time. I was surprised that his presence was such a comfort. But at the same time it was also sort of unsettling, stirring emotions I wasn't entirely ready to face—like moving on, hope for the future, crap like that.

As he walked past me, I caught a whiff of his cologne. He smelled so good, like sandalwood and pine, as if he had showered and run through the forest after. I fought the urge to rub against him and inhale deeply. He was playing with my mind without even trying. Suddenly, I realized that when Richard and I were together, he had to put in effort to evoke these feelings in me, while Ren simply had to exist. I needed to nip this burgeoning crush in the bud before my imagination took it too far.

He turned to face me, his expression softening as he took in my appearance. "You look great, by the way," he said. His voice was warm and genuine, and my nerves flew away.

"Thank you."

"Are you feeling better?" He sipped his coffee as he studied my face. "You look better."

"Yeah, I'm sorry for freaking out on you before. I was stuck in the moment with Richard and couldn't stop thinking I'd never see Cody again. It was irrational, but I couldn't stop the thoughts from coming."

"No apologies. I'm glad I was there. I see a notebook. Are you making plans?" He watched me carefully as if he cared. Like he would listen to whatever I had to say, I mean *really* listen. I could get used to this. If a man didn't look at me like Ren did right now, I didn't want him.

"I'm supposed to be planning the grand opening of the bakery. And I'm really trying to be happy about it."

"Tell me all about it."

"It's called Something Sweet. It's wedding themed—you know, something borrowed, something blue, something old and something new... Anyway, this whole thing is ironic now, since I no longer believe in love and my business partner is the one Richard cheated on me with."

"Ouch. Do you want to talk about it? Should I be in the loop as your date?"

"It would probably be a good idea to cover the basics at least. I went to culinary school with Dana. We were never best friends, but we were friendly. Our goals aligned, and we decided to work together. I won a bunch of baking competitions, and along with that, enough money to fund whatever I wanted to do. She was ready to start her own business as well. So we talked, made a deal, and then made a plan. Then she slept with Richard, and they are currently together.

Richard has been trying to get me to forgive her. Apparently, she feels bad, like boo hoc, right? That's about it. Now, cheer me up. Let's be friends. Can we do that?"

"Absolutely." He leaned against the staircase banister with a mischievous glint in his eyes. "I think we need to establish the ground rules before we do anything together."

"Rules?" I teased. "It's just a few pretend dates, not some kind of secret society we're trying to infiltrate."

"Exactly, but if we're going to pull this off, we need a game plan. We can't have people thinking we're just friends. We need rumors to start flying for both of us. Richard might be comfortable messing with you, but now that I'm here? No one messes with you."

"Oh." I shivered at the thought of having Ren around to protect me. "Good thinking. Okay, so rule number one." I set my coffee on the console table by the door and tapped my pen against my notebook. "We should look like we're having fun. So no sulking in the corner or staring daggers at each other."

His head drew back on his neck, affronted, eyes narrowing in a half-hearted glare. "Easy, I can be fun on occasion. Rule number two: we need to be...affectionate. Hand holding, arm-in-arm, stuff like that."

I flushed. "You mean be touchy-feely?"

"Exactly. But not more than we're comfortable with. Those can be a subset of rules, and we can figure that out later."

I wrote it down. "Got it. Rule number three: witty

banter and/or flirting. We need to maintain the illusion that we're falling madly in love. Right?"

His eyes lingered on mine as he stepped closer, a smile tugging at the corners of his lips. I felt the weight of his attention, and I couldn't help but wish it were real. He looked at me as if he had seen me for the first time and reveled in every detail.

Confused, I shook my head to clear it.

Was he really *this good* at faking?

"That should be easy." His voice was dark, rumbling from his chest as he reached out a hand to brush an errant curl over my shoulder. "Rule number four," he continued. "Compliments."

"I love compliments," I burst out almost hysterically. "Tell me I'm pretty."

His eyes never left mine. "Pretty?" he scoffed. "No. You're fucking gorgeous, Piper. Even when your cheeks were green, I couldn't stop looking at you. You're strong too. You've taken control of your emotions today and will get control of this situation with Richard, Dana, and Cody, too. I know it. I can see it in your eyes."

My mouth opened and shut like a fish out of water as I searched for words. I felt my cheeks go up in flames, sure that I'd turned bright red—a change from the green. Progress, I guess.

"Too much?" He cracked a smile, breaking the mood, and thank god for that; I swear I was about to pass out. Or maybe kiss him or something else equally *touchy-feely* and totally inappropriate.

"I can handle it." I grinned at him, full of false

bravado, but whatever. Turning away, I grabbed my coffee from the console table. "Let's go to the kitchen." I took off, trusting he'd follow. I needed a moment without his gaze on me. He really was listening. It felt like he knew me already.

He sat across from me as we settled in at my table. I took a moment to gather my thoughts and redirect my focus to our plans while he sipped his coffee and watched me fidget with a knowing grin lighting up his face.

"How long have we been together?" he asked, breaking the tension.

"What?" Gah! It took a second, but I came to my senses enough to answer him. "Okay, right. Rule number five: If anyone asks how long we've been together, we say it's three weeks or possibly a month." I paused to write it down. "Three weeks," I mumbled as I wrote. "Yeah, so that's about how long I'll be separated from Richard. And it will be believable because you and I are still getting to know each other. It will be new, so it's okay if we don't know everything. Plus, I don't want anyone to even think I cheated. I am not a cheater. I would never cheat. Cheaters suck. Fuck cheaters."

"Yeah, they do suck. I think three weeks is perfect." His eyes burned into mine. "How did we meet?"

"Aside from our connection to Violet and Jake, we could say that sparks flew at my sister's bookstore," I answered decisively. "We reached for a copy of the same book; our hands touched, and bing, bang, boom. Magic."

"Magic, huh? It's cute. Cliché, but it works."

"Of course, it works." I stole another brief glance and

grinned at him as I wrote. "Clichés exist for a reason. It will plant a familiar seed of truth that nobody will question."

"Good point. Okay, partner in crime." He offered me his hand across the table to shake, and I couldn't help but notice how natural this all felt despite my nerves. He had an easy charm, and he was confident. This thing might actually end up being fun. "Shall we seal the deal again with a handshake?"

I offered my hand, shivering as his big palm engulfed mine. "Deal," I agreed softly just as Smog entered the dining room with a loud *meow*.

"Wow, he's huge," Ren remarked as Smog jumped on the table to stare at him.

"Yeah, he's a Maine Coon; they can get pretty big. Be careful. I don't think he likes men very much. He couldn't stand Richard. He treated his shoes as a litter box."

"Smart cat. Serves him right. Are you friendly?" He held his hand out for Smog to sniff.

But he didn't have to worry. To my surprise, Smog started purring and flopped to his side on the table in front of him. "Okay, do you have cat treats in your pocket?"

"Nope." Ren smiled as Smog rolled over and let him give him a belly rub.

"He likes you, and basically, he only likes me." My eyebrows shot up. "He tolerates my family, but nothing like this."

"Smog suits him." His eyes met mine. "He's a beautiful cat."

"He was a stray, along with Nimbus, who is currently sleeping on the couch. They lived near the dumpsters at my old apartment. It took a while, but I forced them to love me, and now here we are."

"I'll add this to the list of reasons I like you more each time I talk to you."

"You say sweet things." I exhaled slowly, trying to gather my feelings and stuff them back somewhere safe.

As I watched Ren pet my cat, I realized even more that I should have paid closer attention to how they had always treated Richard. It felt as if they could read my inner doubts about him and were trying to warn me.

The bottom line is that I had to start trusting my instincts. And right now, my instincts were screaming that Ren was amazing, and there was nothing fake about how quickly I was beginning to like him.

Chapter 6
Ren

I leaned back in my chair, relaxed now that we had settled everything. I would have told her I was proud of how she had bounced back from her earlier upset, but I was afraid it might come off as condescending, so I didn't and decided to ask her about the bookstore instead.

"Now, about the bookstore where we met. Is it the one on Sycamore? Petals and Prose? I noticed it the first time I drove into town. It looks amazing. Like it's dusty and old and full of weird books."

She nodded, and a nostalgic smile crossed her face. "That's the one. My grandpa opened it ages ago. He's a big reader and a poet as well. My sister, Cara, manages it for him. Our grandparents own several businesses besides the inn. They're kind of like the entrepreneurs of Honeybrook Hollow."

"I love that," I said, genuinely impressed and intrigued. "How many sisters do you have?"

She sighed, and her eyes shifted to the side as if she were about to get into something scandalous. "Paige, plus three half-sisters. Cara and Lucy are the same age, but they have different mothers—you can figure out for yourself what happened there. And then there's Eliza. Our dad is obviously a big, huge cheater. Hence, my totally unhinged reaction to Richard cheating on me and his efforts to control my reaction to it and keep Cody from me. I can't believe I fell for his bull crap—"

I reached out to pat her hand in solidarity. "Not unhinged. Totally justifiable. My father was also a cheater. I have zero respect for men like him."

She turned her hand palm up and laced her fingers with mine. "Paige told me that you are basically a crusader. Violet told me even more about your family, though not in a gossipy way; she adores you. I'm sorry about your dad. No kid deserves to grow up the way you did."

I nodded, feeling a familiar pang of anger.

My father was abusive—a gambler and a cheat. He was always coming and going. When he was gone, we could be ourselves and breathe. But he always came back when he needed money or a place to crash. He kept that up for years until I was old enough and strong enough to make him stay away for good. He died about ten years ago, and he was not missed.

"It's my mission to help any woman stuck with men like my father. It's Jake's, too."

"Now, that I love," she said, her eyes lighting up in admiration. "And that's what Lyla's Place is for—to honor your mom. Let me know if there's anything I can do. I would love to volunteer, or maybe I could organize a cupcake fundraising drive or something. It probably won't bring in as much as the charity dinner donations, but I'd be happy to do it."

"That would be amazing. *You* are amazing."

"Thank you. I think you are, too. I'm glad we are finally getting to know each other. We've been in the same orbit for a while now."

"I'm glad too. I'm trying to slow down. That's one of the reasons why I moved here. That, and to be closer to Jake and the rest of my family."

"You needed to stop and smell the roses?"

I chuckled at the cliché. "Something like that."

"I'm doing that too. That's why I moved into this house. I need to learn to—I don't know, relax or something. I've been working too much lately."

"Exactly. I've never really taken the time to stop and appreciate the little things. Sometimes, I forget how important it is to just...pause. This is why Jake is making me take the rest of the week off. I wouldn't have done it otherwise."

Her grip on my hand tightened briefly, a silent affirmation that she understood me. She smiled softly, a gentle warmth spreading across her face as she released it and picked up her pen. "Well, I am actually growing roses on the side of the house. Feel free to stop and smell them anytime if you ever need to take a pause."

"Thank you. I might take you up on that." I cleared my throat and snapped out of the flirty haze we'd found ourselves in. "Am I holding you up? I know I stopped by unexpectedly."

"Um, no." She grinned at me with a shake of her head. "I'm the one who barged in on you first. And I didn't even bring you any coffee. It's all good. All I had to do today was work on plans for the bakery's grand opening, but I've lost the motivation, if I'm being honest. Richard pretty much wrecked my day. I tried to let it go, but I'm still mad at him."

"Would you like me to go with you to pick up your dog? I'm happy to help you out in any way I can. And I mean it. I'll do whatever it takes."

"You're sweet, but no. I'm going to let it go for today and think it over. He wants me to have lunch with him after we take Cody to his vet appointment to talk things through. I'm going to text him and tell him I'll go. He promised I could take Cody home with me after."

"Are you sure about that?"

"I—no, I'm not. But I don't want to make this get any uglier than it already is, and I really don't want him to sue me or whatever else he can do."

"I think you should talk to Paige."

Her lips quirked at the corner. "So, you're telling me you're in favor of making this ugly?"

"I'm in favor of whatever or whoever helps you stand up for yourself. I'm not trying to push you into anything, but Paige will keep your best interests in mind."

"Paige will lose her mind. And that's not what I want. She's been through enough lately. I can take care of this myself."

"Okay. I wasn't trying to imply you couldn't—"

She met my eyes. "I know enough about you to know that. Don't worry, Ren. I just don't get why he's pushing so hard for me to forgive Dana. He has to know that's never going to happen."

"I think you're amazing. He probably does too. He has to know how badly he fucked up." Afraid I'd revealed too much, I looked away from her gorgeous eyes, shifting my focus back to Smog, who I swear could read my mind by how he looked at me right before he stood and darted out of the room. Yeah, buddy, wanting to be near Piper was entirely too easy.

"Thank you." She breathed, her cheeks turning pink. "I still feel like a fool, though. That's why I didn't mention the lunch thing before."

"I don't blame you for trying to keep the peace. Do I believe he's trying to manipulate you? Yes. You love Cody, and he's taking advantage of that. The issue isn't you; it's him. But you're nobody's fool, and you can take care of yourself. Just don't try to handle this alone."

"I won't. I don't even want to. I just want things to go back to the way they were. I mean, I don't want to get back together with Richard. But I could do without this newfound determination of his to have us all be friends or whatever."

"Honestly? Things can't go back to how they were. But that doesn't mean it can't turn out okay."

"You're right," she murmured, looking at me through her lashes. "Enough about Richard. I'm sick of him. Let's change the topic. Are we really doing this?"

I let out a nervous laugh as liquid heat spread through my chest. "I—yeah. I think we can help each other out."

"Who are we telling? Of course, Paige knows it's fake; it was her idea, but what about Jake? And Violet is my best friend. I can't imagine keeping this from her. And I have three more nosy sisters. And don't even get me started on my mother. God, and my grandparents—"

"We probably shouldn't tell anyone. Can Paige keep a secret?"

"Yes. We keep all of each other's secrets. I'll just avoid the topic with everyone else. Say it's casual, or like you told Richard, we're seeing where things go. It could work. I don't like lying, but the more people who know, the greater chance that we'll get busted."

"That sounds good to me. And remember, this is supposed to make our lives easier. Say the word if it starts feeling too complicated, and we will reevaluate the situation. Promise me."

"I promise."

"Good. Now, when is Cody's vet appointment?"

"Why?" She eyed me suspiciously.

"So I can make sure to be home when you get back to keep an eye on things."

"I'll be okay," she finally replied. "I know I wasn't okay earlier, but I am now. I swear. You don't need to protect me. This isn't part of the deal."

"You're right. It's not part of the deal—"

"Are you sure you don't have a rescue kink? She interrupted. "I promise I can handle this myself. I'll be okay."

I paused, considering her words. "Rescue kink? No. Wanting to make life easier, safer, and better for women in every way I can? Absolutely. I'm a protective guy. I admit it. But I won't apologize for it."

Her head snapped back, and her eyes widened. "Okay. Wow."

"I know you can handle him on your own, but why should you have to?"

"Well then. Okay. Thank you, Ren."

I shrugged in answer, my cheeks heating in awkward embarrassment. If we spent any more time together, I might start to like her, and then every word I said from now on would only serve to make it obvious.

"Okay. Fine, it's Monday afternoon. It is the last appointment of the day, so Richard won't have to miss work. I should be back by five. I appreciate this."

I grunted in response, irritated that she still had to deal with him. "Anyone would do it. He's an asshole."

"No." She looked me dead in the eye. "Anyone would *not* do it. My father never could be bothered with me or any of my sisters. You are a good man, Ren."

I shook my head, not letting her words sink in, trying to dispel the sudden warmth infusing my chest.

"Thanks," I muttered. "You're pretty special yourself. And I'm sorry about your dad. Seems like you wanted yours to stay around when all I wanted was for mine to stay gone. You deserve someone to stand up for you, Piper. We all do."

"Do you always know what to say?"

I gave a half-smile, the corner of my mouth lifting. "Fuck no."

Our conversation drifted into a comfortable silence, each of us lost in our thoughts.

My ability to be near her and function normally was rapidly diminishing. It was then that I knew I had to get out of here.

"I better get going," I blurted.

"Oh." She seemed surprised. "Okay. I'm glad you stopped by. We can talk more about all of this later."

"I'll text you." Texting was safe. I didn't have to look at her while I did it, and I could be very careful about what I said without giving away how attracted to her I was.

With one last look at her, I slid out of my chair, hesitating as I stood by the table.

This was all fake. It was all for show.

But no matter how many times I tried to convince myself of these facts, I still only halfway believed them.

"Hey."

"Yeah?" She looked at me expectantly, and I found myself wanting her to expect things from me. Real things.

Why not. What could it hurt?

"Do you think we should have dinner together tomorrow night?" I should have left it at that and made this real, but I chickened out. "Like a practice date? So we can iron out any kinks before the real deal."

Chapter 7
Piper

Yes. *Yes. Yes.* That's what I almost said.

"That's probably a good idea." Is how I actually answered him.

Cool. Casual. Calm.

So unlike me.

"Do you have a favorite restaurant in town?"

"We could eat at the Inn," I stupidly suggested, forgetting that my family owned it—my incredibly nosy and unafraid-to-ask-embarrassing-questions family.

"The Honeybrook? I didn't realize there was a restaurant there."

"It's the best one around. But maybe we shouldn't go there. My family owns it. I wasn't thinking."

"Right." He cleared his throat.

"I mean, on second thought, we could go there. You'd love it. Everyone does." *Second thought?* I barely even had the first one.

I watched as he hesitated, his eyes searching mine. The moment stretched, hanging in the air between us.

Awkward. Confused. Weird.

Totally like me.

"We could try another place. That would probably be more comfortable, uh, you know, considering everything —" he offered, breaking the silence.

"No, really. It will be fine. The food is awesome. The ambiance is cozy and warm. I can reserve one of the corner tables. It will be quiet and private. My family will be cool—probably." Lie, my family was never cool. Our baseline was overly friendly with a side of blatant meddling. Whatever, they would be nice to him, and that's all that really mattered.

But now I was starting to freak out, thinking maybe he wanted to keep this a secret in town.

His smile returned, genuine this time, and he nodded. "Okay then, the Honeybrook it is. I'll text you tonight."

As he walked out, I felt a weird mix of relief and anticipation. This was probably my dumbest idea ever, but I was excited all the same. I thought about calling Paige, but rejected the idea. Asking her opinion would make this even weirder.

I sat still for a moment, taking a deep breath to let the decision sink in, and wondered if I should call it quits.

No, it would be fine.

I had to stop overthinking everything. Besides, it was just dinner. A chance to get to know each other better, which was vital if we wanted anyone to believe our scheme.

Restless, I stood.

I needed to do something. Anything was better than this anxious silence that descended after Ren left.

I decided to walk to the bakery to plan the opening festivities there. Maybe I'd get inspired if I was surrounded by what I was supposed to be happy about. I stuffed my notebook into my purse, hollered goodbye to the cats as I locked the door, and then headed around the corner and down the street toward Something Sweet, determined to reclaim my freakin' joy.

Sycamore Street was the heart of Honeybrook Hollow. It was lined with small businesses, each with colorful flower boxes and cute window displays that changed with the seasons. The street used to be paved with cobblestones, but they'd since been replaced. Vintage street lamps were hung with planters stuffed with flowers spilling over their sides, and big pots packed full of small evergreen bushes and flowers were placed here and there.

The town square was the preferred gathering place for most of the town's activities. A winding walking trail encircled the area, and people loved to walk or jog amongst the flowers liberally planted along the sides. The trail led to a gazebo, its white pillars and roof festooned with climbing roses and ivy. It was a favorite spot for small weddings, birthday parties, and other community events. Nearby, the playground was buzzing with the sound of children playing, and the dog park was also buzzing, but with barking and excited yips. Too bad joy was not actually infectious because I was not feeling any of it. I missed my dog, damn it. I needed a plan to get him back. I was even willing to get nefarious, as Paige suggested.

The smell of grilled onions and bacon wafted from Pennywhistle Pantry, the small diner directly across from the park. I was tempted to cross the street and stop in for a bite. But I had too much to do, so I kept walking, or really, I was mainly stomping and muttering to myself under my breath. I'd slipped into a bad mood after Ren left, and I knew it was written all over my face. Anyone who caught a glimpse of me could probably tell how I was feeling, which was probably why no one had stopped me to chat or say hi. Oh well. I had time to feel better later. Right now, I was grumpy, and that was okay.

Something Sweet was just up ahead. It was part of a small group of businesses that formed a little strip mall. We'd painted our storefront a pale pink and added a magenta and white striped awning over the door. The place was small, but we didn't need much space for what we wanted to do here. The sight of it should have filled me with pride, but instead, it only heightened the turmoil currently roiling through my brain.

As I approached, I saw Dana sitting at a table inside, and my heart sank even further. I wasn't ready for this confrontation. I tried to compose myself, but my bad mood was already gnawing at my patience.

How could she sit there all calm and collected as if she didn't wreck all our plans with her selfish choices?

Dana was beautiful, a petite brunette; she was pretty much my exact opposite. She was dressed in all white, with a pink and white striped apron, just like a baker straight out of a movie.

The sight of her made me so mad. I probably should have stopped to eat. I could feel myself turning into someone else, and seeing her forced all the anger I'd been stuffing down to the surface. I took a deep breath, trying to shake off the spikes of rage clawing at my chest, but it was no use. I felt like Madeline Kahn in *Clue*.

Flames...

This was happening. Now. Richard wanted the two of us to talk? We were about to freakin' talk.

I hesitated for a moment, trying to summon the strength to engage in another difficult conversation. This place had been our shared dream. Dana would be here for the day-to-day operations, while I would be here to do what I loved: elaborate, showy, special orders. We'd nurtured it together with countless late-night and early-morning planning sessions. Now, it felt like something teetering on the edge of collapse. How could I keep the peace and work with her?

"What are you doing here?" My voice was sharper than intended as I threw open the door and stepped inside.

Taking a deep breath, I stepped forward, feeling the weight of everything that happened pressing down on me. The room shrank as the walls closed in. The tension was unbearable. I felt like I would snap.

She looked up, surprised. "I was making a list of

things we may need for the opening. I wanted to help." A small flicker of hope shone in her eyes.

Unbelievable. "I do not need your help."

Her eyes widened in shock, and she quickly looked at the table. "I know I messed up, but can we at least talk about it?" Her murmured question only made me angrier.

I wanted to leave, but knew I had to stay and at least let her know where I stood. We hadn't spoken since I found out. "I really don't think we have anything to say. I mean, nothing is going to change what happened."

"We still have to work together, Piper." She leaned back in her chair with a heavy sigh.

"We don't have to be here at the same time. Plus, email exists for a reason, okay?"

"We used to be friends."

"Yeah, and then you screwed my boyfriend. What do you want me to say, Dana?"

"Wow." She sat there blinking in shock. "That was harsh."

"Harsh? Really? No. What was harsh was when Noah caught you banging Richard on my new chaise lounge on my back patio. Remember that?"

She looked away without answering.

"I thought you wanted to talk. Let's talk about it. Yeah, I thought we were friends, but I was obviously wrong. Who started it? Did Richard come onto you first? Did you forget your old culinary school buddy when you were sleeping with him? How long did it go on?"

"I—okay, um, Richard, you know how he is. Richard was persistent." Her voice shook as she stared at some point beyond my face. "I didn't know how to handle it because I liked him too. We were just talking one night, and then things escalated." Her eyes met mine, pleading with me to understand. "I never wanted to hurt you. I swear."

"You didn't know how to handle it? You could have said no. You could have walked away and talked to me about it. But instead, you betrayed our so-called friendship."

"Piper, please." Tears filled her eyes. "I wish I could take it all back. I hate that it happened this way. Please believe me. I didn't mean to fall in love with him. It just happened."

"Believing you doesn't change anything. Did you think of me at all when you were pursuing a relationship with him while he was still with me? Did it feel good to know you were sneaking around with him behind my back while we were working together to open this place?" I spun in a circle, fully committed to the moment. Finally, exhaling as I let loose everything on my mind since I found out.

"No! I didn't mean to. It just happened one night. It kind of exploded. We didn't intend—"

"You didn't intend to fuck him? How does one accidentally have sex with someone, Dana?"

"Stop it. It wasn't like that! We fell in love. You're being crude. This isn't like you. Please, Piper. Quiet down. People are going to hear you."

"I don't care who hears, and do not tell me to be quiet. I'm not the one in the wrong here." I glanced behind myself at the window, seeing a few passersby pausing briefly before hurrying on. It didn't matter. I had to get this off my chest. "Apparently, you don't know me at all. Just like I never thought you were the type of person to sleep with another woman's boyfriend. But here we are. And for the record, I'm mad at Richard, too. He is equally to blame for this situation. Unfortunately for you, he's not here right now."

"Why can't you let this go? You weren't right for each other—"

"How would you know that?" I seethed. "You don't know anything—"

"He told me things," she shrieked. "You weren't getting along. You didn't want to move in with him, not really—"

"Oh. My. God. This is unbelievable. I'm done."

"What do you mean, done? We're partners. You can't just quit."

"I'm not quitting," I bit out, shaking with fury. "I'm done talking to you. Like I said before. Email me if you have something to say."

"Email you? Really? That's how you want to handle this?" Her voice trembled as she tried to catch her breath. "I thought we were friends. I messed up. I'm sorry. How can you be so cold?"

"Seriously?" A bitter laugh escaped. "You think we can just go back to business as usual after this? You've shattered any trust I ever had in you."

Tears streamed from her eyes. "I know I can fix this.

Please, Piper. Don't let one mistake ruin everything we've worked so hard on."

"One mistake," I laughed bitterly, turning on my heel toward the door. "This was a series of choices that made it clear that whatever friendship we had meant nothing to you. Don't expect things to go back the way they were."

"We have to work together. Please. Tell me what to do to make this right." Her voice was barely a whisper. She acted like I was the one who had hurt her.

"There's nothing you can do. I can't pretend, and I don't trust you. I'll come in for the big projects like we planned, and we will communicate through email only. I'm not giving up on this place because of you. Don't worry about that. If anyone is leaving, it will be you. I can buy you out. You'll be free."

This was far from over. I knew it. Work had always been my escape. What was I supposed to do now?

"Piper, please." She had followed me outside, tugging on my arm until I turned around.

"Don't push me, Dana. We need boundaries."

"Fine," she snapped back. "But you know this isn't about boundaries. It's about cowardice. You want to hide? Fine. Run away from the hard stuff. I'll email you."

"Good, we agree on emails. I can't do this with you."

She glared at me as if the situation was my fault. "Have the day you deserve, Piper."

"*Me?*" I sputtered. "You're mad at *me?* You are unbelievable. You have the day *you* deserve, you backstabbing, duplicitous twat. I hope the rest of your day is as shitty as you are."

I watched her flounce back inside, slamming the shop's door with a huge bang.

"Great," I muttered. "That went so well."

"Hey, Piper! Everything okay?" I spun to see Lucy approaching, walking Larry, one of the llamas our grandparents kept at the Inn, on a leash. He was also her inspiration. She wrote a popular series of children's books based on him. She was in jeans and a pink sweater, her long butterscotch waves flowing over her shoulder in a ponytail.

Even the ridiculous sight of my sister walking a llama like a dog didn't make me smile. My mind still reeled from the confrontation with Dana. I wiped my trembling hands down my jeans, then my chin started wobbling, and my nose stung. Shit, I was about to freaking cry even more now.

"Yeah," I squeaked. "Everything is just peachy."

She raised an eyebrow, knowing I was full of crap. "Want to talk about it?"

I eyed Larry, who was now eating the plants in our window box like they were part of his own personal salad bowl. He looked up at me and snorted, daring me to make him stop. I shrugged—Dana had planted it. She could suck it.

"Not really. I just had a huge fight with Dana. Richard is still an ass. I don't have Cocy back yet. And I can't just forget them both and move on. I'm stuck. I have to work with her. How am I supposed to do that?"

She tugged gently on Larry's leash. "Quit it, Larry.

Let's go to the park. He's going to cause trouble if we stand still. Want me to kick her ass for you? I'll do it."

"You sound like Paige." Our eyes met as we headed back into the park, and she laughed.

"Sometimes her methods are sound. Honestly, a lot of the world's problems would be solved if some people got smacked around when they were acting up." She held a hand up. "I mean grown people, not little kids, so we don't need to argue about this. Also, I might rethink this later. I'm pissed on your behalf, it makes me ragey."

"No, do not kick her ass. Well, maybe? No." I nodded decisively. "Violence is not the answer. And why are we more willing to stand up for each other than ourselves? That's something to think about."

"Right? But, the offer stands if you change your mind…" She tilted her head with a grin.

"I won't. If there's going to be any ass-kicking going on, I'll do it myself."

She nudged my shoulder with hers. "So, what are you going to do then?"

I sighed, kicking a loose pebble on the path. "Figure out a way to work with her somehow? I don't really have a choice. And Richard—I don't know. I'll just try to keep my distance, I guess." I thought of Ren and felt relief that I wouldn't have to go to the dumb grand opening alone.

"I'm just going to say this because I know it's on your mind. You don't have to worry about Cody. I see him with her at the dog park almost every day when I'm out with Larry. He likes her, and she's nice to him."

"I know. Richard used to give me updates before he

started in on this whole forgiveness thing. I know he's fine, but I'm still not letting him go."

"Of course not. He needs you."

We walked in silence for a bit, the sounds of the park filling the space between us. Larry trotted ahead on his leash, no longer attracting stares like he used to whenever Lucy took him out. People were used to him now.

Finally, I broke the silence. "Maybe I'll try talking to her again."

"Bitches like her don't listen."

I rolled my eyes but couldn't help smiling. "Yeah, but I have to try something. I can't just avoid her forever."

She raised an eyebrow. "True. But don't let her walk all over you. Stand your ground."

We rounded a bend in the path, and the scent of blooming flowers filled my senses, relaxing me. I shrugged. "I have no idea what I'm supposed to do. I've never been in a situation like this. I'm usually a non-confrontational person."

She gave me a sidelong glance, her eyes filled with understanding and a bit of mischief. "Non-confrontational? She needs to be confronted. It's okay to be mad, and you're not fooling anyone. Underneath that calm exterior, you're a fighter.

I snorted, shaking my head. "Yeah, well, fighting isn't exactly my strong suit."

"I know. You want everyone to like you." She slipped her arm through mine. "You're a people pleaser, Piper. Even though you can be sarcastic sometimes, you're sweet on the inside. They don't deserve your grace. I mean it. Don't let her get to you."

"Okay. I'll try to remember that when I feel guilty later for being mean to her before."

"No guilt. She deserves it. There should be consequences for behavior like hers. Like, it's your turn to be the problem. No more taking people's shit then cleaning up after it. Okay?"

I considered her words as we continued walking. Larry bopped along, happily exploring every scent and leaf, just like a dog.

"I never thought of it that way. Why am I always the one to make things work? Being the peacemaker is a thankless job."

"You don't have to be. They messed up. Not you. Look." She stopped to face me. "No matter what happens, you're not alone. You have me and the sisters, and Larry. I'm sure I can get him to spit at her next time we see her at the dog park if I bribe him with a banana."

I laughed, the sound echoing along the trail. "You think Larry is bribable with a banana? He has standards. Also, gross. I've seen him spit before, and no thanks."

"Okay, let's tell Grandma all about it and let her go scorched earth."

"No, that's too much. We don't need that kind of trouble."

"Fine, I'll bring him by the shop when she replants and let him snack on the window box again."

"Every time, Lucy. Bring him by every time she fills that damn box."

She nudged my arm playfully. "You got it."

We did a lap around the gazebo before saying our goodbyes; then I headed home to finish out the rest of this craptastic day alone.

Party, schmarty. I decided to pick up some balloons and grocery store flowers on the day of the event and call it a day.

No, screw that. For now, I was done, and that was okay. I was not about to let that witch steal my dreams away from me.

Chapter 8
Ren

This was not a real date.

Those words were hard to believe when I stood outside Piper's door wearing my best suit and tie, about to pick her up for dinner.

Three knocks and one doorbell ring later, I heard the click of her footsteps approach the door, and my heart surged in my chest.

Fake? Yeah right. Nothing about the way my body reacted to her was fake.

The door swung open, revealing Piper in a stunning blue dress that hugged her curves.

Her hair cascaded in loose waves down her shoulders, framing her beautiful face with an elegance that took my breath away. Her eyes sparkled with a mixture of excitement and adorable nervous energy, and her lips curled into a soft, welcoming smile as she met my eyes.

"Wow," I breathed as, unable to help myself, my eyes roved over her. "You look stunning."

"Thanks. You look pretty good yourself."

I offered her my arm, and she slipped her hand through the crook of my elbow. As we made our way to my car parked in my driveway, the crisp evening air filled with a subtle tension that neither of us wanted to acknowledge.

"We could have walked," she stated as she buckled her seatbelt. "It's close enough."

"Would you rather?" I asked, trying to gauge her mood. She glanced up at me, a small, appreciative smile on her lips.

"Kind of. I'm a bit nervous," she admitted, her voice a soft murmur. "Maybe the walk will clear my head before we get there."

"I'm nervous too," I admitted. "This feels like—I don't even know what it feels like, if I'm being honest."

"I don't either." Her eyes met mine across the console. "But I still want to have dinner with you."

"Let's walk," I decided. "Stay put." Walking there and back would give me more time with her.

I got out, rounded the car, and opened her door, offering her my hand and keeping hold of it as she got out. I didn't want to let go. "May I hold your hand? Like this is a real date?"

"Do you want to?" Shy eyes met mine, then quickly looked away.

I squeezed her hand slightly, feeling the warmth and softness of her skin. "It would be good practice, don't you think?"

"Yeah. Good idea. I reserved the corner table in the

back. It's pretty private. We can ease our way into this thing."

This thing.

Whatever this thing turned out to be, I was into it.

The evening was cool, and the sky was dotted with twinkling stars peeking through the wispy clouds. Our footsteps echoed softly against the sidewalk in a gentle rhythm that soothed our simmering nerves.

We walked in comfortable silence. She was gorgeous in the early evening twilight. It felt almost magical out here. It felt *real*.

The Honeybrook Inn was just down the street, but every step felt significant. I stole glances at her, noticing her hair ruffling in the slight breeze and how the old-fashioned street lamps cast her in a golden glow. The way her lips curled into a slight smile when she thought I wasn't watching sent my heart racing. She was beyond beautiful.

"This place is bigger when you walk up to it," I remarked as we reached the Inn's parking lot entrance. "Driving by doesn't do it justice."

We stopped at the archway that led into the parking lot, and she turned to look up at me.

"Oh, yeah. It's huge, over fifty acres. You're going to love the restaurant. I already know what I'm getting."

"I do too," I said without thinking.

She tilted her head. "I thought this was your first time here."

"Oh, it is. I always look at the menu before I try a new place. Otherwise, I get lost in all the choices and take forever to order. It's embarrassing."

"You're cute."

"I am far from cute. I have a terrible reputation as a grouchy hardass divorce attorney, I'll have you know."

She laughed and we continued walking, our hands brushing against each other, until I grabbed hers again and held it tight.

"If you say so. You've been nothing but sweet to me."

"Of course. Who could ever be mean to you?"

Her face fell briefly before she caught herself and plastered on a smile. "I can think of a couple of people," she murmured. "I need to toughen up."

I stopped and turned to face her, catching the hint of vulnerability in her expression. "There's nothing wrong with being soft. It means you care, and that's a rare quality."

She looked up at me, her eyes searching mine. "Maybe, but it also means people think they can walk all over me. Like I said, I need to toughen up."

"You will do no such thing. You'll stay soft. And I will beat the living shit out of anyone who makes you lose that smile."

Her hand tightened in mine as a small smile tugged at the corner of her lips. "God, Ren. Why do I like that so much?"

"Because it's what you deserve." Her smile widened, and I felt a warmth spread through me, knowing I'd managed to lift her spirits, even just a little bit. "You're perfect the way you are—"

"Piper, sugar, come on in!" Our heads whipped to the side in sync at the sound. I squinted into the dusk to see an older woman on a Segway riding toward us, with three little pugs running along beside her.

"Grandma? What are you doing out here?"

"They have to do their business before bedtime. Grandpa is busy watching the TV. Your table is all ready. Is this him?"

"Oh. Yes. Excuse me. Grandma, this is Ren Moretti. Ren, this is my grandma, Mabel Darlington."

He offered his hand. "Nice to meet you, Mrs. Darlington."

"Nice to meet you in person. I know all about you from Paige, and I like you already, honey," she said as she stepped off the Segway and shook his hand. "Do you like dogs?"

"Love them."

Her eyes narrowed. "Cats?"

"Love them too."

"Sweet girls who need a nice man to take care of business?" She shot me a wink. Subtle, she was not.

"Grandma!" Piper squealed as I burst into laughter.

"Those are my favorite," I grabbed Piper's hand and kissed the back, grinning as her grandmother eyed me speculatively.

"What?" she smiled innocently at Piper. "You need someone to help you get Cody back, and he sure as heck helped your sister get what she needed."

"Ren and I are just seeing where this goes—it's casual. We have reservations, we can't be late. I'll catch you up about Cody later."

"Reservations," she scoffed. "Family is family. You sit

wherever you want, whenever you want. Reservations..." she muttered as she hopped back on her Segway to follow after the dogs. "Have fun tonight," she called over her shoulder.

"She means well. I don't—I don't even know what to say, other than I should have warned you about her and her nosy ways. How did I do, though? Casual? Seeing where things go?"

"Perfect." I grinned at her. "Exactly as we planned."

"Let's go inside." She grabbed my hand and pulled me after her.

As we walked the rest of the way toward the entrance, the soft crunch of gravel under our feet mingled with the distant hum of the pugs barking in the distance. The Inn stood majestically, its old-world, log cabin charm a perfect complement to the mountains dotted with spiky pines against the misty moonlit sky beyond the roofline.

"It's beautiful, Piper. Did you grow up coming here?"

"Yes, it's been in the family for generations. I love it here."

Stepping inside, we were greeted by the cozy, rustic elegance of The Honeybrook. The wooden beams overhead and the big, crackling fireplace in the corner were homey, yet refined. The check-in desk was off to the right, while to the left was the entrance to the restaurant.

The lobby was grand, with multiple places to gather. Leather couches flanked the fireplace, and a sitting area with a huge shelf full of books was in the far corner. I could tell this was a place to spend hours exploring.

I followed Piper toward the restaurant, smiling down

at her as she led the way and shaking the hostess's hand after she introduced us. Flickering candlelight cast soft shadows on the tables and décor as the hostess led us to our booth. I wanted to stop in the middle and look my fill, but figured I could do that once we were seated.

Piper ordered a bottle of wine, then we looked at each other, smiling as the hostess left our table.

"Do you remember the first time we met?" she asked.

My cheeks heated because, of course, I did. I remembered everything about her. "I do. It was one of Violet's coffee shop parties. You wore a bright red dress, and your hair was platinum and rolled up like a 1950s pinup girl. You were stunning. I asked Jake about you."

"You did?"

"I did." The sommelier interrupted to pour our glasses. "Thank you." I waited until she was out of earshot. "Um, yeah. I had to know who that beautiful blonde ray of sunshine was, so I made him tell me who you were."

"I asked Violet about you, too." I sucked in a breath, pleased that she'd noticed me back then. "You want to know something funny?" she asked.

"Always."

"Years ago, after my divorce, Violet tried to set me up with Jake. It was before they got together, of course. We were barely out of college."

I felt a pinch of discomfort. "I didn't know you were married." It wasn't the marriage; the thought of her and Jake is what bothered me. I shrugged it off, it was moot anyway.

"I was barely even married. It lasted about a year. We weren't even at the legal drinking age yet, and we both swore we were ready to be man and wife. Wild, isn't it?"

"Yeah, that's way too young." Tabby flashed through my mind, and I cleared my throat to cover my sudden burst of emotion. Should I mention her?

"Did I strike a nerve? I'm sorry."

My smile faltered for just a moment. "No, uh—I was married. She passed away a few years ago."

"Oh, Ren. I'm so sorry." She reached across the table, her fingers brushing mine. "I didn't mean to bring up a painful topic. I feel terrible for making light of marriage. I knew you were a widower, Violet told me. It slipped my mind. God, I wasn't thinking—"

"No, please. It's okay. She was my best friend." I cleared my throat, not quite believing that I was about to tell her everything. "We grew up together. She was sick, and her husband left her. I married her so I could take care of her. Make medical decisions, things like that. No one knows that part, that it wasn't real."

"How are *you* real?"

"What?"

"The more I learn about you, the more I admire you. You are selfless."

"I'm not," I stammered, embarrassed. "Not really."

"I won't say anything." Her eyes lit up with understanding, and it made me feel seen, truly seen for the first time in a long while. "You said no one knows..."

"I'm not sure why I told you, other than somehow, it felt right. I didn't tell Jake because he always encouraged me to focus on myself. He was the youngest, and with our dad the way he was, I sort of filled that role in the family."

She covered my hand with hers, squeezing lightly. "I'm honored you told me. I think you're amazing. No wonder you don't want to date anyone for real."

I picked up my menu, nodding, unsure if that was true anymore now that I was sitting across from Piper and her big brown eyes filled with sympathy. I desperately needed to change the topic and was afraid that I'd said too much. "Um, what are you having?"

Taking my not-so-subtle hint, a smile unfurled across her face. This dinner was turning into something unexpected. I felt a strange connection to her, like an inexplicable bond was forming between us.

"So, I always get the same thing when I'm here. It's my grandma's recipe, and it's my favorite thing in the world. But you have to tell me what you're getting first." Her eyes twinkled in the candlelight, lighting me up inside.

"Is this a test?" I joked to cover the feelings I was finding it increasingly harder to hide.

"No." She laughed, her cheeks turning pink from the wine. Or maybe it was me. I couldn't help but wish I was affecting her as much as she was affecting me. "Well, maybe it is. Let's see how much we have in common."

"Okay. I decided to order the chicken pot pie and mashed potatoes. What can I say, I'm a fan of comfort food."

She clapped her hands together, then clasped them

under her chin with an adorable tilt of her head. "Me too. The secret is fresh sage from her herb garden out back. It makes it taste kind of like Thanksgiving. I love it."

"So I passed?"

"Tell me you want marionberry pie after, and you pass with flying colors."

"It's my favorite. But I require the vanilla bean ice cream on top."

"Me too. It's the little things, Ren. I firmly believe that the small pleasures in life are what keeps me from losing my shit entirely."

"Right? Where would I be without Coffee Cabin's iced mochas? My morning jog now includes a stop for my fix on the way home."

"Ooh, good choice. Those are great. But whatever you do, don't try a vanilla bean scone or you'll add another habit to the list. It's my favorite."

We ordered, then continued talking about our favorite foods and little quirks between bites of chicken pot pie and sips of the delicious wine she'd chosen. Our connection was effortless, natural, and filled with laughter. I'd never felt like this before, and I didn't want this night with her to end. It felt like a beginning and not a pretense.

I paid the check, and she took my arm as we walked out of the restaurant with no remark or regard for anyone who may be watching. In fact, the subject of being seen together hadn't come up once, even after meeting her grandmother.

The street was quiet, the night enveloping us in cool mountain mist as we strolled along as if we were lost in our own little world.

Turning the corner, we reached Loganberry Lane. Her porchlight beckoned, signaling that our evening together was almost over.

I didn't want to let her go.

I took her hand as we approached the steps leading up to the porch. The air was crisp, and the stars were faintly twinkling through the clouds. Her heels clicked softly across the wooden planks until we reached the door.

"Thank you for tonight," she whispered, looking up at me. "But we didn't really practice anything. And I don't know if anyone noticed us or not. I was having too much fun with you to care, I'm sorry."

"Never apologize for having a good time. I loved every minute we spent together."

"I did too. You're a good dinner date, Ren." She turned to face me fully; she was nearly my height in her heels.

"So are you."

Our faces were mere inches apart, and I wanted nothing more than to kiss her goodnight. The world seemed to pause in this moment as I tried to decide what was appropriate.

We stood still a heartbeat longer, and then her hand tightened in mine. She tilted her head back with a sigh, and I wondered if I could trust myself not to take things too far, beyond the realm of practice or pretense or whatever we were doing. I didn't want to go somewhere I couldn't come back from.

"I haven't even known you a month yet," she murmured. "But it feels like way longer." Her pretty face was all I could see. Big eyes, full, pink lips, and all that golden hair spilling over her shoulders. I had it bad for her, and I didn't think she had any idea what she was doing to me.

"We've been meeting off and on for the last couple of years, Piper. At Violet's holiday parties, the wedding, and the reception, don't forget about that backyard barbeque Jake attempted to throw last summer. So, it's been way more than a month."

"You're right." Her hand drifted up my chest, fingers curling into my tie to pull me closer. "Maybe you should kiss me goodnight then."

"For practice?" I whispered, trying to get some clarity, but finding clarity seemed impossible with my hands skating around her waist and her luscious lips so close to mine.

Her eyes shifted from mine briefly before she answered. "Sure, why not, right?"

"Yeah..." I felt the warmth of her breath against my skin and got lost in an overwhelming surge of emotion. Trying not to overthink it, I gently cupped her face in my hands, my thumbs brushing lightly against her cheeks. She closed her eyes for a moment, leaning into my touch.

This was my cue. Slowly, I lowered my mouth to hers, the anticipation almost tangible. When our lips met, it was like a spark ignited between us. She was soft, so soft.

I deepened the kiss, losing myself in her taste and the way she fit perfectly against me.

When we finally broke apart, our foreheads resting against each other, I opened my eyes to find her gazing back at me with a look that mirrored my own.

Chapter 9
Piper

"What are we doing?" This had been the best date of my life, and it wasn't real. My heart broke a little bit at the thought of not having another night like this.

He looked at me with a tenderness that made my heart ache, yet I couldn't ignore the flashing neon sign in the back of my mind reminding me that none of this was real.

His arm tightened around my waist. "I'm kissing you goodnight," was his soft reply.

"Do it again." I couldn't resist him. I needed more.

He yanked me close and pressed his lips to mine. His lips were insistent and soft, even though he kissed me hard. The heat between us blazed into something undeniable, leaving us suspended in a moment that felt both fleeting and eternal at the same time. It was confusing.

"Like this?" he groaned against my mouth.

"Yeah." My voice was nothing but breath. "But maybe one more time."

"For practice?" He pulled back to whisper in my ear. "Is that what we're doing?"

Practice.

God, what was I getting myself into?

I gave a slight nod, unable to speak, my throat tight with feelings I was too afraid to express or even acknowledge.

"For practice?" he repeated, his voice low and rumbly.

I nodded.

And then he was kissing me again, with a fervor that matched my own.

The night faced away, leaving only the sensation of his lips moving against mine, his tongue in my mouth, the heat of his hands on my body, and the rhythm of our breaths intertwined.

My hesitation, that fear of having my heart broken, faded away in the intensity of this moment that felt so right. All that mattered was this.

We finally pulled apart, our breathing ragged and hearts pounding. His hand lingered on my cheek in a gentle caress that sent shivers down my spine.

"Maybe we should stop," he murmured, his eyes searching mine.

I bit my lip, the taste of his kiss still lingering. "Maybe." My voice was barely more than a whisper. "Yeah, you're right. I should probably go inside."

In this instant, the fear of getting my heart broken

again seemed a small price to pay for the chance to find out what could be, but he was right about stopping. It would be stupid to take this too far tonight.

"Goodnight, Piper."

"'Night."

"Get inside." His voice was pained. "I'll wait for you to lock up before I head home."

True to his word, he waited as I fumbled in my purse for my keys, then went inside. I didn't hear him walk away until my deadbolt slid into place.

By rote, I got ready for bed. Smcg and Nimbus swirled around my feet until we were tucked beneath the covers.

But I couldn't sleep. I lay there, staring at the ceiling, replaying my night with Ren like a movie in my brain. Smog curled up beside me, while Nimbus settled on the pillow by my head, his purring a soothing, yet ineffective lullaby.

Thoughts of Ren, of the way he had kissed me, his touch, the way his body felt beneath my hands, swirled in my mind, battling the notion that this was all nothing but an illusion. It had felt so real.

Morning came sooner than expected, sunlight streaming through the curtains, and with it, that same stupid sense of hope that wouldn't go away.

My phone pinged with an incoming text. My stomach sank when I realized it wasn't Ren. It was Paige.

Paige: Rise and shine, sleepyhead.
We're on the way.

What the hell? I hadn't made any plans with Paige. I rolled over, deciding to ignore her.

I was in an in-between period of my life—between jobs, between men, stuck somewhere between sadness and hope.

Damn it.

Sighing, I tossed the phone onto the bedside table and forced myself out of bed. The room was chilly, and I wrapped my arms around myself as I padded to the window. Drawing back the curtains, I let the sunlight bathe the room, hoping it might chase away the bleak shadows lurking in my brain.

I had no idea what Paige had planned. Part of me wanted to go back to bed and shut out the world, but another part—the part still clinging to that stupid sense of hope—convinced me that if I just tried to face the day with a smile, then maybe I'd see Ren later.

Smog meowed at me from his perch on the dresser while Nimbus sat in the corner, staring at the ceiling.

"Nimbus, quit it, you're freaking me out."

He meowed plaintively at me and pawed at the wall.

"Quit being weird and go find something to do," I told him. "I'll shower and get dressed, then we'll get both of you some breakfast."

I yanked the top drawer open, tossing a pair of

leggings and a matching hoodie on the bed before stripping off my caftan to head to the bathroom for a shower.

The water was a temporary escape, the steady stream lulling me into a semblance of calm. But as I stood there, head bowed beneath the spray, all the restless anticipation washed over me again.

The memory of kissing Ren last night played on a loop in my mind. I swear my lips still tingled.

After drying off, I pulled on my clothes, wondering how to get out of whatever Paige had in mind.

Nimbus wound around my legs as I finally reached the kitchen, and Smog greeted me with an expectant look. At least taking care of them gave me some structure, some sense of normalcy amid this weird limbo I was stuck in.

I was thrown off. I couldn't stop thinking of Ren. As I prepared my coffee, my phone pinged again. My heart skipped a beat, but it was another message from Paige telling me they were outside waiting for me, and *not* Ren telling me something wonderful.

I sighed, giving my coffee maker a longing glance as I snagged a bottle of water and headed to the door.

Paige was standing outside, her face lit up with excitement that could only come from being extremely caffeinated. She waved as I opened the door, then gestured to my sisters standing on my driveway, all in various forms of athleisure, along with Grandma on her Segway in a hot pink jogging suit—I guess she'd left the pugs at home.

"Trust me, you need this," Paige chirped, looping her

arm through mine and pulling me onto the porch before I could gather my wits enough to slam the door and lock myself inside.

I shot her a skeptical look but allowed myself to be dragged along. "Whatever this is better end with brunch and mimosas, or at least a cup of coffee," I muttered beneath my breath.

"Oh, it will. We're having coffee after at Coffee Cabin."

"Great. So, what's the plan?"

"We're going for a walk. Remember? We talked about it the other morning. Mom is still in Hawaii, obviously. But Grandma is here."

She flicked two fingers out in a mock salute as she drove her Segway in a small circle in the driveway. "It's time to start talking, honey," she called. "I've been hearing things about you. You need your family."

"What things?" I hedged as I shot a side-eye to Paige.

"So many things," Eliza answered. "I could blackmail half the town if I wanted to. People spill their guts when I'm making their morning coffee."

"We can walk, but I won't promise to talk. It's too early."

We started walking through the neighborhood, the morning air crisp and filled with the scent of blooming flowers and mountain mist.

The chatter started as a mix of gossip, plans for the week, and playful teasing about Grandma's newfound Segway skills. Paige kept her arm looped through mine.

Clearly, she suspected I'd make a break for it if one of them started grilling me.

"So, what's been going on with you?" Cara asked, her tone casual but her eyes sharp.

"Nothing much," I replied, trying to deflect what I knew she was going to ask about. "Planning for Something Sweet's grand opening, the cats, the usual."

"What about the hazelnut latte hottie, the other day?" Eliza burst out. "He was asking all about you, like what kind of coffee you liked, if he should bring you breakfast. He was looking all kinds of sexy in his gray joggers and that tight T-shirt. Ren, is it?"

"Yeah, he's my new neighbor, and you know who he is. He's Paige's lawyer and Jake's brother. He moved here from Portland."

"Oh, right." She nodded. "That explains why he looked familiar."

"Is this your attempt at some kind of intervention or fix-up? Or what? What is it you are all up to?"

Lucy shot me a knowing look. Did she tell them about Dana giving me shit? "No, I said nothing," she answered as if she'd read my mind. "We just want to make sure you're okay, like in general. You have a lot going on."

"Well, I'm okay. Thanks." I decided to take them at their word, feeling a small sense of comfort being surrounded by my family, even though I knew by the time this morning was over, they'd be all up in my business.

Paige squeezed my arm as we rounded the corner,

approaching the Coffee Cabin. "You know we're here for you, right? No matter what?"

I nodded, feeling a lump in my throat. "Yeah, I know."

"Stop." She held out her arm, and we all froze. "Shit," she muttered, yanking me back behind the bushes along the street. "Richard is here. With *her*. Freaking Dana."

I tried to peek around the bushes. "Is Cody with them?"

"Stay here. I'll check." Grandma buzzed around us on her Segway. "I own this damn place and I'm not hiding."

A few seconds later, Paige's phone went off with a text message.

"Cody isn't here," she informed us. "And Grandma is going home, she has to pee. And one of us should talk to her about texting and driving on that thing."

"Like she'd listen," Cara scoffed.

"She also said not to pull any shenanigans without her."

"Eff that," Lucy said. "I'm in the mood for a good shenanigan. I haven't started any shit since I tossed a Margarita in Skip McFadden's stupid face."

"No," I protested. "We're adults. We're going to get our coffee, find a spot to sit, and I'm going to say hello to them like a grown-up woman. No drink tossing. Promise me."

"Fine. I promise," she grumbled.

"I have to get to work in about ten minutes anyway," Eliza said. "Sadly, I don't have time for trouble today."

I hugged her. "Love you."

"Love you too. For the record, I'm available for trouble and shenanigans after I get off."

"Got it." She jogged around the bushes to go to work, leaving the four of us standing there looking at each other.

"We're really handling this like adults?" Paige asked, raising an eyebrow.

"Yes," I confirmed. "We are perfectly capable of acting like mature individuals."

Lucy rolled her eyes but followed us to the window, where we ordered our drinks and found a cozy table beneath the covered outdoor seating area.

Coffee Cabin was bustling with the morning rush, so Richard and Dana hadn't noticed me yet.

We settled into our spots, Lucy and Paige waiting for me to take the lead.

"So..." Paige broke the silence.

I took a deep breath, steeling myself. "So, I'll just go to their table and say hello and see where it goes from there. No shenanigans, no drama. I still have to work with Dana and share Cody with Richard, and I need to find a way to do that."

Cara snorted. "Drama follows this family around like a demented stalker. We'll be right here when it catches up to you."

Ignoring her, I sipped my coffee and then stood to head to their table.

"You got this," Paige encouraged. "Proud of you."

My heart pounded in my chest as I approached the

corner where Richard and Dana sat. The last thing I wanted was another confrontation, especially in a public place.

"Morning," I said, standing at the edge of their picnic table.

Richard looked up, a flicker of surprise crossing his face, quickly masked by indifference.

Dana, however, smiled warmly. I knew it wasn't genuine. She was up to something.

"I didn't expect to run into you this morning." Richard's tone was flat, foreboding. "How are you?"

"Um, I figured we needed to chat." I tried and failed to keep my voice steady. "About Cody, the bakery, all of it."

Richard patted the bench next to him. "Sure, have a seat."

I slid in next to him, trying to ignore the weight of Dana's gaze on me. "Look, I know things have been tense, but we need to sort this out for Cody's sake."

Dana nodded. "We should be on the same page."

"Dana and I have been talking," Richard began. "You really upset her the other day. She was inconsolable. I don't know how I would have calmed her down if it wasn't for Cody. She had a panic attack, Piper, and you know what a sweet dog Cody is, he helped pull her out of it."

I felt a pang of guilt. "I didn't know it was that bad. I'm sorry, Dana."

Tears filled her eyes. "It's okay. I just—couldn't believe you were willing to ruin our friendship over this."

"This? You mean you and Richard?"

She nodded tearfully as ice flooded my veins.

"What are you talking about? Me? *I* didn't start this. I didn't ruin anything—"

She didn't answer, save for a small hiccupping sob as she reached for a napkin to dab at her eyes.

What the heck was she playing at?

Richard took her hand across the table. "Baby, shh, it will be okay. I promised to take care of you, didn't I?"

"Richard and I are in love," she cried. "You two were never right for each other. You wouldn't have lasted, and you know that. Why can't you understand how I feel?"

"This is all moot," Richard cut in. "The point is, Dana needs Cody. She's fragile right now. I tried to get you to fix your friendship with her. But you couldn't let things go. She's really afraid of working with you, Piper."

"Afraid? Of me? I don't understand, I mean, what—?"

My mind raced as I tried to understand what they were getting at. I had to say something, but the words wouldn't come.

"Listen," I began, my voice trembling. "Let's not be hasty—"

Richard cut me off. "Dana will be going to Cody's check-up with me. When things settle down between the two of you, we can discuss whether you still want to be part of Cody's life and how that will work. But for now, it's best to keep our distance from each other. And about the bakery? We should discuss possibly buying you out. I don't see how you two can work together with how things are going. We wouldn't be here right now if you had only listened to reason. I'm sorry."

I stared at him in disbelief, every word like a blow to the chest. But now was not the time to argue with them. "I see. Um, I'll just leave you to your coffee."

"Thank you, Piper." Dana smiled, sugary sweet. "I'll email you about the shop."

I needed time to think.

But more importantly, I needed to get away from them before I started crying.

Chapter 10
Piper

With my head buzzing and my heart like a weight in my chest, I returned to my sisters' table.

Paige took one look at me and herded us to the back of the Coffee Cabin, threw open the door, and pushed me inside.

Eliza turned toward me, concern etched across her face. I tried to summon a smile, but it felt too heavy to lift.

"What happened?" she asked. "You've gone pale."

Finally, I found my voice. "Richard and Dana want to buy me out of the shop. And they think I should stay away from Cody for now."

"Like fucking hell. None of that is going to happen," Paige bit out.

"What is wrong with them?" Eliza hissed. "They can't just pull the rug out from under your life and go about their merry way. I don't think so."

Tears welled up in my eyes, blurring their faces. The

room closed in around me. I blinked rapidly, trying to control myself.

Lucy and Cara were at the back door. Without hesitation, they enveloped me in their arms.

Paige's fierce expression softened as she looked at me in sympathy. "We'll figure this out," she assured me. "They don't get to dictate your life."

"Yeah, they dropped a bomb, for sure," Lucy added. "But that doesn't mean what they say goes."

"Maybe if I gave up the shop, they'll let me have Cody," I wondered aloud.

"No," Paige hissed. "You were not born to give up your dreams and tolerate selfish assholes like them. You've worked too hard."

"Whatever they said to you is bullshit. I know it," Cara added.

"Now isn't the time to make decisions," Lucy said. "We'll talk to a lawyer if we have to. They can't do this to you."

"I'm not deciding anything right now." I heaved out a sigh. "It's just—why am I surprised? This is me. I'm not a woman who has good things happen to her—I'm just not. Richard looked at me like we hadn't spent nearly two years together, and he looked at her like—I mean, it's obvious he never cared about me the way I cared for him. I think I'm just not a grand gesture kind of girl. Dana doesn't have the money to buy me out, but he does. He's doing everything for her, buying my shop for her, and taking my dog for her. He never offered to help me. I didn't need it, but it's the thought that counts, right? He never even asked me about my plans for the bakery. But he's all in with her."

"Oh, Piper, no. Plenty of good things happen to you and you deserve way more than a selfish prick like him—"

"That's not it. I don't want him back. I want—"

"You want what he's giving to that cow, Dana," Eliza deduced. "But not from him."

"Love like that is not for me. I'm just going to have to accept that I'm never going to be swept off my feet. I'm always going to be a step on the road to someone else's happily ever after. This is my life."

"Please, you're breaking my heart." Paige pulled me into her arms. "Stop torturing yourself. We can fix this."

"Hello?" I pulled back. "I would love to stop torturing myself, but I don't seem to know the safe word."

Cara's expression was soft. "You don't need a safe word. You'll remember your strength once the shock wears off."

"Lucy nodded in agreement. "And we'll be here."

"I'm being negative right now, I know that. I'm not in a good headspace. I want to go home."

"My car is at my place. I'll go get it and drive you, okay?" Lucy lived behind the Honeybrook, in one of the forest cabins they rented. Some were long-term rentals, and the rest were for tourists and skiers.

"Thank you. I don't want to see anyone, especially them."

"I know, I totally understand. I'll be right back."

Lucy drove me home, insisting that we stop to pick

up lunch for me to eat later when I declined her offer to stay with me.

It was ratty robe and caftan time for this girl. My brief foray into hopeful optimism had been foolish, and it was all because of Ren. It was nice to let my little crush on him bloom—to fantasize, to dream of maybe having something real with him someday, but I had to go back to reality. Some things were not meant for me. Like love, romance, a man who would do anything to make me happy, shit like that. I could have a nice life without those things. I could be content, and I would be after I allowed myself a few days to get over it and figure out what to do for the rest of my life.

I texted Ren that the vet appointment was off and he didn't have to worry about me, then reentered hermit mode.

I spent the next few days in a haze of self-pity, alternating between binge-watching old *Friends* episodes and napping. My phone was a constant source of anxiety; the notifications were piling up, but I ignored them all. It was easier to avoid everyone, to pretend that the world outside my house didn't exist.

Lucky for me, I had plenty of groceries and cat food. Smog and Nimbus were thrilled by my constant presence, and napping was their favorite thing to do, so we were getting along just fine.

After a few days, the fog began to lift. I took a long, hot shower and let the water wash away the remnants of my mopey despair. Sometimes, I required solitude and silence to cope.

I had no desire to even think about Something Sweet or Dana and Richard, so I didn't. I could deal with that later; there was still plenty of time left until the bakery was scheduled to open anyway.

And as for Cody, maybe I'd ask Ren to help me find good legal advice. Ultimately, I could open a new bakery if I had to, but Cody was irreplaceable.

I was feeding Smog and Nimbus in the kitchen when I heard a knock at the door. My heart skidded to a halt in my chest, and I glanced at the clock. It was early, and I wasn't expecting anyone.

I moved cautiously toward the door. Even though I was rejoining the land of the living, I didn't want to talk to anyone about it.

Through the peephole, I saw Violet, holding baby Lyla—the namesake of Ren and Jake's mother. I threw open the door, and Violet greeted me with a warm, yet slightly knowing, and a little bit smug smile. We'd been best friends since kindergarten, and if anyone could get me to spill my guts, it was her, and she knew it.

"I'm not here to force you into talking to me and butt into your business. I know how you operate, and you'll tell me everything when you're ready. Here, take her." An attempt at reverse psychology—nice. She thrust Lyla into my arms, and my heart melted. It had been too long since I'd held this little angel. "I brought coffee and breakfast from the shop. It's in the car. I'll be right back. Oh, and Jake is on the way." Violet owned a coffee shop in Sweetbriar, the next town over. I used to step in and run the shop for her along with her sister, Holly, when she'd been too pregnant and miserable to work, and I'd often bake with her in the morning whenever I was free.

She darted off, down the porch steps toward her car, leaving me standing in the doorway with Lyla. I cradled her soft, tiny form against my chest and felt a soothing sense of calm wash over me.

I settled on the couch, with Lyla nestled comfortably in my arms. The smell of fresh coffee and pastries permeated the air as Violet reappeared, balancing two steaming cups and a paper bag. She placed it all on the coffee table with a look of sympathy on her face.

At first, we sipped our coffee in companionable silence, broken only by Lyla's adorable coos. But soon enough, I felt words bubbling up inside me, the need to confide in Violet like I always had, but I couldn't make them come out when it was only more of the same. Nothing good ever lasted for me and I didn't want to dump any more of my self-pitying bullcrap on her.

For now, my life was a mess, and pulling myself out of it would be a struggle.

"You don't have to talk," she said. "I'm just here to let you know that I love you. Jake is on the way from his office. I know this is a hard time, but he can help you get rid of Dana and probably get Cody back too. I want you to let him."

"I love you, too, and I'm not in the mood to talk about anything, so thank you for being here. Silent comfort works too. And, about Jake, yeah, I need help, and I'll take him up on it. I might be a pacifist at heart, but I'm not stupid."

"You're not stupid. You're a fighter. And I'm here for you. Always." She shot me a sidelong glance as she sipped her coffee. "You know you're not the mess you think you are."

"How do you always know what I'm thinking?" Despite my grim mood, I burst into laughter. "Quit reading my mind."

She shook her head, her expression still warm but insistent. "You know I can sit here all day if you'd like. We're in no rush. I know you too well, and I know you're worried and stressed out. I also know you don't want to be a burden when you think I'm busy with the baby."

"Well, yeah. You just gave birth; it hasn't been that long. That isn't easy. You must be exhausted."

"I'm doing great. Jake is wonderful with Lyla. So, I'm plenty rested. But you don't have to tell me anything. I made you a promise when I got here."

"I'll snap out of it," I assured her." I always do. I just need to reassess my expectations, so I stop setting myself up to get hurt."

"I get that. Just don't give up."

What I didn't tell her was that I already had given up. I was never falling in love again—ever.

Violet had a way of making me feel seen, even when I felt most invisible. As the minutes ticked by, the silence between us grew comfortable and comforting.

Jake stopped by after we'd finished with our coffee. Lyla had fallen asleep in my arms, so Violet got up to let him in.

"Hey," he whispered. "I can only stay a minute. Did you have a chance to talk?"

"She's on board," Violet informed him.

"Yes," I agreed. "I want to hire you. I know I need help. I have no idea where even to begin to fix this."

"Good, I do, so don't worry. For now, and I know this will be hard, just steer clear of them. No contact. Let them keep Cody for now. We want as much of what we do to be a surprise." His smile was reassuring and so much like Ren's, it was uncanny. "I'm going to turn around and get back to the office. Piper, you're family and we will get you through this. I promise."

As he left, I felt a deep sense of gratitude and relief for their friendship.

"He's right, you know," Violet said softly, breaking me out of my thoughts. "We're family. I'm glad you're letting him help. I don't want them taking advantage of you. You're too kindhearted sometimes. That sounded terrible." She laughed lightly. "How is being too kind a problem?"

"No, I get what you mean." I smiled. "I need to stick up for myself more. And thanks, Vi. I appreciate you two more than I can say."

Lyla stirred slightly in my arms, her tiny fingers curling around a strand of my hair, and I sighed.

I could handle this, and I would be okay.

Chapter 11
Ren

She didn't know I'd heard almost everything.

I'd been sitting at a table beneath an awning at Coffee Cabin, indulging in my iced mocha addiction, when I saw her talking to Richard and Dana—I didn't hear that part. Still, I knew they'd upset her because of the way Paige rushed her to the back of the building with her sisters. But I was just close enough to hear what was said through the open back door. Somehow, I knew she wouldn't want me to see her that way; we weren't there yet. So, I'd stayed out of sight until they left and then went home.

Jake had insisted I take some time off before starting work at the office, so I was stuck here fighting the urge to text her or bring her some coffee or do something to cheer her up.

Instead of doing any of that, I changed into my running clothes and took off on a jog. The fresh air and the rhythm of my feet on the pavement cleared my head

—until I reached the park and spotted Richard and what could only be Cody.

Fighting the temptation to knock his ass out and take Cody to Piper, I slowed my pace to watch them. The dog park was alive with activity as usual. Cody was the picture of canine exuberance, his fluffy golden coat gleaming in the sunlight. He was adorable, all tail wagging and infectious energy; he darted from one end of the park to the other, chasing after a ball and greeting every dog he encountered. He was clearly happy and well-loved, even with Richard, which was a relief to see.

"Hey! Ren!" I turned to see a pretty butterscotch blond walking a llama heading my way and had to do a double take. A llama?

"Hi." I stopped and waited for her to catch up.

"I'm Lucy," she greeted me. "This is Larry. I'm Piper's sister." Once we were up close, I recognized her from the Coffee Cabin earlier.

I held out a hand. "Nice to meet you, Lucy. Ren."

She tipped her head, gesturing to Larry, and gave me a look.

"Nice to meet you, Larry," I quickly added.

He tipped his head to match Lucy and whined. Okay then. My curiosity was more than piqued; I waited for her to speak.

"I know who you are. And I saw you the other day."

"Oh yeah?" I hedged, not wanting to give myself away.

"Yeah, the day Piper lost her shit with Dana—that

day. You were listening to us talk in the back of Coffee Cabin, weren't you?"

Embarrassed, I let my eyes drift closed. "I was and I'm sorry. I'm not proud of it."

"Why not? I watched you. I could see you care about her. That's a good thing. Obviously, I know all about you from Paige, and I approve."

Approve? Of what? I decided to let that slide and address her implied question.

"I do care. I like Piper a lot. But it was rude of me to listen in like I did."

"Screw that. Piper needs people like us on her side. She's too sweet for this world. I was surprised when I heard her screaming her head off at Dana. She finally stood up for herself a little bit, you know?"

I nodded, mulling over her words. "Yeah, I noticed that. Like she has a backbone but doesn't always show it?"

"Exactly. She has a temper. But it takes her an eternity to lose it, like way too long." Lucy confirmed. "She's all about peace and harmony but screw that. Some people need a swift kick in the butt, or a drink tossed in their face."

"You aren't wrong..."

Just as I was about to ask Lucy for more insights about Piper, Richard sauntered up, a smirk playing on his lips as he approached us with Cody trotting happily alongside him. Cody was eager to reach Lucy; his tail wagged furiously, and his eyes sparked joy when he saw her.

"Watch out for this one," Richard said to me instead of a polite greeting. "I assume you're still dating Piper. Lucy is a protective little viper. They all are when it comes to her."

"Nice to see you too, Richard." She drawled and handed me Larry's leash. She bent to pet Cody, who was immediately all over her, wiggling like mad as he licked her face and whined. "I know, boy. I love you, too."

"Watch your mouth," I snapped. "That's my woman and her sisters you're talking about."

He laughed in response, and his amusement made my anger flare.

"What is your problem?" I glowered at him, trying to keep my temper in check.

His smirk widened, and he shrugged nonchalantly. "I'm not being serious. It's all in good fun."

"Yeah, well, try having fun without being an asshole."

"This is great," he snarked. "Piper sure can bring the protective side out of people."

"Except for you, right?" Lucy stood, glowering at him. "You treated her like shit."

"You don't know her like I do." He insisted. "She's unforgiving. I deserve what I got, I accept it, but Dana does not."

Lucy was incensed. "Who the hell do you think you are? Both of you betrayed her."

I held up a hand to silence them both. "You don't know Piper at all," I ground out. "And you sure as fuck don't know me or you'd be on the opposite side of the park keeping your fucking mouth closed."

Lucy grinned, with a glint of mischief shining in her eyes. "Ooh, I like you." She took Larry's leash from my hand and smacked the side of my arm. "A lot."

I grunted in response.

"Gotcha, come on, boy. Time to go home, *mama* is waiting for you." Richard's smirk returned as he patted the top of Cody's head and walked away. Cody hesitated, torn between following him and staying close to Lucy, but eventually, he trotted after Richard, casting a forlorn glance back in our direction.

"That stupid asshole," Lucy muttered. "He knows how much Piper loves that dog."

"I do not like him," I stated.

"You made that obvious." She drew her head back as she studied my face. "And in case you were wondering, I don't either."

I glanced down at her, a smile tilting my mouth up at the corner. "Nope, it's pretty clear where you stand, too."

"Good. To hell with him and to hell with making peace. Screw that guy."

We stood for a moment, watching as Richard and Cody faded into the distance.

I heaved out a sigh, wondering what I could do about the situation, other than chasing him down to beat the shit out of him and take Cody home with me.

"So, you and Piper, huh?" Lucy's eyebrows raised as she aimed a satisfied smile my way.

Shit.

I might have gone a little too far. We were supposed

to create simple fake dating rumors—not what I'd just done.

Damn my temper.

"You don't have to answer that. I'm just nosy." She laughed. "But you are invited to the weenie roast. Catch you later, Ren."

"Yeah, later," I answered distractedly, wondering how in the hell I would bring this up with Piper. "Wait, weenie roast?"

"Yeah, weenie roast. I'll tell Piper I invited you."

She was already walking away, so I decided to forget about the weenie roast—was that a metaphor, or a barbecue? Never mind. I had bigger problems to figure out now, like how to tell Piper what I'd just done.

"Come on, Larry, you have a planter box to snack on," she muttered as she led him toward Something Sweet.

I turned to head home, then felt the first raindrop hit my forehead. Great. Just what I needed. I broke into a sprint, hoping to get home before the skies opened up completely. My luck, of course, was nonexistent. The rain started to pour, each drop feeling like a cold slap to my face. I hunched my shoulders, grumbling to myself about how this day couldn't get any worse.

The streets were nearly empty, with only a few poor fools like me outside scrambling for shelter. The rain quickly soaked through my clothes, making me shiver in the growing chill of the evening. I sped up, my shoes splashing through puddles and sending water up my legs.

As I turned the corner, still fuming and cursing under

my breath, I saw Piper sitting on her porch. Her presence would have made me smile if I wasn't drenched to the bone and freezing my fucking ass off. I hesitated, my mind racing with a million thoughts about what I should say to her. I decided to cut across her lawn to reach her quicker. I had to tell her what I'd said to Richard before she heard it from anyone else.

Bad idea.

My foot hit a slick patch of grass and I went down hard, my feet flying out from under me. I landed with a thud, the wind momentarily knocked out of me, and the rain continued its relentless assault. I groaned, both from the pain and the sheer embarrassment. This day was shit. I should have never left my damn house.

Piper rushed over, her concern evident even through the curtain of rain. "Ren! Are you okay?" she called, her voice cutting through the storm.

I tried to muster some dignity as I pushed myself up, wincing at the mud caking my hands and clothes. "Yeah, just perfect," I muttered, flinching in pain as I stood up. "Never fucking better." The gravity of the situation and the pain were momentarily forgotten as my annoyance and grumpiness surged to the forefront. I had trouble deciding what was more irritating—the rain or the fact that Piper had to see me like this.

"Oh my god, you're all muddy!"

"Yeah, thanks for pointing that out," I drawled, trying to brush off some of the mud. "I slipped."

Piper extended a hand to help me up, her grip strong and steady despite my awkwardness. "Come on, let's get you cleaned up. You can't stay out here in the rain forever."

As much as my pride protested, I let her help me to my feet. Once I was up, she took my hand and walked me to my house and damn it, I let her.

Once inside, the warmth from the heater started to seep into my cold, wet bones, and I sighed with a mixture of relief and exhaustion.

"Where's your bathroom?" She demanded.

I grunted and pointed toward the hallway. With an amused side eye, she tugged me toward it, shoving the door open and yanking me inside. "Sit," she ordered, pointing at the edge of the tub.

I sat. This bossy side of her was intriguing and weirdly, also kind of hot.

She handed me a towel, and I began to dry myself off, shivering slightly. "Thanks," I muttered, feeling a bit sheepish.

She nodded, her eyes filled with a mixture of concern and amusement. "You look like you've had a rough day."

"You could say that," I replied, running the towel over my hair.

"Take a shower. I'll be in your living room, and then we'll examine your hands and elbows. You're bleeding."

I glanced down at my hands and elbows, noticing the streaks of blood for the first time. "I'm bleeding?" I murmured, more to myself than to Piper. The realization hit me like a ton of bricks, and suddenly the dull throbbing in my hands intensified, transforming into a sharp, stinging pain. "Shit," I exclaimed, instinctively clutching my hands together.

"I know. That has to hurt. Go wash up, get warm. I'll wait."

"Thanks. But I can take it from here. You don't have to take care of me. I'll be okay."

"All right. If you're sure?"

"Yeah, I'm sure. I got this. Thank you for helping me up. I'll be okay."

"Of course. I'll see you later."

She stepped out of the bathroom, closing the door behind her, and I turned the water on. I was freezing and fucking miserable. I stepped in with a huge sigh.

The hot water cascaded over me, washing away the grime and blood, and the warmth began to soothe my aching muscles. I stood there for a while, letting the steam envelop me, feeling the tension slowly ebb.

My mind wandered to the day's events, the chaos with Richard, the rain, the fall, and how Piper's presence in my home felt right. I liked her here. Her assertiveness was strangely comforting and only a little bit embarrassing.

When I'd used up all the hot water, I turned off the shower, dried myself off, and stepped back into the hallway, feeling slightly more human.

Piper was waiting in the living room with a small first aid kit on the coffee table.

"It's later," she said with a smirk. "Do not argue with me. I can see your elbow, and you can't. Trust me, you need my help."

My mouth fell open, and suddenly I was acutely aware that I was wearing only a towel.

"Piper, I—" I began to protest, but she silenced me with a look.

"Sit down," she said firmly. "You need to be taken care of."

I hesitated for a moment before dropping onto the couch beside her. Piper's presence had a way of making me feel both vulnerable and safe at the same time. It was a strange duality. What was also strange was that I did what she said. No one told me what to do.

She grabbed the first aid kit and began to clean my wounds with a gentle yet determined touch. The antiseptic stung, making me wince, but she was quick and efficient, moving with a grace that belied the sternness in her voice from before.

Her focus was unwavering, her hands steady as she worked. I couldn't help but feel a sense of gratitude for her assertiveness, for her willingness to step in and take control when I was too weary to do so myself. I was just going to go to bed and change the sheets if I got blood on them.

After wrapping the bandages around my hands and elbows, she leaned back and inspected her work. "There," she said, a hint of satisfaction in her tone. "You'll be right as rain. Pun intended." Her laughing eyes met mine for a moment, and I smiled.

After she finished tidying up the first aid kit, I noticed her gaze lingering on me a bit longer than usual. Her eyes traveled from my elbow to my shoulders, and I could see a faint blush creeping across her cheeks. She quickly averted her gaze, but the moment didn't escape me. It was a subtle sign that she found me attractive, and it made me feel—it exhilarated me, which also kind of freaked me out.

"Thanks," I mumbled, pulling the towel tighter around myself. Piper's eyes flicked back to me, and for a fraction of a second, I saw a mix of embarrassment and something else—something that made my pulse quicken.

Was this a sign that she maybe wanted more with me? More than just friendship and a few fake dates?

She cleared her throat, trying to regain her composure. "Ummm, so, yeah. Just keep the wounds clean, you know what to do."

"I do. So, listen. I need to tell you something before you go. I ran into your ex today. Lucy was there too, and her llama, which is weird, but okay."

"Yeah, I had a run-in with Dana recently, too. I suspect they might be planning to steal my bakery out from under me." She shook her head; it seemed like she was resigned to the fact that they would keep messing with her, and—*no*, not under my watch.

I was immediately incensed, angrier than I was after my encounter with Richard before. "I do not like him," I all but growled. "He's too free about running his fucking mouth about you. We need to be seen together. Tonight."

"What?" Her eyebrows shot to her hairline. Clearly, she was not used to someone who was ready to throw down for her.

"What's his favorite place in town?" I demanded.

"The Pennywhistle," she answered breathlessly, with her eyes big. "He's addicted to their burgers."

"Good. That's *our* place now. Go home. Put on something pretty. I'm taking you to dinner. I'll pick you up in ten minutes."

"Um." She shrugged lightly, "If you want pretty, I'll need at least twenty."

I allowed myself another good look at her, sitting prim and proper on my couch, wearing another sexy as fuck caftan—this one in a red silky material that I wanted to feel against my skin. My skin, which I was becoming increasingly aware of, was mostly exposed.

"We can leave right now for pretty, golden girl. But I doubt you want to go out wearing that caftan."

"Oh." She turned bright red. "Right."

I watched her, taking in every detail—the curve of her neck, the way her hair fell softly around her shoulders. The light in her eyes that seemed to dance with every thought and emotion.

I wanted to be near her.

My pulse quickened, and my heart raced with feelings I hadn't experienced in far too many years to count.

She had taken care of me—insisted on it.

Didn't listen to my bullshit and bandaged me up. So, I was sure as fuck going to protect her from that motherfucker spreading bullshit about her around town.

"I'll see you in twenty minutes. Okay?" I said softly.

"Okay," she murmured.

Chapter 12
Piper

Twenty minutes. Yeah right. If I were already wearing makeup, then maybe.

I shuffled rapidly from Ren's house to mine, not wanting to run and end up falling on my ass like he had just done.

I made it to my porch, threw open the door, and holy hell, now I only had about nineteen minutes.

"Not now. You have plenty of food," I tossed over my shoulder to Smog and Nimbus as I dashed up the stairs, refusing to think about why my heart was racing so fast and I couldn't seem to catch my breath.

"Eighteen minutes!" I mumbled as I made it to my bedroom, then jolted to a sudden stop by my bed.

"This is all for show." He had a run-in with Richard. This was part of our deal, nothing but a fake date so word would get back to Richard, damn it. He wasn't even part of my life anymore, but he was still freaking ruining it, the jerkface loser. No, not ruining. He could try, but I would always be great. Fuck him. No one could ruin my life except myself, and I always managed to come out on top. This time would be no exception.

A glance at the clock on my nightstand told me I had sixteen and a half minutes. I wrinkled my nose. I wouldn't need it.

After a brief rummage through my closet, I tossed a pair of jeans and a sweater on my bed along with a pair of winter boots. Cute and casual would be fine. More than that would be overkill.

In the bathroom, I ran a brush through my hair and quickly applied mascara and a slick of soft red lip gloss. "Pow!" I grinned at my reflection. "You got this." Laughing at my positive affirmations, I quickly dressed, grabbed my purse, and made it back downstairs in time to hear Ren knock on the door. "Perfect."

He greeted me with a wide grin. His messy hair and relaxed demeanor made my heart flutter, despite my resolve to keep tonight strictly business. This wasn't about him; it was about proving to everyone that I could move on from losers like Richard, and Ren was going to help me do it.

"You look great," he said, his eyes sparkling with genuine admiration.

"Thanks," I replied, trying to match his enthusiasm. "Ready to get this over with?"

"Get it over with? Ouch." Ren laughed, a warm sound that eased my anxiety. "Let's make this fun instead." He held his fist out for a bump.

I bumped it back with a smile. "I can do that."

We walked to his car, chatting about inconsequential things, the banter light and easy. The drive to the Pennywhistle was short, and the town was beautiful under the rain-drenched, misty moonlight.

The Pennywhistle Pantry was a charming relic of a bygone era. As Ren and I walked through the door, the bell above jingled, announcing our arrival. The warm glow of vintage neon lights bathed the room in a nostalgic hue, casting soft shadows on the polished chrome stools and the checkered black-and-white floor. Booths lined the walls, their red leather seats inviting us to sink into their squeaky comfort.

The air was filled with the aroma of frying bacon, fresh coffee, and the sweet hints of milkshakes being blended behind the counter. A jukebox stood in the corner, softly playing tunes from the 50s, adding to the ambiance.

Servers in classic uniforms, complete with aprons and jaunty caps, bustled around, serving plates piled high with pancakes, burgers, and golden fries. The place was lively but cozy, filled with the hum of conversations and the clatter of dishes.

Ren gestured towards a booth near the window, and we settled in, the worn leather creaking slightly beneath us. I took a moment to absorb the surroundings, feeling a wave of comfort wash over me. This diner, with its timeless charm, was the perfect escape from the drama and tension that had plagued my thoughts earlier. And I was going to have fun if it killed me, damn it.

I'd been here with Richard a million times, but it felt different tonight—time to exorcise some more freaking demons.

Ren caught my eye and smiled. "Feels like stepping back in time, doesn't it?"

I laughed because his meaning and mine were totally different. I was remembering being here with Richard, and he was probably thinking of a 1950s TV show or something like that. "Yeah, it's nice. I've always loved it here."

He picked up the menu. "What's your favorite?"

"I don't know yet. I'm choosing a new favorite tonight," I looked up at him, my lips tilting at the corner. "Moving on to new things." His eyes were so gorgeous, warm and sparkling as he looked at me. "Better things," I added in a soft whisper.

"I like that. You deserve some peace."

Our server came by with coffee, tilting her head to the cups already on the table, and eyeing us curiously as she poured. I guess we were being *seen*. Score one point for Piper and Ren and the fake dating plan. We told her we needed a few more minutes to order, and she headed back to the kitchen.

Our hands brushed against each other as we both reached for the cream at the same time. "You go first," I offered.

"Thanks," he poured a scant amount of cream in his coffee, then added a spoonful of sugar. "How do you feel about chicken fried steak?" he asked.

"I love it. But you should let me make it for you some-time and get something else here. I have my grandma's recipe, and it's untouchable."

"Ahh, I'll take you up on that. It's one of my peren-nial favorites. I order it whenever it's on a menu."

Did I just invite him to dinner? What the hell is wrong with me?

For someone determined not to get into another rela-tionship, when it came to Ren, it felt like I was practically throwing myself at him. Whatever.

"I'm getting a BLT," I declared. "I've never had one here, but I've had the bacon and it's excellent. In fact, I sometimes come here just for the bacon. I'll order break-fast with extra bacon and just eat that, then take the scrambled eggs home for Nimbus and Smog." I grinned, looking up at him through my lashes. "Look at me revealing shameful secrets."

"Next time, just get a plate of bacon." His eyes were earnest, then he winked, and I swear my heart stopped beating for a second. "Never let anyone bacon shame you, Piper."

"You're right. But I'm starving and I want extra crispy tots, so I'm going for the whole shebang."

"That sounds good. Sign me up."

We ordered our food—both of us getting BLTs. He asked for extra bacon on the side and gave me half of it. Was he trying to make me fall in love with him? Because, hello? It was working.

We made small talk while we ate, chatting about

Honeybrook Hollow, places he wanted to try and hadn't yet, the events the town had listed on the marquee in the park, and oohed and ahhed over our new shared favorite: The Pennywhistle Pantry's BLT.

But I hardly remembered any of it when all I could think about was that I was sitting with the sweetest, kindest, sexiest man I had ever met in my life.

I was in trouble—big fat trouble shaped like tall, dark, and handsome Ren.

"This is my new favorite place. Sorry to your grandparents and the Honeybrook, but I love it here. I might see if I can rent a booth and move in."

"Told you." I grinned at him. "It's all about the bacon."

"How is the dessert? Want something?"

"I have a better idea—"

"Immediate yes," he cut me off with a huge smile. "After the BLT, I trust you implicitly."

As I laughed, I felt something change inside me. The sound of my own laughter—real and not forced or faked to make someone feel good—was like an old favorite song I hadn't heard in far too long, and it was all Ren who was bringing it out of me. I glanced at him, and my heart fluttered with unmistakable attraction. His smile was infectious, his eyes twinkling with mischief as he talked about the bacon that had become our inside joke.

Every moment spent with him felt like discovering a new favorite song, each note sweeter than the last. I wanted more of it—more of him. My laughter wasn't just an expression of joy; it was a bridge to something deeper, a connection that was growing stronger with every shared smile and every playful tease.

I was beginning to like him more than I ever thought possible. His charm was undeniable, and the way he made me feel was something I couldn't ignore. Spending time with him was wonderful, and I found myself wanting to linger in his presence, soaking up every bit of this newfound happiness.

I was drawn to him, not just by his looks, but by the way he made me feel.

"Come to Something Sweet with me," I invited. "I'll show you around, and we can make cupcakes for dessert. Any kind you want." Was it stupid to invite him deeper into my life like this? Probably, but I wanted to see how he would react.

Would he realize I was bringing him into my dream with me?

Would he grasp the importance?

Like a fool, I was testing someone who wasn't even mine, but it felt right, so I brushed my fears aside and went with my gut.

"I would love that," he said, his voice steady but betraying a hint of enthusiasm, like he didn't want to appear overly eager.

"Okay then." I nodded, trying not to be too eager as well.

We paid the check and then made the short drive to Something Sweet.

When Ren and I walked inside, I couldn't help but feel a sense of pride as I saw his reaction. The bakery was decorated in pink and white, charming, and pretty in every corner.

The kitchen, my pride and joy, was immaculate. Gleaming countertops reflected the soft light from the pastel-painted walls, and everything was in its perfect place. The scent of sugar and spices lingered in the air, making the space feel warm and inviting. Ren's eyes widened slightly as he took in the surroundings, and I could tell he was impressed.

"This is amazing, Piper," he said, his voice filled with genuine admiration.

"Thank you." I smiled, feeling a flutter of happiness. "It turned out exactly as I envisioned. Let's get started on those cupcakes. What's your favorite?"

"Chocolate. Always. I may or may not be a legit chocoholic."

"Birds of a feather..."

"You too?"

"Yep." I moved around the kitchen, gathering ingredients as I spoke. "We're making my quadruple chocolate cupcakes. Chocolate cake, chocolate ganache filling, chocolate cream cheese frosting, then either curls, mini chips, or sprinkles. I'll let you choose.

"Chips. Please let me know when I can help. You're the pro I don't want to get in your way."

Ren watched as I measured out the cocoa powder, his gaze warm and intense. I could feel the electricity between us, a subtle but undeniable attraction, as I let him sift the dry ingredients together. We exchanged playful smiles and meaningful glances, the air around us buzzing with an unspoken chemistry. It took everything in me not to shove everything off the counter and have my way with him.

The cupcakes went into the oven, and I moved on to the ganache.

"Here," I said, handing Ren a spoon coated in rich chocolate. "Taste this."

He took the spoon from my hand, his fingers brushing against mine, sending a shiver up my spine. He closed his eyes as he tasted the ganache, a soft moan escaping his lips. "Delicious," he murmured.

Unable to resist, I dipped my finger into the ganache and tasted it myself, savoring the smooth, decadent chocolate. Ren's eyes met mine, and in that moment, I felt a magnetic pull drawing us closer. I leaned in, my lips brushing against his, tasting the sweetness of chocolate on his breath.

"You're delicious," I whispered.

Our kiss deepened, and his hand on my waist pulled me closer, backing me up until my back was against the wall and we didn't have a single inch between us.

I couldn't breathe. I couldn't think. All I could feel was him. I lifted onto the balls of my feet and ran my hands into his hair so he couldn't pull away. His tongue slid against mine in a soft swirl. He made my head spin until I was in a drunken state of anticipation, waiting to see what he'd do. He could do anything, as long as he didn't stop kissing me.

His mouth dropped to my neck, tongue darting out to taste the hollow of my throat as he cupped my breast with his palm. He traced my nipple with his thumb, slowly, back and forth, then pressing gently.

"Is this okay?" he asked.

"Yes," I moaned, eyes drifting closed as I leaned into his hand. "More."

Arms around my waist became hands lifting the hem of my sweater as I raised my arms over my head, and his mouth replaced his fingers as he tugged the cup of my bra down.

"You're so pretty, sweetheart. So soft." He flattened his tongue, then grazed the peak of my nipple with his teeth. Waves of desire pooled inside me as he trailed his lips to the other breast and unhooked my bra.

"I want to touch you too." I untucked his shirt and pulled. Smiling when he reached his hand behind his neck and took it off.

The muscular plane of his chest was irresistible. I ran my hands up and down, the light dusting of hair tickling my palms. "Kiss me again," I murmured.

He slammed his mouth against mine, stealing my breath and sending shivers down my spine as I rose on my tiptoes again and flung my arms around his neck.

We went out of control, hands touching everywhere we could reach, tongues and teeth clashing. It was like this was our only chance to learn everything we could about each other before we ran out of time.

He pulled away, resting his forehead against mine. I could feel his panting breath against my mouth. "Piper—"

I met his eyes with mine. His were dark with desire. A muscle ticked in his jaw, and I traced it with a fingertip.

"What's wrong?" I asked. "Why did you stop?"

"Nothing's wrong. Everything feels too right. Way too right." He ran a hand down his face and looked away.

"Okay…" I took a step back, crossing my arms over my chest.

His hands balled into fists at his side as if he were holding himself back. "I don't want to push you into something you aren't ready for. We're supposed to be pretending. Aren't we?"

I looked away, then bent to pick up my sweater and bra. "That's fair. I guess."

"I—trust me when I say I would like nothing more than to bend you over this counter and finish what we just started."

The timer went off for the cupcakes. But I was still focused on the thought of being bent over the counter by Ren.

"Crap." I slipped into my sweater and grabbed the oven mitts to get the cupcakes.

"Are you okay?" He picked up his shirt and put it back on.

I took a deep breath and turned to face him. "I'm fine. Just needed to get these cupcakes out before they burned."

He nodded, his eyes still smoldering. "Alright then. Let's not let these cupcakes go to waste."

"Yeah. I promised you dessert." I felt awkward. But

his smile, though hesitant and unsure, made me feel a bit better.

We both laughed, breaking the tension, though the heat between us still simmered just beneath the surface.

He helped me place the cupcakes on the cooling rack, then into the fridge so they'd cool faster. His hands brushed mine occasionally, sending little sparks of electricity through my fingertips.

I glanced up at him, and he was watching me, a mixture of desire and restraint written clearly on his face.

"Maybe we should clean up," he suggested.

I nodded, feeling the awkwardness settle. We started cleaning up, moving around each other with a careful choreography. The space between us felt charged, like a taut wire ready to snap.

We stacked dishes, wiped counters, and exchanged glances that said more than words ever could. Ren's presence was steady, grounding me as I tried to sort through my tangled emotions.

When the kitchen was spotless, he turned to me, his expression softening. "Do you want to talk about it?"

I nodded. The mood was broken. "Are we okay? I didn't mean to lead you on—"

"You didn't lead me on. And I'm okay as long as you are."

"Good. I want to be okay."

"See? I know you're going through some shit, Piper. What kind of an asshole would I be if I rushed you into more than you're ready for?"

"You're a good guy, Ren."

It was for the best. Complicating my life when it was already in a precarious place wasn't wise. I needed time before moving on, and that was okay.

He drove me home and walked me to my door, waiting outside until I was safely inside and had locked the door.

Chapter 13
Piper

I awoke abruptly to the sound of Nimbus yowling in the corner of my room. My heart pounded as I tried to shake off the remnants of sleep to see what he was going on about.

The room was dimly lit, shadows dancing on the walls from the moonlight outside. It didn't make sense, but I was too afraid to turn on the light. What if I saw something terrible?

I squinted into the darkness. Usually, he just stared and maybe scratched at the walls a little bit. But this was different. His back was arched with his fur standing on end, eyes wide and fixed on something I couldn't see. His ears were flattened against his head, and his low growl sent chills down my spine.

Smog was acting weird, too. He sat at my feet, alert as if he were guarding me.

My initial grogginess faded quickly as I became more aware. I strained to hear any other sounds amidst

Nimbus's yowling. That's when I heard a faint, almost imperceptible noise coming from within the walls. It was a soft scratching, accompanied by a low, rustling sound.

My pulse quickened, and an uneasy feeling settled in the pit of my stomach. I had to get the hell out of here.

Yeah, I joked about this house being haunted, but I never thought it really was, or I would have moved the frick out at the first sign. What the hell was going on?

I threw back the covers and swung my legs over the side of the bed, my feet touching the cold floor. With each step, I felt a growing sense of dread. Nimbus continued his vocal protest, his eyes never leaving the corner, drifting up and down the wall as he pawed at the baseboard and softly growled.

As I approached him, the scratching noise grew louder and more insistent. Nimbus hissed and lunged at the wall, scratching at it furiously as his growls turned into trilling yowls, a sound I'd never heard from him.

I turned, searching for Smog. He was still perched at the foot of the bed, alert and keeping an eye on everything.

"We're getting out of here." I gathered Smog in my arms, then bent to grab Nimbus, but he darted under the bed, hissing, spitting, and growling his fluffy brains out.

"I'll come back for you." He was completely freaked out, fur standing on end. If I tried to catch him, he'd probably scratch the hell out of me. "Shit, shit, shit," I chanted as I darted out the door and down the stairs.

I threw open the front door and was met by the crisp night air. I shivered in the dark as Smog twisted in my arms, but I held him close as I hurried down the steps and onto the walkway.

I took a few deep breaths, trying to calm my racing heart as I stood there. The faint glow of the streetlights cast long shadows across the yard. I turned to look at the house, the scratching sound still echoing in my ears. Nimbus's yowling could still be heard faintly as I'd left the front door open.

Just then, the headlights of a car swept into the driveway. Ren stepped out, concern etched on his face as he took in my disheveled and freaked-out appearance. I stood there shaking, my cat held tightly in my arms.

"What's going on?" He asked, voice low and steady.

"There's something in there," I replied, my voice shaking. "I heard it... scratching and rustling in the walls. Nimbus went wild. I've never seen him like that—"

"I'll check it out."

"No! What if it's a ghost? Wait, I have to get Nimbus. I can't leave him in there. Oh my god—"

"Get in my car. I'll go inside, yeah?"

"But what if it gets you? You could be killed!"

"There's no such thing as ghosts. It's probably an animal, an insect nest, a beehive, I don't know, something like that. There's a rational explanation. This house is old, Piper. Not haunted. I was just teasing you the other day." He gestured to his car. "Get inside, get warm. I'll be right back. Promise."

"No, I'm coming with you. I can't ask you to go in there by yourself. You shouldn't die alone, rescuing my cat, who has gone out of his mind..."

He smiled softly and held his hand out. "We'll be okay."

"Okay..." I took his hand, only slightly embarrassed that I held it in a vice grip. I was scared out of my mind.

We entered the house, and I opened the downstairs half bath, and put Smog in there. He protested loudly.

"Just for a minute, I promise. *Shh,* we have to rescue your brother."

"Where was the noise?"

"In my bedroom. Nimbus woke me up, scratching at the walls and yowling. None of this feels real. Am I awake? Are you really here?"

"I'm really here, sweetheart." He chuckled. "Let's go upstairs."

I followed him up the stairs, sticking close to his back, wishing I could call *Ghostbusters* or Sam and Dean, anything to avoid confronting the noise in my room.

We stopped in the hallway right outside my open door. Nimbus was back in the corner, staring at the ceiling where we could hear the same light scratching as before. But now that I was calm, I could hear it in the hallway above our heads as well.

"Tell me you hear it too, and I'm not stuck in a bizarre, haunted house-themed lucid dream."

"I hear it," he confirmed. "There's definitely something up there. What's above your room?"

"The attic," I answered, with my eyes glued to the ceiling. "But I don't go in there."

He looked at me like he thought I was cute, and a smile played about his lips. "Why not?"

I met his eyes, glad for the dim light since my cheeks had gone up in flames. This night was embarrassing on so many levels. "Because it's dusty and scary and old. Mrs. Fenwick, uh, the previous owner, left her porcelain doll collection up there when she moved out. She said I could keep it, but I don't like how they look at me. I don't want anything to do with them. I was going to hire someone to clear it out up there, but I haven't gotten around to it yet."

"God, I've never met anybody as fucking adorable as you are, Piper."

"Well." I exhaled a surprised puff of air, completely charmed. "Thank you."

"You're welcome." He reached out his hand and I took it, shivering softly as he clasped my fingers, pressing our palms tightly together. "Shall we?"

"Weirdest date night ever," I said, cracking jokes to cover my nerves as usual. "But I guess so."

We entered my room. "Wait here."

"Huh? Where are you going?"

"Keep an eye on Nimbus while I check the attic."

"What? Wait! No! I don't want to be alone in here! Wait, no. I'm fine. I'll be okay," I couldn't stop the panicked rambling words from falling out of my mouth. I'd need an entire journal to document all the different ways I'd embarrassed myself tonight. "Go ahead. I'm fine, I promise."

"There's nothing to worry about."

"It's the door next to this one."

"Thought so." His eyes softened on mine. "It'll be fine. Wait here."

I looked around the room, spotting my phone on the bedside table. I swiped it up and got ready to dial nine-one-one. I trusted him, but one couldn't be too careful.

I took a deep breath and listened as Ren's footsteps echoed in the hall along with the scratching.

Nimbus must have accepted that something was being done about the noise. He snapped out of his kitty-cat rage fest and hopped up to join me on the bed. I scooped him up and cuddled him close but he was having none of that. He hopped out of my arms and sat next to me instead.

The hinge squeak told me Reb had opened the attic door, and I slammed my eyes shut in anticipation. Of what? I had no idea, but something was up there.

"Shit!" He yelled as his footsteps pounded across the hall.

I peeked out the doorway.

Raccoons.

So many raccoons.

One of them ran through my legs and into my room. Nimbus jumped from the bed to chase it. Around and around they went, knocking my bedside table to the floor before I managed to shoo Nimbus into the bathroom and close the door.

The raccoon ran out. I stumbled to the doorway, trying not to trip over the contents of my bedside table drawers as I made my way toward the hallway to check on Ren.

At the top of the stairs, I saw him open the front door

and then run toward the kitchen, probably to open that door too.

"Is Nimbus okay?" he shouted.

"He's in the bathroom."

"Good, I'm going to try and herd them out of here."

I watched him dart back and forth from the top of the stairs, trying to corral the raccoons through the open doors as I leaned against the banister, wondering how best to help. He was like a blur of determination, and the chaos seemed never-ending. I grabbed my broom from the small utility closet and joined him. Meanwhile, Nimbus's desperate yowls echoed from the bathroom, adding to the cacophony. Smog, as usual, was quiet.

We walked through the house, checking all the corners and closets, pausing in the kitchen for a moment to rehydrate.

Ren insisted on going up and checking the attic and gave it the all-clear.

Finally, it seemed they were all gone. We closed the doors and met up in the foyer.

"That was something," he said, huffing and puffing for air.

"I know it was only raccoons. But I don't think I'll ever sleep again."

He let out a sigh of relief and leaned against the wall. "I guess we can let the cats out now," he said with a smile, wiping sweat from his brow.

"Yeah, I think it's safe."

"Want me to stay here tonight? I can crash on the couch. Or I'll sleep outside your door. This was a lot. You need some rest." He tucked my hair behind my ear, his touch lingering as he slowly let the strands drift from his fingers.

"I, uh, yes." Forget trying to be brave. There was no way I could sleep tonight. "Please. I can't face being alone right now. But you don't have to sleep outside my door. That's silly."

"The couch?"

"Do you mind? Are you sure?" My pulse fluttered so rapidly, I wondered if he could see it. I slid my hand up my throat just in case.

"I'm happy to."

"Okay, help me let the cats out, then I'll grab some blankets and a pillow for you. I appreciate this a lot. You have no idea."

"It's no trouble at all. I'll check on Nimbus. I don't want him to hurt you accidentally. He was pretty worked up."

His gaze was warm and reassuring. And I was so, so glad I wouldn't be alone tonight. I couldn't help but notice how his eyes lingered on me. It wasn't just concern, there was something more, my heart raced, and my cheeks flushed. It was magnetic. A connection hummed in the air between us. A lingering hint of something deeper.

"Thanks." I headed downstairs to the half bath. Smog sauntered out as if an army of raccoons hadn't just overrun us. I watched him head to the kitchen, probably to check on his food bowl. "Nice talk," I muttered. "Glad you're okay."

"Oh shit." I cringed and ran for the stairs, remembering my overturned bedside table and its spilled contents—spilled *private* contents.

Damn it, damn it, damn it.

Too late.

Ren was already standing in the doorway, his cheeks tinged with pink as he saw my collection of vibrators strewn all over the floor.

"Uh...nothing to see here," I cracked, better to make a joke than die of humiliation. "Just my drawer full of fun. Hopefully, it will help me stick to my no-more-dating and never-falling-in-love-again-ever plans."

"Ahh, I see." He seemed relieved that I was joking and not embarrassed.

I fumbled to gather the scattered items; my face probably as pink as Ren's. "Can we pretend this never happened?"

He righted the bedside table, and I managed to stuff everything back into the drawer. "Thanks," I mumbled, maybe dying of humiliation was a good idea now.

"Sure," he said, chuckling. "This never happened. No dating, no love, gotcha. But our fake dates are still on, right?"

"Of course," I replied, closing the drawer with a decisive thud. "I never go back on my word."

His smile was a mixture of genuine amusement and the kind of understanding that made my embarrassment slowly fade. He leaned against the doorway, watching me with those steady, thoughtful eyes.

"Seriously," I finally said, once I had managed to

compose myself somewhat. "Thanks for not making this even more awkward."

"Hey, everyone has their secrets," he replied lightly. "Yours just happen to be a lot more...colorful. Raccoons in the attic and an impressive collection of—fun."

"Colorful." I laughed, taking a slow step closer to him. "I guess you could say that."

"By the way, about those fake dates, a gala at a children's hospital is coming up."

"You're so amazing." I tried to be cool, to ignore the fluttering in my stomach at the thought of another evening spent in his company.

"Thank you, but not really. I—um—like to help when I can, I guess. Anyone would."

"No, I mean, look at what you did tonight. You drove right into my driveway, no questions asked, and single-handedly defeated the covert army of raccoons living in my attic. Where were you anyway?"

He huffed a laugh. "I couldn't fall asleep, so I went on an ice cream run. It's probably melted in the bag."

"I'm sorry."

"You're more important. I couldn't leave you, standing in your driveway, nowhere to go but back into a potentially haunted house. What kind of man would I be if I did that? Good thing it was only raccoons."

"Wait. Stop. I think I've figured you out. Your love language is acts of service. But that's totally obvious to anyone who knows you. You say you're grumpy, which is a contradiction. I don't think you're grumpy at all. I think your job forced you to see the worst in people, and you closed yourself off and hid behind a gruff exterior for protection. You're like a classic eldest daughter stereotype, if she were to take the form of a buff, badass, almost silver fox, grumpy-on-the-outside divorce attorney. You take care of everyone you know, Ren. So, yeah, you're amazing. I will accept no argument on that fact." I ran my fingers over the gray hair at his temple, then touched the tip of his nose, grinning when the cute pink flush reappeared above his stubble.

"I don't know what any of that means." His laughter was deep and rich, a sound that could fill a room and make everyone within earshot smile. It was infectious. And I felt pretty special because I knew he didn't let many people see this side of him.

It was like a pressure valve releasing, the tension melting away as we realized we were more alike than we thought. Silence hung between us for a moment, comfortable and warm as we each realized that we were absolutely going to become—friends. Just friends, damn it. I was *not* dating anyone for real. No matter how amazing and kind and good-looking and built and—gah!

Forget it.

No.

Bad, Piper.

"Well, I think you're pretty awesome, Ren, and I'm glad you're here."

"Thank you. And I think the same about you. You're one of the sweetest people I've ever met." He grew serious. "I think about you more than I should."

A flutter of emotions swirled in my chest, each one

more confusing than the last. His words shimmered in the air, and I felt a magnetic pull toward him, like something was nudging us closer together, rewriting the lines between what was real and what was pretend. Or maybe I was just pretending this wasn't real when deep down I knew that it could be.

"I do too. I mean, I think about you, too, Ren. Entirely too much for my own good." I confessed, my voice barely above a whisper.

"What should we do about it?"

My pulse quickened at his words, and I took a deep breath to steady my racing heart. I didn't want to lose whatever we had by not being honest.

We stood there, the silence wrapping around us like a cozy blanket. His eyes held a depth of sincerity that made my heart skip a beat. It was as if we were both acknowledging the delicate balance we were walking on, the fine line between friendship and something more.

Without breaking eye contact, I took a step closer, my breath catching slightly. "Show me."

"What?"

"Show me what you think about when I'm on your mind."

His gaze softened, and he reached out to gently tuck a stray lock of hair behind my ear.

The air between us shifted.

Uncertainty was replaced by possibility.

Pretense by chemistry.

His lips met mine in a tender kiss.

Chapter 14
Piper

"**M**ore," I whispered against his lips. "This is what I think about, too, and I need more."

"Are you sure?"

I nodded, thinking to myself that I'd always want more from him.

For a moment, we stood there with our words hanging between us like a fragile thread. Then, we moved closer, breaths mingling in the small space that separated us.

He reached out a hand, hesitated, and then gently took mine. The warmth of his touch sent a shiver down my spine.

"I guess we need to decide if we want to cross that line again," he whispered, his eyes searching mine for an answer that I wasn't sure I was ready to give.

I squeezed his hand gently, the answer forming on

my lips. "Maybe we should just kiss," I suggested. "Just see what happens when we do what we feel."

"I'd like that," he murmured, his thumb brushing over my knuckles. "I'd like that a lot. No pressure."

"Right. No pressure. No definitions. Just us, doing whatever we feel like. That's okay, isn't it?"

"Yes." His voice rumbled from his chest as the space between us seemed to vanish.

He leaned in, and our lips met in a soft, exploratory kiss. His hand moved to cup my cheek, his fingers threading into my hair. The kiss deepened, our movements growing bolder, fueled by the unspoken understanding that this was right, even if it was still undefined.

Each touch, each caress, sent sparks through my veins. His hands found my waist, pulling me closer and anchoring me to him. I melted into his arms, exploring the contours of his back and the broad expanse of his shoulders.

When we finally pulled away, breathless and smiling, there was a new certainty between us.

No labels.

No promises.

Just the beautiful, intoxicating present.

His forehead rested against mine, and we stayed like that. Savoring the connection we had made.

"Wow." I breathed, my heart racing.

"Yeah," he agreed, his voice a soft rumble. "That was..."

"Amazing," I finished for him, and he chuckled softly.

"Yes, amazing."

His fingers traced the line of my jaw, and warmth spread through me. We didn't need words, not when our silence spoke volumes.

"I'm going to the living room."

"Stay," I whispered, the word slipping out before I could stop it. His eyes searched mine, and the corner of his mouth lifted in a smile.

"For practice," he asked, teasingly, though there was a hint of something earnest beneath his tone.

"For practice," I echoed, trying to match his lightness, but my heart betrayed me, beating a staccato rhythm in my chest.

"I've been dying to do this again since the other night."

He leaned in, his lips capturing mine in a kiss that was familiar, electrifying, and all that I could ever hope to feel.

He backed me against the wall, his leg slipping between mine. He had mentioned our kiss from the other night, but this kiss was nothing like that one. This time it was dominant, like he knew what he wanted. He'd gotten a taste before, but now he wanted it all.

His hands drift down my sides to grip my hips, pulling me tighter into his body. I was overwhelmed in the best way possible.

He stilled and inhaled hard, pulling away.

As if he could read my mind, he brushed the hair over my shoulders and kissed my forehead. "Tonight was a lot, sweetheart. Maybe I can just hold you while you sleep?"

I nodded, feeling the weight of the day settling over

me. "Yes, I would really love that," I murmured as he wrapped me in his arms, like a cocoon of safety and comfort. "Are you sure?"

"All I want is to be close to you, however you need me to be."

He kicked off his shoes and we climbed beneath the covers, lying there as minutes turned into hours. I drifted off, feeling his hand occasionally smoothing over my back, a soothing gesture that lulled me further into sleep until I was out.

Practice...the word echoed in my dreams as his arms tightened around me, and I felt him relax against me.

Chapter 15
Ren

I woke up in bed with two cats and no Piper.

The sun streamed through her gauzy pink curtains, casting a warm glow over the room. Smog and Nimbus were curled on either side of me asleep. I stretched slowly, careful not to disturb them.

The scent of coffee reached me before I heard Piper's footsteps in the hall. She appeared in the doorway, a tray in her hands and a smile that made my heart skip a beat on her gorgeous face. "Good morning," she said, her voice soft and soothing. "They like you. I love this."

"Morning," I replied, propping myself up on one elbow. The cats stirred but remained comfortably nestled against me.

The ratty old bathrobe was nowhere to be found. Not a caftan in sight either. I'd barely had time last night to process what she'd been wearing when I drove up let alone when we were dealing with all the raccoons, but I was sure as fuck processing it now.

A tiny red tank top skirted the edge of her waist, riding high above a skimpy white pair of soft cotton sleep shorts with a strawberry print. Her legs were long, her hips were made for my hands to grip—

Fuck me.

I needed a cold shower. Or to shoo the cats out of the room and find some way to get her beneath me.

Frantically, I bunched the covers over my dick so she wouldn't see what she was doing to me as she approached the bed to place the tray on the nightstand. "I made breakfast. I hope you like blueberry muffins. They're homemade because that's me, a baker." She closed her eyes, shaking her head. "And a dork."

My stomach rumbled in response, and I grinned. "I love blueberry muffins, any kind of muffin, really. But what I love more is waking up here with you. Thank you, you didn't have to go to all this trouble."

"It's my turn to take care of you now." She laughed softly. "It's no trouble at all. I enjoy it. Besides, you deserve a little pampering after last night.'

She handed me a steaming mug of coffee, and I took a sip. As I settled back against the headboard, she joined me on the bed, carefully arranging the tray so we could both reach.

"I have to tell you something—" I started, but she cut me off.

"No, I think I already know what it is. I talked to Lucy earlier." She took a sip of coffee, her eyes twinkling into mine as she looked at me above the rim of her mug. "She was thrilled that I have a new sexy-hot, protective boyfriend. And she told me she invited you to the weenie roast. And she brought up the Richard thing. Ugh."

"Is everything okay?"

"So far, yeah, it's just typical Richard. I'm sorry you had to deal with him, but I appreciate it."

"No, I'm sorry I got carried away. It took all I had not to knock him out and get Cody back for you. If I messed things up, I'll fix it. But I'll fix it even if I didn't mess anything up. You just have to let me."

"I have it under control. Jake is preparing paperwork for me to buy Dana out, or to fight it if she actually makes an offer to me first, and if you know of any dog custody experts, we need a list. Thank you for standing up for me. You have nothing to be sorry for."

"I'm glad to hear that, Jake is the perfect person to go to about the bakery, and I'll get him a list of people he can consult with about Cody ASAP. You're in good hands with him."

"I just hope this can all be done before we open. Violet thinks I'll have to make Dana miserable first, then she'll cave. But I'm not too sure about that. Especially because Jake told me to avoid her as much as possible."

I chuckled at the thought of Piper making anyone miserable. She was so damn sweet. "So, what's the weenie roast all about? Do I need to bring anything?"

She laughed. "No, just bring yourself. My grandpa sets up a small bonfire out back. We get potato salad and pie from the Pennywhistle Pantry because those are his favorites. We eat off paper plates, so there's nothing to clean up. Then, we drink beer and shoot the shit for a couple of hours. Rain or shine, every other week, it happens. You're on the roster now. But don't worry, there's another newbie besides you—Lucy's boyfriend, Spencer. Remember him? From Christmas, when he picked you and Jake up in Portland in his tow truck? He saved Lucy from a snowbank right before New Year's Eve, and now they're together."

"He's a good guy. I'm happy for her. Are you okay with me being there?"

"Yes." Her smile lit me up inside. "I would have invited you myself after this morning. So, yes. I'm more than okay with it. Plus, it'll be good practice for us, don't you think?"

Practice. The word hit like a little jab in my heart, but I let it go.

"It couldn't hurt. I'm not used to stuff like this. My family was never big on gathering together. Until now, with Jake and Violet."

"We didn't either at first—because of my dad. But Grandpa said he wouldn't have five granddaughters who didn't talk to each other, so the weenie roast was born. We're an odd bunch, but it works. All our moms, except Eliza's, are friends now, and Dad is off, who knows where, with his latest girlfriend. He would never show up anyway."

"What happened to Eliza's mom? Stop me if I'm being nosy."

She waved her hand around as she took a sip of her coffee. "I'm an open book." She laughed lightly. "Plus, after you've been in town for a while, the local gossips—

my grandma being the biggest—will find a way to let you know all about my family."

"So, I'm getting the story straight from the source. Nice."

"Exactly. Dad left her. No one knows where he is most of the time. Grandpa says he's always chasing the next big thing, but it always ends up being just one heartbreak after another. Eliza's mom is still picking up the pieces. He strung her along for years, and now he's gone again."

"That's terrible." I took a bite of a blueberry muffin and moaned out loud. "Piper, these are amazing."

Her smile was radiant. "Thank you! It's only a matter of time before Grandpa gets her to come."

"He sounds like a great grandfather."

"He's the best, and I know he'll like you. You're cut from the same cloth."

"I'll take that as a compliment."

"It's definitely a compliment."

Smog stirred, then headbutted my side and started purring. Nimbus was still out like a light. "Does Nimbus usually sleep this long?"

"I think he exhausted himself trying to scratch through the wall to get at the raccoons. He'd been obsessed with that corner since we moved in. I should have taken him seriously."

"Like when they were pooping in Richard's shoes?"

She laughed, the sound bright and infectious. "Exactly."

"And what are they telling you now?" I stroked

Smog's soft fur as he leaned against me, nuzzling into my palm.

A thoughtful expression crossed her face, and her cheeks turned a cute shade of pink as she watched Smog melt into my side. "They're telling me something I'm not ready to hear yet."

"Fair enough," I answered, keeping my voice gentle, not wanting to break this peaceful moment. Her gaze met mine, and for a moment, I saw hope mingle with fear. But then she looked away. I could be patient. I had no other choice. She snuck up on me and I didn't want to lose this feeling.

Smog's purring grew louder, a soft rumble of contentment that filled the room. I glanced over at Nimbus, now stirring slightly in his sleep.

"I'm sorry, Ren, I—"

"Sweetheart, no. I love your honesty. Demands and pressure leave a path of destruction in any relationship— family, friends, all of them. I'd never want to push you. What we do or don't do can only be on your terms since you're the one not ready for more."

She sighed deeply and looked at me through her lashes. "I know I asked this before, but how can you possibly be real?"

"You learn a lot about relationships in my line of work," I joked. "I'm constantly adding to the list of what not to do. One that I started early by observing my father."

"Okay, but your terms count, too, Ren. Don't let me

push you." Her eyes were earnest and beautiful as she met my gaze.

"Don't worry. I already know you won't."

"Okay, good." She breathed. "But promise to tell me if something changes. I don't want to push you *away*, either."

"I promise, you won't."

"I'm just not ready for—"

"I get it. You don't have to explain. You just got out of a bad relationship, I understand, and I think we're on the same page. I'm hesitant to dive into anything as well. I never thought I'd—" I held back, not wanting to spill my guts this early. I'd scare her off by telling her I never thought I could feel like this for anyone, that I wanted her, that I could fall for her, and I probably was already falling. I knew her enough to know that now was not the time to tell her.

"It's okay. I never imagined I'd be interested in anyone this soon after what happened with Richard and Dana. This is new territory for me, too. Sad that at this age I finally—never mind."

"This is new for both of us. We'll navigate it together," I reassured her, taking her hand across the tray.

"Does this even count as fake dating anymore?" Her cute nose crinkled up. "What is this?"

"Something entirely unexpected." I chuckled softly. "And I guess it depends on how you define fake dating," I mused. "But either way, I'm glad we're doing it together."

She smiled, a hint of relief in her eyes. "I guess the fake part is not our problem. What people think we do and what we're doing are two different things. Nobody has to know our business."

"Exactly. The image we project to get what we need is one thing. But what happens behind closed doors is only for us."

"I like that. Tell me about the children's hospital gala."

"It's black tie. It's not like the dinners we usually attend. This will be mainly for meeting people and getting our name out there, making contacts so we can partner up on events in the future, things like that."

"So, dress to kill and get ready to socialize?"

"Yep. Is that okay?"

"Totally. I'm happy to go with you."

"But can you pretend?"

"Of course." Her brow furrowed. "What do you mean?

"Pretend that you want me?" *Shit.* What was I saying?

"I won't have to pretend, Ren."

Her words sparked a mixture of relief and longing. For a moment, I was lost in the depth of her gaze; the fear in her eyes from before was gone. I reached out, taking her hand in mine, feeling the softness of her skin.

My heart skipped a beat, but I quickly masked my reaction with a smile. I searched her eyes, trying to unravel her thoughts.

I wanted to kiss her again, but should I?

I leaned close, over the tray, feeling the warmth of her

breath against my skin as the room seemed to shrink around us.

"Do you mean that?" I asked softly.

"Yes," she whispered.

The tension was palpable, and I couldn't resist any longer. I closed the distance between us and pressed my lips to hers. She responded instantly, kissing me back and running her hands up my chest.

Smog and Nimbus hopped off the bed to run out of the room, and we broke apart.

"They'll be okay. Their breakfast is ready too. I already filled their bowls." She stood, grabbing the tray to set on her dresser, then shut the door before climbing back into bed with me to sit at my side, with her back up against the headboard.

This was what I'd been missing in my life. Togetherness, simple and easy.

She was what had been missing.

The electricity between us was irresistible. The thrill of not knowing what was coming. This fucking desire I had for her—stronger than I'd ever felt for anything or anyone. I wanted her. I had to have her. I had to find a way to make her mine.

For the first time in my life, I couldn't think.

I didn't want to.

All I wanted was to keep this feeling I only had with her.

This wasn't safe. I knew my heart was on the line, and she wasn't ready to be with me in a real way, but I didn't care.

Her eyes heated on me, and my stomach swirled as my heart started beating so hard, I could hear it echoing in my ears.

She smelled so good, like vanilla and blueberries, and fucking joy and light and sunshine and everything I always wanted but never had in my life.

Her eyes dropped to my mouth before lowering to half-mast, with her lashes fanning against the top of her high cheekbones.

A whimper fell from her mouth right before her tongue darted out to wet her lower lip. Then she bit it, and I was done for. No more resisting. No more *not* kissing her. No more denying what we both wanted.

"Maybe we should practice," she said, and I then was hers.

My entire body trembled, and I grew hard as a rock. This was happening.

I wrapped my hand around the back of her neck and crashed my mouth against hers.

Chapter 16
Piper

His lips touched mine, and all the thoughts flew out of my head.

Caution was boring.

Stopping was stupid.

And most of all, nothing about the heat that existed between us was fake. I had a feeling that things would explode between us sooner rather than later, and now here we were.

This was our third kiss, and it was nothing like the first two. The progression from *wow, he's attractive*, and *I must have him inside me immediately*, was like going from zero to sixty.

"Tell me now, if you have any doubt about this, Piper and I'll stop. No questions asked, and no feelings hurt. I swear. And if you need to tell yourself this is practice or pretend, or whatever else you need to do to protect yourself. Do it. I understand."

"God, Ren. I don't even know what to say right now."

"You don't have to say anything. All I want is you." The words were hot against my mouth as he spoke.

"I want you too. Right now. I'm saying yes."

I tugged at the hem of his shirt, grinning when he reached behind his neck and yanked it over his head. His body was insane, nothing but planes, angles, and sharply defined muscle. He was beautiful. I dipped forward to lick the little dent at the base of his throat, where his pulse fluttered.

He moved his hands to my back, tugging at the hem of my tank top, I lifted my arms and let him pull it over my head, falling to my back on the bed as he covered me, and bent low to suck a nipple into his mouth with a sharp pull.

My hands slid into his hair, pulling him close as my legs fell to the sides. I felt him through his pants, huge and hard, as I ground myself up against him and wrapped my legs around his back.

He pulled back, hair wild from my hands, cheeks flushed, pupils blown wide with pleasure. "I've never felt like this," he growled. "You're magic, I swear."

"I've never felt this way either. Only with you."

"Good. Are you sure?"

"I'm sure."

He moved lower, sliding his fingertips in the waistband of my shorts as he placed a kiss right below my belly button. Down they went, along with my undies as he slid off the bed to his knees and pulled me along with him until my ass was at the edge.

Oh god.

"I'm dying to see if you taste as good as I imagined," he murmured hotly against my skin.

Oh crap.

I closed my legs as best I could, cringing as I bumped the side of his head with my knee. But that little embarrassment was nothing when I knew if he went down on me, it would go on forever, and he'd end up annoyed when he couldn't get me off.

"No, it's okay. I have condoms in the bedside table. You don't have to do this. You can stop."

His head jerked back, and he gripped my outer thighs to steady my legs. "What's wrong? Did I do something?"

"No," I leaned toward him, propping myself on my bent arms. It's just—I can't come like this. I never have. It's okay."

His eyes lit up with understanding. "Do you want me to stop because you don't want it? Or stop because you think I don't want to do it?"

"Is this part of your rescue kink?" I joked to hide my embarrassment. "Save the woman who can't orgasm from oral?"

His eyes dropped low, between my legs, for a second before returning to mine. "No, sweetheart. This is an entirely different kind of kink. May I try?"

"Oh god."

"Tell me you want it because I sure as hell want to do it to you. I promise."

"Okay," I squeaked. "I mean, yes. Why not, right?"

He chuckled, and I shivered as I felt his breath hot against my inner thigh as he bent forward, moving my legs apart with his broad shoulders. "Say the words, tell me what you want." He darted his tongue out, flicking it against my clit before sliding his lips up in a grin. "And before you start to worry. I fucking love this. Look at how pretty you are."

My mouth fell open, but I couldn't speak.

"Tell me you want me to taste you, lick you, suck on that sweet little clit of yours until I make you scream."

"Oh god. Yes, please."

"When I got here last night, I didn't think my morning would start inside you." He grinned as he entered me with a finger, then licked a circle around my clitoris. "I've been thinking about how you'd taste since the day I first saw you, do you know that?"

"No," I moaned. "I did not know that."

I begin to unravel as he did exactly as he said, licking, sucking, fucking me with his fingers...

I let go, shifting and writhing against the relentless movements of his fingers and tongue.

"You're doing so well," he whispered, his breath blowing hot against my sensitized skin. "I wish you could see how gorgeous you are, all pink and slick with my fingers buried inside you. You're so wet, so hot, and so fucking sweet. You taste like heaven. You need to come, I can feel it. Tell me how bad you want it, sweetheart. I'd do anything for you, do you know that? Let yourself go. I'm here to catch you."

I arched my back, shoving myself against his face, unable to answer. I flew apart as he increased the pressure, spearing his tongue into me while he swirled his fingers in circles over my clit, holding my hips down so I couldn't move. He made me feel things I'd never, ever felt, and I got lost in it.

"I never knew it could feel like that. Oh my god, Ren. I have condoms," I breathlessly informed him when I came back down to earth.

"I want to take you on a real date before we go further. Is that okay? Then we'll talk about maybe starting something real together, can we do that?"

"Yes. But first…" I pushed him onto the bed and dropped to my knees. "I'm going to return the favor, if that's okay with you." I unzipped his pants and freed his erection while I waited for an answer, licking up the underside and kissing the tip after he nodded an emphatic *yes*."

"It's more than okay. Fuck, keep going."

This was not usually my favorite thing to do, but now that he'd just gotten me off so spectacularly, I wanted nothing more.

Making me feel good mattered to him, and I wanted to show him that I cared about him too so I sucked him to the back of my throat and grabbed onto his hips, holding on so he couldn't back away.

He was a gentleman. I doubted he'd be okay with the thought of me tearing up and gagging on him.

"Be careful. Don't choke yourself. You can probably get me off just by looking at it," he joked. "Baby, please…"

I was right.

His hands went into my hair, stroking it softly and

holding it out of my face as his thumb brushed my cheek. His gaze was gentle, even reverent, as I looked up at him.

"Touch yourself. Come again, with me," his voice was growly and deep and sexier than anything I'd ever heard so I did it, spreading my knees wide so I could circle my clit with my fingertips.

He groaned, biting his lip as he watched me. Then his head fell back, showing me the sharp outline of his jaw, the strong column of his throat as he shivered, and tightened his hands in my hair, shuddering as he released down my throat.

He helped me up, then pulled me down next to him on the bed, wrapping me in his arms and kissing the top of my head.

"Fuck, sweetheart. You're so goddamn perfect." His gravelly, undone exhalation sent goosebumps dancing across the skin of my neck where his words hit warm and true.

We hadn't gone all the way, but what did that matter when it felt like I'd just given him part of my heart?

Caution was smart.

Waiting was wise.

What had I done?

My heart still wasn't fixed from the last time it broke, and he wanted to start something real with me.

He pulled me closer, and I let out a small sigh, snuggling into his embrace. I closed my eyes, savoring the moment, wishing it could last forever.

But my mind, ever restless, refused to let me be.

Doubts and fears crept in, reminding me of the times I had been hurt before.

He seemed to sense my unease. His hand gently stroked my back, and he pressed a tender kiss to my forehead. "You're safe here," he murmured. "With me, you'll always be safe."

"I know," I whispered. Rationally, I knew he was telling me the truth. But that deep place in my heart, the one that held onto all the hurt in my life, pushed his words away.

"Hey." His soft voice lifted me out of my spiraling thoughts, and I pulled back to look at him. "Come closer. It's okay."

I wanted to believe that this time could be different, but deep down, I couldn't—not yet. At least I knew enough to realize that these feelings had nothing to do with Ren. The fear of rejection loomed large in my heart. My thoughts were a mess, weaving in and out of my hopes and fears.

Oh, how I wanted this time to be different. I didn't want this chance to end up like the others, and I'd end up gutted and hollow.

Was I ready to be real with Ren?

I wanted to be.

But could I be with him without hurting or driving him away when it seemed as if no matter how hard I tried with someone, I never seemed to be enough?

Chapter 17
Ren

My heart had run away from my brain.

No, that wasn't it.

My dick had taken control of everything, and all logic had been lost.

Everything felt confusing and tangled. My emotions were in a whirlwind. Sometimes it seemed like I couldn't differentiate between real and pretend.

It had been about a week since my time with Piper. We'd seen each other each morning before I left for work.

We shared quiet conversations and stolen moments, yet my insecurities lingered like shadows, whispering doubts into my mind.

Despite our daily interactions, I found myself pulling back a little bit, afraid that she would break things off if I pushed her too hard for more.

I knew my feelings for her were real, but I'd trapped myself in a labyrinth of my own making. I needed clarity, but my body was driven by desires that overshadowed reason, and I was stuck in a tug-of-war between my heart, head, and primal instincts. If I didn't get my shit together, it would tear me apart along with any possibility I had to be with her.

Each moment with her felt more real than the last, pulling me deeper into a space where I almost didn't know how to act around her.

We needed to talk, that much was clear. But I didn't want to scare her off. She'd been through a lot and was still stuck in a terrible situation.

I wished Paige hadn't suggested we pretend to date each other. I should have said no and asked her out the proper way. Then maybe this would be real right now. Then maybe I'd spend my nights with her, naked, buried inside of her sweet little body instead of alone in my bed, wondering what I should do.

Maybe I'd be with her right now, instead of in my car driving to meet Jake, where hopefully he could help me sort out the mess in my head. How could I live without her now that I'd gotten a taste of what I wanted?

As I pulled into his driveway, I tried to steady myself. I knew this conversation could go one of two ways. Either Jake would confirm my fears, or he'd help me find a way forward.

I took a deep breath and stepped out, the cool evening air grounding me momentarily.

Violet greeted me at the door with a hug. Jake was already waiting for me in the living room, a look of concern on his face.

"I can see it all over you, man," he said, leaning forward, his eyes searching mine. "You've got it bad."

I ran a hand through my hair, frustration bleeding into my voice. "I'm a mess. I don't know what to do. One minute, everything feels perfect, and the next, I'm drowning in doubts, and I'm afraid I'll scare her off."

He nodded, taking a sip from his mug of coffee. "You've got to stop overthinking it. Just be genuine and follow her lead—"

"There's something you don't know."

His eyebrows shot up. "Go on."

"We were pretending. Paige suggested I bring her as my date—"

"Ahh, I get you. Is that why you're back on the RSVP for the gala this weekend? By the way, thank you for that. I did not want to go."

I ran a hand down my face, embarrassed. "Yeah, I went to Twilight Tavern after the last dinner and ranted about it. Paige suggested Piper go with me, and I jumped at the opportunity."

"Treat it like it's the real thing. Show her you're there for her, no matter what. Use the gala as an opportunity to show her how you feel. Or at least show her how a man should treat a lady."

I took in his advice, rolling it over in my mind. "Alright, it couldn't hurt, right?"

I was ready to face the truth. I wanted Piper, not just as a fake girlfriend, but as the real deal.

"It's been a long time for you, hasn't it?"

"What?"

"You know, dating, falling in love, all of it. You've been alone since Tabby died."

"I was alone when she was alive, too," I blurted.

"Yeah, she was so sick for so long—"

"I mean—" I closed my eyes, finally ready to tell him the truth. "We never loved each other. I mean, we did, but not romantically." I continued, feeling the weight of my confession. "But now, with Piper, I feel—everything. I haven't felt this way in years, maybe ever."

A shocked expression settled over his features before he bit out, "Damn it, Ren. Why didn't you tell me? You know I wouldn't have judged you." He ran a hand down his face, nodding as his eyes filled with understanding. "You're too good for this world. Tabby's husband ran off. That's why you stepped in. My god, I'm sorry I didn't figure it out back then. I could have helped. You didn't have to marry her—"

"I wanted to. She deserved to be taken care of. She deserved love and protection. She was my best friend. She deserved the world and it fucking sucks that cancer robbed her of it."

He placed a comforting hand on my shoulder. "You gave her everything you could. But now it's time for you to find your own happiness, and it isn't easy, not when you've spent your life taking care of everyone else."

I looked down, taking in his words. He was right. My whole life, it felt like I was living for other people. My family, Tabby...

Could I really allow myself to pursue something for myself for a change? The thought of it was exhilarating.

"I want to be happy," I confessed, feeling a surge of vulnerability. "But I don't know if I remember how. Actually, I don't think I ever knew how."

He smiled. "You looked happy when you were talking about Piper. Feelings are real, even if the circumstances are not."

"Okay, but she's not ready, I know that. Also, what if she doesn't feel the same way about me? What if she doesn't want to go with me anymore?"

"She does!" Violet rushed into the room. "I only heard the last part, I swear. I wasn't trying to listen in. She still plans on going to the gala with you. She asked me if Jake and I were going." A smile tugged at the corners of her mouth. "We shopped for a dress together. We filled up carts all over the internet. She ended up borrowing one of my dresses, but I won't tell you what it looks like. It'll probably be bad luck."

Jake and I exchanged glances, then he laughed. "They aren't getting married, not yet anyway."

"She likes you, Ren." Violet placed a soft hand on my shoulder. "I'm not saying anything more than that. But please go with your gut and be patient, okay?"

"I don't want to give up on her, but she told me straight to my face she doesn't want to date anymore, and she's never falling in love again—ever."

"She's been hurt. It's self-protection, okay? Listen, she likes roses, red and pink, just like the ones she grows on the side of her house. And she has a good heart, just like you do." Her eyes bored into mine. "I have no idea why I would tell you any of this."

I chuckled. "Gotcha. I'll give her the most expensive bouquet of roses I can find. Is that a good plan? And I'll check out that yarn store across from the post office."

"Perfect, and a box of mocha truffles from See's couldn't hurt either, just saying," Jake added. "The two of them are obsessed with those."

I nodded, feeling a glimmer of hope. "Thanks, Vi. I'm going to take your advice and go for it. Should I pick up some truffles for you too?"

She shrugged lightly. "I mean, if you want to keep your best brother-in-law title." A satisfied grin lit up her face. "I can't wait to see how it all unfolds. I'm just sorry I wasn't the one to make this match. Having a new baby threw me off my game. Paige and I will have to grab some coffee and compare matchmaking notes."

"She wasn't trying to matchmake us," I protested.

"The two of you are only perfect for each other, but okay." She rolled her eyes. "I'm sure you're right." Her laughter was not convincing.

I thought it over, trying to recall the night Paige suggested we fake date each other.

Jake laughed softly. "Just be yourself and let things happen naturally."

I sighed, feeling the weight of uncertainty and the fear that I'd push too hard again. "I just hope she feels the same. It's hard not to overthink everything."

"Trust me, Ren. She's thinking about you, too," Violet assured me. "Just take this one step at a time."

"I can do that."

We said our goodbyes, and then, as I started my car, I

decided to stop at the local flower shop on my way home, hoping they'd have some peonies or at least something pretty and pink to give her. I was in luck. I chose a bouquet of red and pink roses mixed with daisies and baby's breath and headed home. The drive felt longer than usual, my mind wandering with thoughts of Piper.

Pulling into my driveway, I saw her knitting away on her porch, wrapped in a gorgeous baby pink floral caftan that matched the flowers. Her presence brought a sense of calm, as if the sight of her could chase away all my doubts.

"There's my golden girl," I called out as I approached.

She looked up, a warm smile spreading across her face when she spotted the flowers I was trying to hide behind my back.

"All I'm missing is the green mask." Her smile lit up her entire face. It was all I could do not to sprint up the porch steps to get to her. "Whatcha got back there?" She set her knitting to the side and eagerly slid forward on her porch swing.

"Someone may have mentioned that roses were your favorite." I held the massive bouquet of fluffy pink and red roses out to her, smiling as she reached out to snatch them, holding them to her face to inhale deeply.

"They are. Thank you. You're too good to me, I love them."

"You're welcome." I sat next to her on the swing and swiped up her knitting. "I don't know what you're working on here, but I like it."

"It's definitely an original, right?"

As I settled next to her on the swing, our thighs pressed together, sending a spark of warmth through me. Her scent enveloped me—floral and sweet, just like the bouquet I had given her. It was intoxicating. I couldn't help but steal glances at her. She was so beautiful, with the sun casting a golden hue over her features, making her look almost ethereal. The way her eyes sparkled with delight and her smile radiated warmth made my heart ache. I wanted to reach out and touch her, to pull her close and never let go. But for now, I was content to simply be in her presence, enjoying the feeling of being close to her.

"Yes. Original. Exactly," I answered as I finished the row she was working on. "Is it a scarf?"

"I don't know." Her nose crinkled up adorably. "Do you think it looks like a scarf?"

"It could. Eventually," I teased.

"Then it's a scarf. Maybe I'll give it to you for your birthday. Someone may have mentioned that it's coming up."

"Oh yeah?"

"Yep. How was your day?"

"It was... enlightening," I replied. "Got some good advice from Jake and Vi."

"They're excellent when it comes to that," she agreed. "What kind of advice?" she asked, curiosity lighting up her beautiful face.

"Mostly about enjoying the small moments and not stressing too much about the future." I looked at her, feeling a sudden rush of affection and wishing she were mine for real. "You know, like this moment right now, with you."

She smiled softly, her eyes shining in the early evening twilight. "I like that. We should do more of this. Sitting out here is everything I hoped it would be when I bought the place."

"We definitely should," I agreed, feeling warmth spread through me. I returned the knitting to her lap and leaned back in my chair. "What's your plan for tonight?"

"Well, I didn't have any plans at all until you walked onto my porch looking all sexy and bringing me my favorite flowers."

"Ahh, and now?"

"I plan on kissing the hell out of you. If you don't have any pressing engagements, that is."

"I think our plans are in alignment," I teased, reaching forward to touch her cheek, feeling the soft warmth of her skin. She leaned into my palm, her eyes fluttering closed for a moment.

She tilted her head slightly, her lips parting in antici- pation as I closed the gap between us, pressing my lips gently against hers.

The kiss was slow, deliberate, and filled with the promise of many more moments like this. I knew all I had to do was be patient.

"I love this with you. You make me feel—" Her eyes brightened with unshed tears before she blinked them back. "Well, you make me feel again. And I didn't think I would. I thought Richard had killed the last bit of love and hope I had left in me."

"Me too, Piper. I never thought I would ever feel this way," I admitted, brushing a stray hair away from her face.

"I'm glad you came over tonight," she murmured, her voice barely above a whisper.

We sat together in companionable silence, the only sound the distant chirping of crickets and the occasional rustle of leaves in the breeze.

She slid to the side, patting the spot next to her on the swing.

The stars twinkled above us, casting a soft light over the porch. Her fingers intertwined with mine. "Maybe we should make this a regular thing," she suggested softly. "Just me and you, right here."

"And another kiss?"

"Obviously."

I wrapped my arm around her shoulders and drew her into my side, kissing her temple, then resting my head against hers.

"I don't know what to do with you, Ren," she whispered. "I want so much, but I'm afraid that I—"

"Don't be afraid, sweetheart. I have all the patience in the world when it comes to you. No need to rush things."

"This is different. You and me, Ren. This is everything, and I just need some time, so I don't mess it up."

"I know, baby. Anything you need."

We sat there, letting the night envelop us as the

gentle sway of the swing matched the rhythm of our breathing.

A small smile slid across her lips before she raised her face to mine and wrapped her hand around my neck, pulling me down to meet my lips with hers in a reassuring kiss.

At first, it was slow, like before, but then a quiet little moan vibrated from the back of her throat, and I pulled her closer, unable to resist.

No one had ever kissed me like Piper. The earth moved when her lips were on mine. She didn't just make me feel good, she made me feel like I had somewhere to belong. Everything felt right whenever I was with her.

"I think you're going to change my life, Ren."

"I hope so," I whispered. "You've already changed mine."

She pulled away slightly, her gaze locked onto mine as if searching for reassurance. "Tell me we have a real chance."

I brushed a stray strand of hair from her face, my fingers lingering on her delicate jawline. "We do. As long as you want me around, I'm here."

"I know I have no right to ask this of you, but can you promise me something? Promise you won't hurt me."

"I promise," I affirmed, sealing it with another kiss. "I'm not the hurting kind of man, golden girl. I don't have that in me."

She buried her face in my chest, wrapping her arms around my waist to hold me tight.

"Thank you," she murmured. "You have no idea how much I needed to hear that."

We stayed like this, holding each other, letting the sky grow dark as we rocked together in the swing and watched the night fall over the street.

It was late when I went home, and I fell asleep dreaming about her.

Chapter 18
Piper

I t was time.

Fake date night at the gala.

We'd made the rules and set the boundaries, but we'd broken them all over the last week. I saw him every morning and evening on my porch where we'd rock on my swing and kiss until we reached the point where he either had to go home or inside with me. So far, he always went home. He respected that I wasn't ready, and it made me want him even more.

I took a deep breath, attempting to steady my nerves. The significance of the evening weighed heavily on my mind.

With my heart pounding in my chest, I glanced in the mirror, trying to convince myself I could do this. We were supposed to put on a show, but obviously, we'd moved past the illusion.

With her hands on my shoulders, Paige turned me

around, studying my face with a critical eye as she set the lip gloss down on my vanity.

"My work is flawless as always. You're gorgeous. Shower her with compliments, my lovelies. Take it all in."

"You look pretty, Auntie Piper," my niece, thirteen-year-old Briar, confirmed.

"This feels like prom night," sixteen-year-old Lark agreed. "Mom did the same look on me. Totally classic. You look stunning. And I covet that dress. Can I borrow it for the Spring Fling Dance coming up?"

"It's Violet's," I told her. "But I'm sure she would let you. One doesn't have a need for formal wear that often around these parts. I'll ask her when I give it back."

"Nice! Thank you."

"My winged eyeliner skills are unparalleled." Paige nodded as she tipped my head side to side to catch the light. "Beautiful. No one question me. I am the queen. It has been declared."

Turning away from the mirror, I grinned at Paige. "I never went to prom, remember? Justin Bradley dumped me for Jackie Douglas the week before, so I stayed home. Fun times. Story of my life, right?"

Paige tilted her head toward mine. "I remember. Who do you think egged their houses when you were moping around in your room and crying into your pillow?" Her eyes shot guiltily to Lark and Briar, who were sitting on my bed, and I burst out laughing. "It wasn't me," she squeaked. "I would never do such a thing. Egging houses is probably some kind of crime. Plus, it's a waste of food."

"Really, Mom." Lark rolled her eyes. "We *have* met you, you know. You would totally egg someone if they crossed you. Please."

"Okay, fine. They never knew what hit them. No one messes with family."

"Someone had to stand up for my honor," I teased her. "Right, girls?"

"Tonight is a prom redo," Paige insisted. "You look fab, you have an amazing dress, and Ren won't know what to say when he sees you. Plus, there will be no awkward attempts at slow dancing or questionable bad punch to worry about."

"Prom redo? I wouldn't go that far," I protested.

"We need to get some pictures before you leave," she said, brandishing her phone. "Girls, get into position!"

We gathered together, posing and laughing as the camera clicked away. Briar and Lark made funny faces, and Paige insisted on capturing every single moment.

Just as Paige was about to take another picture, my phone rang. I picked it up and saw Ren's name flashing on the screen, and my heart did a little flip.

Fake? Yeah, right. My reaction to him was more than real.

"It's him," I said, my voice barely above a whisper.

"Well, answer it!" Lark urged. Her eyes wide with excitement.

I swiped to answer with trembling fingers. "Hey, Ren," I attempted to be cool but failed.

"I hope I'm not calling at a bad time."

"No, not at all. I was just getting ready."

"Great, I wanted to let you know that I'll be there in ten minutes."

"See you soon." I tried to keep my voice steady, but knew I failed.

As I hung up, Paige swooped in to give me a final once-over.

"Okay, girls, it's time to clear out of here."

They hugged me goodbye and headed downstairs to wait for Paige.

"You got this," she reassured me, with a quick hug. "So, this is day—wait, how many days has it been since I suggested the two of you fake date each other?" Her eyes were sharp, and her grin was full of mischief. "Anyway, it's day, whatever, of me waiting for you two idiots to fall in love."

"What?" I shook my head, hiding my smile because little did she know I may already be halfway there. "I can't believe you sometimes. What did you do?"

She burst into laughter. "Nothing. I did nothing but make a small suggestion." She popped up an eyebrow. "Don't you worry about it. Time heals all wounds, and Ren will be there when you're ready. Am I right?"

I grabbed my handbag and a dressy jacket. Then we went downstairs. The girls were on the couch with Smog and Nimbus.

"Right? Paige, you're unbelievable, that's what you are. This isn't prom or anything like it. I only asked for your help because it's fancy, and I didn't want to embarrass myself with my basic makeup and hair styling skills. This is not a big deal."

"Gah! Don't be boring. It *is* a big freaking deal! It's huge! What happened to romanticizing your life? Casual or not, real, pretend, who cares? You look pretty, go have some fun. Am I right, girls?"

"Totally," Lark agreed while Briar just watched us talk, her eyes bouncing to each of us as if she were taking notes for the future. "I saw him at Coffee Cabin talking to Auntie Eliza the other day. He's hot for an old guy."

"Old? Ouch." Paige clutched at her chest dramatically and collapsed onto the couch with the girls. "Pretty sure we're the same age."

"Sorry." Lark burst into laughter. "I just call it like I see it."

"Ew, Lark." Briar nudged her side. "What if they get married? You just called our potential future uncle hot."

"Yeah, I said, hot *for an old guy*. That doesn't count, it's just being nice."

"Stop digging the hole, honey. You'll just make it worse," Paige said with a laugh.

"Whatever." She rolled her eyes. "This is what I get for trying to be nice in this family. I see how it is."

Paige rolled her eyes right back and tickled her side. "Kids these days. No respect for their elders."

"See?" Lark teased. "She just admitted she's old."

"Straight to jail!" Paige shouted in mock anger. "Okay." She clapped her hands together. "Let's go! Your Auntie Piper needs to be alone when her hot old-man date arrives."

The girls ran to the car while Paige hung back to hug me again. "Have fun," she whispered in my ear. "Don't think of anything, no worries, no insecurities, just you, living your best life because you deserve it. Ren is not like the assholes you were with before. I only see good things for you. I love you."

As Paige hugged me, a whirlwind of emotions swirled in my chest. Nervousness gnawed at me, making my heart race. This was the first time I'd be stepping into Ren's world, and the gravity of it all was just overwhelming. Our relationship had always felt topsy-turvy but tonight was important.

I had never been this deep into anyone's life before, and the thought of seeing Ren in his element both thrilled and terrified me. Would I fit into his world the same way he had effortlessly woven himself into mine? Or would I feel out of place, like an impostor trying to play a role that wasn't written for me?

Paige's words echoed in my mind, calming some of my fears. I deserved this. I deserved to be happy, to let go of my insecurities, and let myself experience this fully. Ren was different—he wasn't like the others who had only left bruises on my heart. He was kind, gentle, and unwaveringly supportive, someone who made me want to believe in love again.

With tears shimmering in my eyes, I pulled her in for one more hug. "I love you, too. Thank you for making this a special night. I had fun with you and the girls."

She pulled back, smiling. "Call me tomorrow. Swear it. I have to know everything."

"I swear."

"Good. You will have fun. I demand it."

As she turned to leave, the sound of Ren's footsteps on the porch made me catch my breath. He was effortlessly stylish in a tailored suit. The fabric hugged his tall frame perfectly, emphasizing his strong build. The way he carried himself, coupled with the sharp cut of his suit, made him irresistibly sexy. I was halfway tempted to tug him inside and suggest we forget the dinner so I could strip it off him and see what he was hiding.

Paige looked back at me one last time, her face lighting up with a knowing smile. She walked past him, giving him a playful wave. "Take good care of her."

He nodded, his gaze locking onto mine with an intensity that sent a shiver down my spine. "Always," he replied softly, his voice full of promise.

"You two have fun tonight," she called as she got into her car.

He waited a beat for Paige and the girls to pull out of the driveway, then his eyes were all over me. "You look stunning." He moved closer, his eyes hot and filled with admiration. "Are you ready for tonight?"

"I think so. You look amazing, Ren."

"Thank you." He extended his hand toward me, and I placed mine in his, feeling reassured by the warmth and strength of his grip. "Shall we?"

We walked hand in hand to his car, then he opened the door for me with a flourish, his manners impeccable as usual. "Your chariot awaits," he said with a playful grin.

I laughed softly, appreciating his effort to lighten the mood. He could always tell when I was getting nervous.

"Thank you," I murmured, sliding into the passenger seat.

He joined me in the driver's side, then leaned over me to fasten my seatbelt for me. "You're welcome." His dark gaze trained on me, sending shivers across my skin where he touched me.

"Still playing hero, I see," I whispered.

"I can't seem to stop it when you're around."

He started the engine and left Honeybrook Hollow. The rugged mountain terrain gradually gave way to pine trees and mist, then transformed into bright lights and tall buildings. The distant hum of the city grew louder, and the sky overhead transitioned from a blanket of stars to the electric illumination of Portland.

Ren's hand rested lightly on my knee, sending tiny electric shocks of excitement through me. He glanced at me, his eyes filled with the same intense admiration.

"I can't believe I get to spend tonight with the most beautiful woman in the room."

My cheeks warmed as I turned to him, catching the mischievous gleam in his eyes. "We're not even there yet."

"Doesn't matter. You'll always be the most beautiful woman in any room I'm in."

"Thank you." I placed my hands on my heated cheeks to cool them. "Can a person die from a blush?"

He chuckled, steering the car smoothly into the parking lot. "I don't know, but your pink cheeks make you even more gorgeous. Don't fight it."

I knew he was being sincere, but rule number four

flashed in my brain: *Compliments*. Despite my better judgment, it got to me.

Knock it off.

Like Paige said, I had to find a way to shut my brain off. I was about to spiral into a cloud of my insecurities and couldn't let that happen.

"Wait here." He pulled into the valet area and then stepped out of the vehicle. Moments later, he was at my side, opening the door with the same flourish as before. "After you, m'lady," he said with a grin, extending a hand to help me out.

"Thank you," I murmured, thankful for this deliberately dorky chivalrous side of him that had come out to play again. It was the only thing keeping my sudden surge of nerves at bay.

I took his hand, and our eyes met as he helped me stand. The world around us disappeared for a brief moment, leaving only the two of us bathed in the soft glow of the parking lot lights.

I felt a rush of warmth and steadied myself, determined to keep my emotions in check.

He led me up the stairs and into the lobby. I followed, our footsteps echoing softly against the polished floor as we crossed through the gorgeous space.

The lobby was a testament to luxury, every detail meticulously designed to exude opulence. Marble floors gleamed beneath the soft lighting, and towering columns framed the space with an air of majesty. Crystal chandeliers hung from the vaulted ceilings, casting a warm, shimmering glow across the room. Elegant arrangements of fresh flowers filled the air with a delicate fragrance, while plush seating areas invited guests to relax in comfort and style.

People were dressed to the nines, the men in tailored suits and the women in gowns that could only be described as masterpieces. Diamonds glittered at throats and wrists, catching the light and reflecting it in dazzling bursts. Designer dresses flowed gracefully as guests moved, each one a unique statement of fashion and elegance. The soft hum of conversation mingled with the gentle strains of classical music, creating an atmosphere both sophisticated and welcoming.

But I was just a girl from Honeybrook Hollow wearing a borrowed dress. Holy crap, how was I supposed to pull this off?

As Ren approached the check-in desk, I couldn't help but feel overwhelmed by the sheer grandeur of the surroundings. Despite my nerves, I knew I had to play my part, to blend in with this world of wealth and glamour. The weight of the deception we carried settled over me, but for now, I focused on the beauty around me and the reassuring presence of Ren by my side.

My mind drifted as Ren approached the check-in desk. I stood beside him, barely absorbing the gorgeous opulence of the lobby, the fancy decor, and the soothing hum of the soft music. Instead, I fixated on the feeling of our hands intertwined, the solid warmth of his big palm holding mine, grounding me while my thoughts threatened to scatter.

I let go of his hand and smoothed the fabric of my

dress as we stepped into the grand ballroom. The soft hum of chatter and the clinking of glasses filled the air. The dinner was in full swing, with elegantly dressed guests mingling and laughing under the glittering chandeliers.

He offered me his arm, and I took it, feeling the weight of our deception settle over us like a cloak.

Reality faded away as I took it all in. We were under the guise of a date, and I was determined to play my part, no matter how real it felt.

Damn it, it *was* real. *We* were real, I knew that. But I also realized I was out of my depth. I'd never attended anything like this before. Charity galas were not my thing.

"You can relax, sweetheart. You're doing great." He whispered as he guided us to our table.

"Thanks," I replied, my voice barely audible over the din.

Inside the ballroom, the atmosphere was electric. Tables adorned with crisp white linens and elaborate floral arrangements filled the space, while a string quartet played softly in the corner.

As we headed further inside, a pretty older woman in a shimmering gown approached Ren, her eyes sparkling with mischief. She emanated confidence and allure, clearly accustomed to being the center of attention. Ignoring me entirely, she leaned in close to Ren, her hand resting seductively on his arm as she spoke in a low, sultry voice.

I stood there, blinking rapidly, not quite sure I was

seeing what I was seeing. I mean, what the hell? I'm standing right here.

"Ren, darling, it's been far too long," she purred, her gaze fixed on him with an intensity that made my stomach tighten. "You must join me for a drink later. We have so much to catch up on."

I tried to steady my breathing, feeling a wave of insecurity wash over me. Did she not see me, or did she simply not care? Before I could react, Ren gently but firmly removed her hand from his arm.

"Thank you for the offer," he replied, his tone polite but unmistakably clear. "But I'm taken." As he spoke, he slid his arm around my waist, pulling me close. The warmth of his touch was reassuring, grounding me amidst the whirlwind of emotions.

The woman glanced at me briefly, her expression a mix of surprise and disdain, before she turned away with a huff, leaving us alone.

Ren's arm remained around me, a protective barrier against the world. "You okay?" he whispered, his voice low and filled with concern.

I nodded, a smile tugging at my lips. "Yes," I murmured, feeling a surge of gratitude and affection. "Thank you. That was—that was something, all right."

Ren found our table and guided me to it.

"Everyone, this is Piper." He greeted the other guests and introduced me with the practiced ease of someone born to be in this world. He mentioned that I was opening Something Sweet and hinted we were together. His words were perfectly measured, giving just enough to pique interest without revealing too much.

We settled into our seats, and I couldn't help but be in awe of his ability to navigate this with such grace. I watched him, struck by how natural he seemed, and wondered if he felt any of the same anxiety that was gnawing at me. I'd be lucky if I didn't have to go to the restroom soon—that's how nervous I felt.

"You are so beautiful tonight." He leaned in, his voice low and intimate, as he slid his hand around the back of my neck and dropped a kiss on my temple. Rule number two: *Be affectionate, AKA touchy-feely*.

I turned, leaning into his touch with a flush creeping up my cheeks again. I wondered if his words were part of the performance, yet I was still unable to suppress the giddy feelings they brought.

"Thank you," I replied, managing a genuine smile. "You clean up pretty well yourself." Rule number three: *Flirty Banter*.

I decided that sticking to the rules would get me through this. I was determined to be here for him, and I could figure everything else out later.

As the meal progressed, I found myself relaxing into the role. The wine flowed freely, and the conversation at our table became more animated. Ren's laughter was infectious, and I started to enjoy myself despite the undercurrent of tension still radiating through my body. I felt out of place and insecure, but realized it had nothing to do with Ren. It was all me.

The speeches began, and I listened with half an ear.

Ren was so confident and charming, and it made me question everything. Was this the real him or just part of the roles we were playing?

"Dance with me?" He asked.

I nodded, needing to get away from the table.

Ren led me to the dance floor, and the string quartet began to play a delicate, romantic melody. He pulled me close, one hand resting on the small of my back, the other holding my hand. I could feel his warmth through the fabric of my dress, and it sent a shiver down my spine.

We swayed gently to the music, our movements in sync as if we had done this a hundred times before. I could feel the strength in his arms and the steady rhythm of his breathing. Being this close to him, I was acutely aware of every sensation—the pressure of his hand on my back, the brush of his cheek against mine, the scent of his cologne mingling with the evening air.

My heart raced, a mix of nerves and attraction making it hard to focus. Was this another part of our performance, or was there something real in the way he held me? I glanced up at him, searching for answers in his eyes, but they were tender and unreadable.

"You're doing great," he whispered in my ear, his voice sending a thrill through me.

"Thanks," I murmured, trying to keep my voice steady. "You're not so bad yourself."

He smiled, and I felt my own tension ease a bit. Despite the nervous fluttering in my stomach, I found myself leaning into him, letting the music and the moment carry us. For now, I decided to let go of my doubts and just be present with him.

We continued to dance, lost in our own little world amidst the sea of other couples. I knew the night would eventually end, and with it, this fragile illusion of certainty. But for now, I was content to hold him close, swaying to the gentle strains of the string quartet, trying to let myself believe in the possibility of what we could be.

But I couldn't help but feel like Cinderella at the ball. Out of place, like it was all going to end at midnight, and I'd end up back at home in my ratty old robe with green cheeks and a broken heart.

As the evening wore on, the air filled with laughter and applause. The room buzzed with conversation, and Ren's deep and genuine laugh resonated through me. I realized he wasn't grumpy. He had said he hated these dinners, but it didn't seem that way at all tonight.

Dinner concluded, and as we mingled with the other guests, I was in awe of his ability to navigate the room with such charm. He was in his element, and I realized that I was not.

"You did amazing." His words broke through my reverie. "Are you ready to go?"

"Yes." I needed to think. Or maybe I shouldn't think. We were in two realities—the reality where we were faking our way through social obligations, and the other where we were falling for each other. It wasn't his fault that I was confusing the two of them tonight.

He approached the front desk to retrieve our coats

and the car from the valet, and finally, we stepped out into the cool night air. His hand found mine, and we walked in silence toward his waiting car. My mind spun with emotions, all tangled up in the night's events.

As we were settled in and ready to go, he turned to me, his eyes searching my face. "Are you okay?" he asked softly, and the genuine concern in his voice nearly undid me. "You're quiet."

I nodded, trying to smile. "Yeah, just a lot to take in."

He squeezed my hand gently. "You were incredible tonight. Thank you for being there with me."

I felt a rush of affection for him, but also a pang of uncertainty. "Can I ask you something?" Seeing a new side of someone I was dating was usually the beginning of the end, and I didn't want that to happen with Ren. My past—my insecurities and old hurts wouldn't stop creeping into my present tonight, and I wanted it to stop.

"Of course." His gaze was steady, calming, and I felt silly for feeling this way.

"Do you really hate these dinners?"

He looked surprised by the question and then thoughtful. "Tonight was different. With you there, it felt... easier, like I could be myself. Like you were my beautiful buffer, like I was safe with you there. I appreciate you coming with me more than I can say. Sometimes being alone is too much."

His words touched me deeply, and I realized that maybe both of us were in uncharted territory. When it was just the two of us it was easier; we only had our own expectations to meet. Being around others is where I started to question things.

As we drove home, the hum of the engine and soft music from the radio kept the silence between us comfortable.

I kept sneaking glances at him, wondering if he was as lost in thought as I was.

Finally, he pulled into my driveway and turned to me, his expression a mixture of weariness and warmth. I hesitated for a moment before speaking, unsure of what to say.

"Thank you for tonight," I said softly, my voice carrying the weight of all the emotions I couldn't quite articulate.

He reached out, brushing a strand of hair behind my ear. "You're up next," he murmured. "Something Sweet's grand opening is coming up soon."

"Yes, it is. I'm going to get through it, then celebrate for real once Jake gets Dana to let me buy her out. Like, have a grand re-opening once she's gone. I let her take over for now. I emailed her to order whatever she wanted for decorations and food, and I'd pay for half. Which reminds me, I need to check in with Jake in the morning."

"I'm so sorry. But I'll be there with you for the first grand opening, no matter what. Don't worry. I will be at your side the entire time. No one will hurt you. I won't allow it." He looked down at me with a devastating smile —it held promises and truth. He meant every word. The pang in my heart was undeniable.

I wanted to kiss him immediately, but instead, I

invited him inside, as if our relationship or whatever we were doing wasn't already complicated enough. "Come inside with me?"

"Absolutely." Without hesitation, he opened his car door, stepped out, and rounded the vehicle to open mine.

As I got out, the light breeze made me shiver, and he wrapped an arm around my shoulders.

We walked up to the front door together. The porch light cast a warm glow over us as I fumbled with my keys, my hands trembling slightly. He noticed and gently took the keys from me, unlocking the door with ease.

I flipped on the light and spotted Nimbus and Smog asleep on the couch in the living room. "Shh," I whispered. "If they wake up, they'll expect to come up to bed with me."

"Ahh, am I coming up to bed with you?" He eyed me carefully.

I felt the heat rise in my cheeks as I nodded, words failing me, as they often did whenever I was near him.

"Then let's not wake them."

We moved quietly through the house, his hand never leaving mine.

He paused at the top of the stairs, looking at me with a question in his eyes. I answered by gently pulling him along and leading him to my bedroom.

I turned to face him, my heart pounding hard in my chest. He reached out, cupping my cheek with his hand, his thumb brushing lightly against my skin.

"You are so beautiful." His voice was thick with emotion. "I know I keep saying it, but I can't help it. I feel it in my heart whenever I look at you. You take my breath away."

"Ren..." I couldn't help but smile and step closer to close the distance between us. "Do you want to stay the night with me again?" I whispered, trailing my hands up his chest.

He chuckled softly, pulling me into his arms. "Yes, and I find the fact that you asked me that hilarious. There is nowhere else I'd rather be than wherever you are."

The warmth of his embrace made me feel safe, like nothing else could. His lips descended toward mine, and every fiber of my being seemed to come alive with anticipation.

When our mouths finally met, all the fears and worries from the evening dissolved into the background, and for a moment, I wondered why I'd had them in the first place.

He was gentle at first, a soft press that sent warmth flooding through me. Then he paused, allowing me to catch my breath before deepening the kiss. His fingers threaded through my hair, and I melted into him.

"Are you sure?" he whispered against my mouth as he pulled back.

I nodded, pulling back in for another kiss.

"Say it. Tell me what you want. Say the words."

"I want you, Ren. I'm telling you yes."

Chapter 19
Ren

She had made all the difference tonight, giving me the confidence to get through the gala without second guessing myself. But it also made me realize how alone I had felt for most of my life. We were two of a kind, always putting others first, but it wasn't like that with Piper, and I didn't want to lose her or how she made me feel like it was possible to have someone who truly understood me.

I opened her bedroom door, nudging her inside and then closing it softly. With a hand braced on the door-frame, I leaned down to kiss her.

She took a step back, her eyes never leaving mine, the air seemed to hum with the electricity between us as she smiled, tender and inviting.

I reached out, my fingers tracing the curve of her cheek, and she leaned into my touch. Her eyes closed as she inhaled softly, and I pulled her close again as we stood there, wrapped in the silence. Her breath was warm against my neck, and the steady beat of her heart matched my own.

"I want you so much," I whispered. "All of you, Piper."

Her eyes met mine, filled with an earnestness that took my breath away. "I want you too, but I don't know how to do this with you, Ren. I don't know how to feel this way anymore without being afraid that I'll lose it."

"Just be with me tonight, no pressure, no expectations. You don't have to be afraid. Let me make you mine so I can finally be yours."

"I want to be yours, so much. Please. Yes, Ren."

It was like I'd been unleashed. I'd wanted her for so long, the word *yes*, uttered from her beautiful lips, detonated something inside of me. I stared at her, biting my lip as I decided where to begin.

I leaned in, our lips meeting in a slow kiss that seemed to last for an eternity. The taste of her lips, the feel of her body pressing against mine, was everything I had ever wanted.

We moved toward the bed, the moonlight casting a silvery glow across the room.

She reached out, loosening my tie and slipping it over my head, then our clothes fell away piece by piece until there was nothing between us but the heat of our bare skin and the pounding of our hearts.

"I've dreamed of this," I groaned. "Every fucking night." I slanted my head to kiss her deeper as I boosted her up with my hands on her ass, smiling against her open mouth when her legs wound my waist. "I'll never get enough of you. Ever."

"Good. I've thought of this. Being with you. More than I want to admit. There are condoms in the drawer. No more waiting. I want you now." I let her go, groaning as she slid down my body until her feet touched the floor.

Opening the bedside table drawer, I grabbed one, spotting all the toys that had spilled all over the floor the other night. "Almost forgot about those." I chuckled.

She shrugged, with a sexy little smile decorating her pretty face. "Next time," she murmured. "All I want right now is you."

I bent, sliding my lips down the delicate column of her throat, my hands at her waist, pushing her backward until her legs met the mattress and she fell to her back.

Her open arms beckoned me, I sheathed myself then joined her, covering her body with mine. Inhaling a sharp breath as her legs fell to the sides and my cock rubbed against her wet heat.

I slid inside her, moving with deep strokes, hard and slow, smiling into her neck when she arched into me and wrapped a leg around my back.

"Tell me what you want." My voice was gravel. I couldn't think. I could only feel. This is where I belonged, buried deep inside her, making her mine.

"This. Just like this. Don't stop," she moaned in my ear.

Then we were silent, speaking with sighs and moans,

her hands running up and down my back and my thumb rubbing circles around her clit.

This was a body and soul experience. Her smell, taste, the sweet slide of her slick skin enveloping me as I thrust into her became all I knew. She was everything, and I would never let her go.

"Roll over," she whispered, pressing her hands against my shoulders.

I obliged, inhaling a sharp breath when she straddled me, then slid down, taking me all the way inside, throwing her head back, as her hands ran into her hair, then down her body.

Our eyes met as she pinched her clit between her fingers and squeezed me tight.

"Just like that, sweetheart. Don't you dare fucking stop."

"You feel so good." She was gorgeous, riding me with all that beautiful blond hair spilling down her back, and her gorgeous breasts bouncing every time she moved. "You're so big it almost hurts."

I grabbed her hips hard, digging my fingertips into her soft curves as I slid my eyes down to where we were joined. The sight of her stretched full of me almost sent me over the edge.

I slammed my eyes shut. It was too much. The sight of her was undoing me, and she had to come first.

Fireworks burst behind my closed eyes. Tingling erupted up my spine as my body tensed for release. I knew she was close. I felt it each time she squeezed me deep.

Then she ground herself down, rubbing her clit against the base of my cock, shuddering, bucking up wildly until she came in a fluttering wave.

About to go over the peak, I opened my eyes. I had to see her. I needed to watch her as I fell apart.

I flipped her onto her back and rocked desperately into her tight heat. Once, twice, before falling over the edge. I gave her my weight for a second, then rolled to my side, gathering her in my arms.

"I've never felt like this in my life," I whispered into her hair.

"Me either." She snuggled close, resting her head on my chest. "Stay. Please."

"Yes." I would stay tonight. I would stay forever if she wanted me to.

"You make me feel hopeful again, Ren."

My arms convulsed around her. "Same. For the first time in years, Piper."

We lay there in silence, listening to each other's breath, feeling the warmth of our bodies as we held each other. I kissed her hair gently, breathing in her scent, and she sighed contentedly. "I'm glad you're here with me," she whispered, her voice barely audible in the quiet room.

"There's nowhere else I'd rather be," I replied softly, my heart swelling with the truth of my words. "Goodnight, sweetheart."

"'Night, Ren."

I woke to her sprawled across my chest. I liked her

cats, but I much preferred this. Her hair was soft as I brushed it aside to kiss her forehead.

She was peaceful in sleep, her features softened, beautiful and serene. I traced the outline of her jaw, and she sighed softly, leaning into my touch, even in her sleep. She was meant to be with me; there was no doubt in my mind.

"I want this every morning," I whispered, my voice barely audible, not wanting to disturb her. "You and me, just like this."

I tightened my arm around her, feeling her body's gentle rise and fall against my side. At that moment, I knew I'd never give up on her or what we could have together.

We were better together, and I was determined to keep it that way. Her eyes fluttered open, and she looked up at me with a sleepy, contented smile that made my heart skip a beat.

"You *are* here," she whispered, breathy and soft. "For a minute, I thought it was a dream."

"Maybe it was," I whispered. "It felt like one."

She nestled closer, wrapping me up in her arms and legs. "Good morning."

"Good morning, sweetheart," I replied, my voice husky with sleep.

She closed her eyes again and inhaled a soft breath. "Ren," she murmured. "I feel like I've waited years for a moment like this."

The emotion inside me was so pure and intense that I felt like my heart might burst. "So have I," I replied, moving to cup her face as I leaned in to capture her lips in a good morning kiss.

Her eyes darted to the clock on her bedside table. "I know you have to go to work soon, so we don't have time for breakfast. But can I make you dinner tonight?"

"You mean, no more evening porch swing make-out sessions?" I teased gently. "I get to come inside?"

Her hands met my side in a playful shove. "Yeah, something like that."

I buried my face in the soft skin where her shoulder met her neck. "I can't wait. Can I bring anything?"

"No, I have it covered."

"I'll probably bring you flowers anyway. Sometimes I'm not good at doing what I'm told."

"Thank god for that." She leaned back, giving me a radiant smile that I felt deep in my bones. "I'm really glad you're here, Ren. Last night felt like a dream, but waking up like this feels even better."

I kissed her softly on the lips, savoring the warmth of her breath and the softness of her skin.

"I'm not going anywhere, Piper. I'll be here tonight, and every night you want me to be."

She looked at me like she was memorizing every detail of my face. "Tonight then," she said with a small smile. "Dinner, just you and me."

"And Smog, and Nimbus, and soon, Cody too."

"Yeah. God, that sounds like perfection—it sounds like a dream."

"It's coming true, sweetheart. And I wouldn't miss it for the world," I added, feeling a surge of emotion.

We lay there for a few minutes, wrapped up in each other, before reluctantly pulling apart. I dressed quickly, stealing glances at her as she moved about the room, her presence filling the space with a lightness I never wanted to lose.

"See you tonight," I said, leaning in for one last kiss before I left for work.

"Yeah." She breathed. "Tonight."

Chapter 20
Piper

Ren and I were practically inseparable now. Of course, he'd go to Lyla's Place and his office in Sweetbriar for the day to work, while I spent my remaining days off before Something Sweet opened, trying to figure out how to handle working with Dana until she hopefully agreed to let me buy her out. Jake was still working on the bakery buyout and the Cody custody/ownership situation, so even though I wasn't taking any action myself, I felt like progress was being made. He told me to stay away from her and Richard and let him handle everything, so that's what I was doing.

Ren and I had dinner together every night, sometimes at my place and sometimes at his. He'd stay the night if it were my place, but I always went home when it was his because of Nimbus and Smog. I couldn't help but feel that one day, he'd come for dinner at my place and never leave. More and more, I felt like Ren and I ending up together was inevitable.

Last night was dinner night at my place, so he stayed with me, but he'd gone home to get ready for the day, and now I was here in my bathtub—just me and my wandering thoughts—yuck. I was a doer, not a thinker. If I couldn't distract myself with work, or a book, or whatever my latest hobby was, then I got restless.

Something Sweet was finally opening today, and I was losing my mind with anticipation. I also had no idea what I would be walking into since I'd let Dana be in charge of everything.

I heaved a sigh, using my toe to turn the hot water back to a steady trickle. I was in a tub full of bubbles, trying to relax, and it was not working. Smog and Nimbus were staring at me from the counter, heads tilted to the side as I heaved a sigh and tried to settle my thoughts.

I was off every routine I'd ever had. Wonderfully loving sex, coffee mornings, and make-out evenings on my porch with an angel of a man telling me he would do anything to make me happy were not how I usually lived my life, and I was thrown off by the too-good-to-be-true vibes filling my head with wonderous possibilities. The fact that I was imagining the future rather than dwelling in doubt was a sure sign of progress.

I don't know how long I had been soaking in the bath, but I suddenly heard the front door creak open and close softly. My heart skipped a beat as I realized Ren must have come back. I listened intently, recognizing the familiar sound of his footsteps as he walked up the stairs.

My breath hitched in anticipation as each step brought him closer.

The door to the bathroom opened slightly, and Ren's face appeared through the crack. His eyes smoldered, expression darkening as he took in the scene of me submerged in bubbles, my toes still resting on the faucet.

"Hey," he said with a smile that could melt all my worries away.

"Hey, yourself," I replied, feeling a wave of warmth wash over me that had nothing to do with the bathwater.

He stepped into the room, closing the door behind him, and walked over to me. I watched him, my heart swelling with affection, blatant lust, and the desire to pull him into the tub with me. Ren had that magical ability to make everything better just by being there.

"Are you ready for today?" he asked, kneeling beside the tub and brushing a bit of damp hair away from my face, before swirling his hand in the warm water. Oh, how I wished he'd move that hand a little to the right and higher. Damn.

"Not really. But you coming with me will make it all better." I sighed, leaning into his touch.

"Do you want me to tell you you're running late? Or do you want to be late? I'm fine either way."

"I love it that you ask." I heaved a massive sigh, not wanting to move. "I'll get out now."

Ren chuckled softly and stood up, retrieving a large, plush towel from the rack. He held it up for me, his eyes never leaving mine, filled with a tenderness that made my heart ache in the best way. As I rose from the bath, the bubbles cascading off my skin, the cats scrambled out of the room, startled by the movement, and splashing water.

"You're too good to me," I murmured, my voice barely more than a whisper.

I watched his throat move as he swallowed, biting his lip as his eyes roamed over my body, dark with desire.

He bent low, starting at my feet, working his way higher to dry every inch of my skin before holding the towel wide to wrap me up in it.

He brushed a strand of wet hair away from my face. "You deserve it, Piper. You deserve all of it."

Ren leaned in, and as he did, everything else seemed to fade away. His lips met mine softly at first, gentle and exploring.

I responded, tilting my head slightly, and the kiss deepened, our tongues moving against each other. His hand cupped the back of my head, fingers weaving through my damp hair, and I felt a shiver run down my spine. With each moment, the kiss grew more passionate, more insistent. His other hand slid around my waist, pulling me closer, and I melted into his embrace as my towel fell to the floor and his hands moved down to my ass.

"You need to get dressed, baby," he groaned into my mouth before breaking the kiss.

"Huh?" Dazed, I studied his face.

"Something Sweet," he said with a grin. "Grand opening."

"Crap! Okay." I snapped to attention, standing

straight. "Yes. I need to get ready. No more procrastinating. I won't take long."

"Take as long as you like," he murmured. "Today is your day. If you need me to push you to help you be on time, tell me and I will. If you want to be late or blow the whole thing off, that's okay too. I'm here only for you."

I nodded, appreciating his unwavering support more than I could express. "Thank you, Ren. I don't think I could do this without you."

I quickly dressed, choosing a simple yet elegant little black dress. As I applied my makeup, Ren sat on the edge of the bed, watching me with a thoughtful expression. The room was filled with a comfortable silence, punctuated only by the occasional rustle of Nimbus and Smog as they settled back into their favorite spots.

Once I was ready, I turned to face Ren. "How do I look?"

"Beautiful. You always do." His smile was warm and genuine, making my heart flutter.

"Except I need you to zip me up." I turned, giving him my back.

His fingers traced up my spine, leaving a trail of shivers in their wake. He lingered at the straps over my shoulders, then leaned down to kiss my neck. "I don't know if I want to zip you up or slide this pretty dress down and kiss you all over."

"God, Ren. How about you unzip me later tonight?"

"You got yourself a deal, sweetheart." He zipped me up, then spun me around with his hands on my shoulders.

I took a deep breath, feeling more prepared to face the day with him by my side. "Okay, let's do this."

He offered his arm, which I took gratefully.

We walked down the hallway, the faint sound of our footsteps blending with the soft purr of the cats. As we reached the front door, Ren paused and looked at me, his eyes searching mine. "I'm here for you, no matter what. I don't give a shit about anyone else or how they feel. Only you."

"I know," I replied, squeezing his hand. "That's the only thing making me feel okay about going."

"Good girl. You got this. And I got you."

"Let's drive, please? I want to have a car handy in case I need to make a dramatic exit."

Ren chuckled softly. "Drama queen. Let's get you in the car and on the road," he said, his voice a soothing balm to my anxious heart.

The drive was serene, the hum of the engine blending with the rhythm of my thoughts. Ren's hand rested reassuringly on my thigh, a silent reminder of his unwavering presence. As we drove through the familiar streets, I couldn't help but feel a sense of dread creeping in.

"You're still worried, aren't you?"

"I don't like confrontations, and the last time I was alone with Dana, I let her have it, which is why I don't have Cody right now. I ruined everything. I can't afford to rock the boat more than I've already done. I could lose him."

"You won't lose him. I won't let that happen."

"I've been trying so hard not to think about him and let Jake handle it, but it's all coming up for me today and I—"

"Do you want me to listen or distract you?"

"Oh god, distract me, please. I can't keep thinking this way."

"Spread your legs."

"What?" I breathed as I did what he said.

His big, warm palm slid up my thigh to rest high with his pinky nestled against the seam of my undies. I inhaled sharply as he ever so slightly moved it side to side, wondering if he'd get upset if I grabbed his hand and rubbed myself against it.

"Do it." He chuckled. "I can hear you thinking about it from here. Take them off so I can feel you."

With a shimmy, I did what he said, folded them neatly, then held them awkwardly in my lap above his hand, wondering where to put them.

Ren's demeanor shifted as he turned the corner and maneuvered the car down a winding road, away from the town's bustling streets and prying eyes. The trees grew denser, their branches creating a canopy overhead, filtering the sunlight into mottled shadows that danced across the windshield. He drove with a focused intensity, his eyes scanning the surroundings for the perfect spot.

Finally, he found it—a small, secluded clearing just off the road. The gravel on the ground crunched under the tires as he pulled in, the car coming to a smooth halt. He cut the engine and turned to me, a mischievous glint in his eyes, as the tension began to melt, replaced by a tangible anticipation.

"I'm going to make you come, then we'll go, okay? Then all you'll have to worry about when we get there is people wondering why you're blushing."

"Okay." I breathed. "But what about you?"

"This isn't about me." He took my undies and stuffed them into his jacket pocket. "But if you're worried about reciprocity, you can let me fuck you in that bathtub of yours when we get home tonight."

"'kay..." If this was his plan, it was working. I couldn't seem to catch a thought. Heat rushed through my body, pooling between my legs. All I could think about was getting his hands back on me.

"Close your eyes and relax."

I did what he said, inhaling sharply as his hand slid between my legs again.

"You're so soft. Are you ready for your distraction?"

"Yes," I whispered, hiking up my dress. I was more than ready. In fact, I was willing to beg him for it because, for now, this was all I could think of.

He slipped a finger into me, then out to circle my clit but it's awkward with the console between us. Panting, I spread my legs wider to give him better access. Trembling, I bent my knee, placing my foot on the seat so I could rock my hips with the rhythm of his hand.

With his other hand, he yanked me close by the back of my neck and kissed me hard, his tongue thrusting inside along with the tempo of his hand and my hips. In no time at all, I was coming. Exploding into pieces as he held me together, whispering how beautiful I looked, how wet I was, and how much he couldn't wait to get inside me later tonight.

I broke away, pulling back to look at him. "You're so hard. I can see it and I need it. Get out of the car. Now. We'll be quick."

One second later, he was out of the car and running around to open my door before I could even finish the thought. Then after another second, I was bent over the hood with his hand spread across my lower back, holding my dress up.

The sound of his zipper and the tear of the condom wrapper had me moaning, and then he was inside of me, hard. Holding my hips tight and pounding into me fast and wild. I spread my arms wide, arched my back with my palms down on the hood, and shoved myself back to take him even deeper as I tried not to moan too loud.

"You're going to come again," he growled, banding an arm around my waist to press his thumb against my clit.

"Yes, yes, yes..." I chanted in a whisper as he hauled me up for one last brutal thrust. He shivered against me as he bent us forward over the hood, covering me with his body and groaning in my ear.

"We're still taking a bath tonight," he whispered before lightly biting the lobe. "I haven't had enough of you yet."

I laughed lightly. "Anything you want."

Breathless and still tingling, we straightened ourselves up and climbed back into the car. The engine roared to life, and as I settled into my seat, I glanced over to find him watching me with a satisfied grin. I found myself wishing I could feel like this every day for the rest of my life.

The short drive to the bakery was a blur of shared glances and stolen touches. He pulled into the lot across the street and reached over, giving my hand a gentle squeeze.

"Feel better?"

"Absolutely." And I did.

For now.

Chapter 21
Piper

We crossed the street to Something Sweet, and I could already tell Dana had nothing to do with the decorations. I'd already paid her for half of what she spent, and the sign and flower arrangements on the sidewalk had definitely cost more than I had given her.

The new handwritten chalkboard sign welcomed us into the doorway, spelling out "Welcome to Something Sweet! Grand Opening Today!"

Ren and I exchanged a glance and smiled, feeling the excitement bubbling between us.

I let go of his hand as I stepped inside. I was in awe. I spun around, taking in the soft glow of fairy lights strung across the ceiling as they cast a warm and welcoming glow to the space.

We had a few small tables in the front area for cake tasting. Each was adorned with delicate lace tablecloths and elegant floral arrangements bursting with pastel roses, my favorite pink peonies, and baby's breath. The sweet fragrance of the flowers mingled with the rich aroma of freshly baked cake. It was like heaven in here.

The centerpiece of the bakery was a wedding cake display that Dana and I had chosen together before everything went to shit.

Weeks ago, I had created an elaborate, multi-tiered fake cake with intricate sugar flowers and delicate piping as an example of what we offered, and it sat proudly in the center with more miniature cakes and pastries, that Dana must have baked, arranged artfully around it, each one a mini masterpiece of its own.

I had chosen the color palette of blush pink, ivory, and gold for the bakery, and the temporary opening day décor enhanced it.

Soft instrumental music played in the background, and I saw Dana behind the counter preparing trays of tiny cake samples and small shot glasses filled with chocolate milk.

No one else was here. We had arrived first, though this wasn't a scheduled party with invitations and such. It was just a day to show off our new business with free samples to lure in Honeybrook Hollow locals and show them what we could do.

"Who did all of this?" My whispered question was answered when my mother entered through the open front door. "You?" My eyes filled with tears. "Mom? You're back?"

"Surprise." She rushed toward me, pulling me into her arms. "I couldn't miss your opening day, could I?" She pulled away, gesturing to the decorations. "But this was all your sisters' doing. They snuck in here last night. It's gorgeous, isn't it? But, honey, why didn't you call me? I would have rushed straight home if I knew what was happening with Richard and—everything."

"You were finally on your epic Hawaii girls' trip. I was not about to interrupt it. I'm fine."

Her eyes found Ren, and she smiled as she introduced herself. "I'm Marilyn, Piper's mother. You have to be Ren. I've heard all about you from Paige. Call me Marilyn, honey, please. After what you did for my Paige, I'll love you forever."

"Nice to meet you, Marilyn. I've heard a lot about you, too."

Mom beamed, her eyes shimmering with pride. "It's wonderful to see this place come to life finally. You've done an incredible job, Piper."

I felt a lump form in my throat as I looked around the bakery, my heart swelling with a mix of emotions. "Thank you, Mom. It means the world to me that you're here."

"Me too. Let's focus on the positive. This is your day. I want you to remember that." She hugged me again and then wandered off to explore the rest of the place.

"Maybe Richard won't show up," I whispered to Ren once my mother was out of earshot. "God, I hope he doesn't."

He leaned in, sliding an arm around my waist. "I'm not worried about your ex, sweetheart. I'll shake his hand with the same hand I just got you off with. He's nothing, and if what Jake has planned works—which it will, he never loses—they'll both be out of your life for good very soon."

"Your hands. Oh god, you have to wash your hands," I pulled him down to hiss in his ear. "I mean, I'm glad we did what we did, I don't regret it, it was fun, and awesome, and amazing, and I want to do it again—but— oh my god, Dana's back there. Should I go talk to her? Jake told me to be cordial but distant. Should I say hi? What am I even talking about?"

"No. You're okay. Stay with your mom, and I'll go to the restroom and wash up. I meant to do that first anyway. I don't want anything to worry you today. I'm at your command."

"Thank you." I knew my cheeks were red, and I took a huge breath to try and calm myself down before I spiraled out of control and went into orbit.

Violet walked in with the baby, and Ren steered me in their direction. "Hang out with Violet," he whispered in my ear. "And try to forget that I still have your panties in my pocket."

"Oh crap." I yanked him close by his lapels. "Can you tell I'm not wearing any underwear?"

He laughed darkly. "No, lucky for you, you chose a long dress today."

"Who even am I?"

"A siren, tempting me to take you with me to the bathroom to make out with you and possibly get you off again with my magic hand."

"You're a nut and a horndog, and I love it."

"Piper!" I watched my grandparents and sisters walk through the door, their faces beaming with joy.

"Good, there are plenty of buffers. I'll be right back." His laughter faded as he headed off to the restroom. I tried to shake off the embarrassment and focus on the guests arriving. The room was filling up, and there was a buzz of excitement in the air as the familiar faces of my hometown waved and smiled as they circled around the room, taking it all in.

Violet approached me, shifting the baby in her arms. "It's so pretty in here, Piper. I'm happy for you! Jake is working, he said to congratulate you and keep you away from Dana."

One of my grandma's friends walked up, joining our impromptu circle. "Hey, sugar! When are we going to see you with Cody at the dog park? We miss you."

I forced a smile. "Soon, I hope. Things have been busy lately, with the bakery opening and everything."

She nodded understandingly, her eyes scanning the room. "I totally get it. This place is going to be great, Piper. Everyone in town will love it. I'm going to grab a sample. It smells so good in here."

"Gah! I'm sorry," Violet whispered. "Jake will have this all handled soon, I know it."

"I hope so. He told me he's filed papers and thinks I have a good chance—oh shit."

Richard appeared at the door with Cody, and my eyes welled with tears. "Violet. Oh. Look. It's Cody." Tears filled my eyes, and I blinked several times to get them to stop. "What's wrong with me?" I laughed to cover my emotional response. "He's okay. I know I don't have to worry, but—"

"Call him," she bit out.

"What?" I swiped a hand beneath my eye, sending Paige and my sisters a tremulous smile as they headed my way.

Dana rushed from behind the counter, making sure I saw her as she headed to greet Richard and Cody. "Thank you, Richie! You brought my baby to see my big opening day!"

"*Her baby?* That witch," Paige muttered, wrapping an arm around my waist.

"*Her* big opening day?" Lucy snarked. "I'm bringing Larry by later for a snack."

"Do it, Piper. Call Cody," Violet repeated.

"Oh yeah," Grandma agreed. "Call him now. Or I will."

As friendly as ever, Cody stood at Richard's side, looking around the room with his tail wagging furiously as he recognized many of his human friends from the dog park.

"Cody," I called, smiling when he started excitedly barking. "Cody!"

He barked louder, started whining, and tugged at the leash. He yipped frantically until he got away and made a beeline for me, the leash trailing behind him.

My heart leapt at his enthusiasm. He was my doggie soul mate, and I had missed him so much. I knelt, holding my arms wide as he bounded toward me. He jumped, wiggling and bopping around me, licking my face with his tail wagging so fast it was a blur.

"I missed you, too, boy!" I laughed, hugging him tightly as the room filled with warm laughter.

"Guess we'll be seeing you tomorrow at the dog park, sugar!" Grandma's friend hollered.

"You sure will," I called back. There was no way I would let him go home with Richard. It was my damn turn now.

"It was so nice of you to keep Cody while Piper set up the bakery," My mother said, sidling up to Richard's side. "Especially after everything that happened. I love how you're keeping it classy."

"Uh, yeah. It was no big deal," he muttered, exchanging a glance with Dana.

At that moment, Ren returned to my side. "Hey, Cody." He knelt next to me to pet him.

Cody barked happily at Ren. As he scratched behind his ears, I stood up and brushed off my knees, feeling a calmness in my heart that had been gone for far too long. I'd missed him so much.

Ren rose to his feet, giving Cody one last pat as he picked up the leash and held it firm, signaling to Richard not to argue. "We've got him now," he addressed Richard. "It's time for you two to relax. Take it easy."

"Yeah." I smiled at Dana. "Thank you for watching

him for me. And thank you for making opening day so lovely."

"We've got it from here," Lucy chimed in.

"Yeah," Eliza added. "Why don't you two take the rest of the day off?"

"Go get some lunch or something," Cara suggested. "The Pennywhistle has spotted *dick* on special—it's a British theme today. I think you'd love it."

"Nice, Cara," Richard grumbled as Paige burst out laughing.

"You stole my line," Paige said through her giggles.

"What?" Cara shrugged innocently. "They do."

"Let's go, Richard," Dana said, grabbing his arm as she shot daggers at me with her eyes.

Richard nodded, covering her hand with his as he guided her towards the door. "Fine. Lunch it is."

As they walked away, my whole body seemed to sigh. I was almost giddy with relief. This is what today should have started like. Dana had no place here anymore, and maybe now she would finally see it and let me take over.

I spent the next few hours serving cake samples and chatting with people who came in to check the place out. My family and Ren stayed with me for the duration while my sisters took turns watching Cody. Lucy was currently taking him for a walk at the dog park.

Ren smiled at me through his mouthful of cake. He leaned back against the counter, eyes shining with amusement. "You know, you're great at this. People love chatting with you. They love your enthusiasm. And the cake is excellent."

"It will be even better once I'm the one baking it. Although she used my recipes." I grinned. "This is almost exactly what I wanted."

"So, you'll be here tomorrow?" he asked.

"No, but I'll be here all the time once Dana is gone for good."

Paige laughed. "Piper will do all the big orders, that's her favorite. Like, when someone wants to spend a few grand on a cake, now they know where to go."

"What?" His eyes grew big. "People really spend that much?"

"Yep." My mother beamed with pride. "Piper's cakes require architecture and sometimes smoke and lighting effects. She's come a long way from her cupcake cart days."

"Really?" He wrapped an arm around me, tugging me into his side. "This I have to see."

"Oh, you will." I arched an eyebrow, as thoughts of what I could bake to impress him entered my mind. The blueberry muffins I'd baked the other morning were child's play compared to what I could do.

"What about the cake samples? Are they going to be a regular thing?" Eliza asked before stuffing a piece of chocolate cake into her mouth. "I'd come here every day for a tiny piece of cake."

"The samples stay." I grabbed a tiny piece of lemon chiffon from the tray. "The best part of a wedding is the cake. And the best part of planning is the samples—it's what everyone talks about. Like, some of us never want to get married, right?" I joked. "Now we have a place to go."

Ren pulled away, his smile fading at my joke. And I cursed myself for being so careless.

I needed to watch what I said, especially since I wasn't even sure I felt that way anymore. The idea of getting married again wasn't as scary as it once was. Meeting Ren was tearing down the walls I'd built.

Chapter 22
Ren

Her words stung. Was I ready to propose? No, it was way too soon for that. But I'd like to think she might say yes if I did someday, that having forever with her wasn't impossible.

I watched her, her face still radiant despite her words that had just stabbed at my heart. I wanted to reach out and tell her that I understood that we were both recovering in our own ways, taking things one day at a time. But I swallowed those words, unsure if they would be a consolation or push her further away.

"Do you think you'll ever want to?" Cara asked Piper, interrupting my thoughts.

Piper looked at Cara, and then at me, her eyes softening just a little. "Maybe. Someday, I might," she said quietly, and for a moment, I felt a glimmer of hope.

The conversation drifted to other topics, but I couldn't stop thinking about Piper's words. I knew we had a way to go, but I believed there would be a future for us where Richard and what he put her through were no longer a factor. I just had to make her see it was possible.

Day faded into early evening, and it was time to close up. Almost everyone had trickled out, leaving me, Piper, and Cody here to finish up.

"I think this went well," I said, looking around. Her sisters had helped us clean up; all that was needed was to set the alarm and lock up.

"I agree, and I can't wait to get Cody home." He was currently asleep under one of the tables.

"Soon enough, he'll go home with you, and you'll never have to worry about him leaving."

"I hope so. Sharing him was hard." She bent down, stroking her hand down his side. "I guess all this excitement wore him out."

"He'll be full of energy when you get him home, I bet."

She glanced around the bakery. "It was a good day. Better than I expected."

"It was amazing. Would it be condescending to say that I'm proud of you?"

A grin lit up her face. "No. Thank you. It was hard, but you made it better. It meant a lot to me that you were here." Her expression was tender as her smile softened. "And, um, about what I said earlier?"

"Yeah?"

"I'm sorry for being insensitive." She bit her lip and looked down at Cody. "It wasn't even completely true. I cover a lot of my feelings with jokes. I really need to stop it."

"I get it." I reached out to take her hand. "We all have our ways of coping. Plus, everything that happened is still fresh in your mind. Seeing the two of them brought it all up. I know that."

"Exactly, today brought up a lot of feelings that I'd been stuffing down for a long time." Her eyes darted from mine again as she smiled sheepishly. "So yeah, I'm not good with feelings and confrontation. Sometimes I don't want to deal, so I, uhhh, I don't know, develop hobbies such as bad knitting and bird watching. Or I make stupid jokes and have sex on deserted side streets." She shrugged her shoulders, shaking her head.

"I see." I turned her face to mine with a finger beneath her chin. "Don't forget about raccoon hoarding, and caftan collecting."

"See?" She burst into laughter. "You get me."

"I do." I chuckled. "I'm not that great at dealing with my feelings either. I'm a workaholic and can be pretty closed off sometimes. Or I go to the other extreme and take care of someone until I drive them away with my smothering ways."

"You're not like that with me. I don't feel smothered at all. Ever." Her eyes met mine again, a flicker of vulnerability in her gaze. "And you've never shut me out. I like that."

"No, you're different. I don't want to shut you out, but I also don't want to scare you off."

"You're different too." A small smile formed on her lips. "I would never admit any of what I just told you to anyone else. And you won't scare me off, Ren. Being cared for like you do is what I've always secretly wanted."

"I'm honored. And I'm glad you don't find me over-bearing."

"I like my independence, but I also want to be babied. I'm a complicated lady, Ren."

She was a fascinating mix of vulnerability and playful confidence, with an irresistible hint of shyness in her eyes. She was absolutely complicated, and I was falling in love with it.

"Have I cracked your code?" I asked her, hoping she'd tell me that I had. I wanted to know her. All of her.

Her laughter was sweet and familiar, and I loved how open she was with me, how she revealed pieces of herself she had hidden from the world. I wanted to protect that part of her, to cherish it.

"I think maybe you have."

My heart swelled at her candor. I leaned in closer, feeling the warmth radiate from her. Our breaths mingled, and after a brief pause, I gently cupped her cheek with my hand, my thumb tracing soft circles on her skin. She closed her eyes, and I took it as a sign to bridge the space between us.

Our lips met in a kiss, soft and sweet, yet filled with an unspoken promise. "I see you, Piper, and I don't want to lose this."

When we finally parted, our foreheads rested together, breaths intermingling again. Her eyes fluttered open, and her smile was full of warmth and something more profound. It gave me hope.

"Let's go home, okay?"

Home. She felt like home. Her including me when she spoke of home made my heart soar.

I held Piper's hand as we returned to the car, the evening air cool and crisp. As we got into the car, Cody jumped into the back seat, his excitement palpable. Piper looked at him and laughed, her eyes sparkling with joy. I couldn't help but smile; her happiness was infectious.

The drive back to Piper's place was filled with quiet contentment, the kind that comes from knowing you're exactly where you're meant to be. Piper's hand rested on my leg, her touch grounding me in the moment. I glanced at her, and she met my gaze with a smile that spoke volumes.

When we pulled into the driveway, Cody was the first to leap out, bounding up the steps like he felt what I did—like he was home, and I hoped that one day this house would be my home too.

Chapter 23
Piper

My heart was full as we drove. I knew Cody's was too, as he happily panted out the back window the entire time like he knew where we were going.

He bounded up the front steps, tail wagging like mad, his excitement evident. Nimbus and Smog approached cautiously at first, their tails puffed up in curiosity. As gentle as ever, Cody lowered his head, sniffing them tentatively until they recognized him and began rubbing themselves all over his sides.

Ren bent down to pat Cody's head. "Welcome home, buddy."

"I'm so happy right now," I wrapped my arms around Ren's waist, cuddling into him as I watched my little fur babies get reacquainted. "Look at them. Back together. Finally."

He kissed my temple. "I know," he murmured, his

voice a gentle caress against my skin. "I'm happy for you. I'm going to call Jake and talk to him about what happened, okay?"

"Oh." Her face fell. "Do you think this will cause a problem? He told me to stay away from them, but I thought—"

"No. It should be fine, but I always like to err on the side of caution, so I'm going to make sure. I'm just going to see what he thinks."

"Okay. I'll go run that bath."

He pulled me closer. "I won't be too long," he whispered softly, his breath tickling my ear.

"I'll be waiting." Slowly, reluctantly, I let him go and started up the stairs.

Ren watched me at the foot of the staircase, a smile dancing across his lips. "I'll be right up. Do you want me to set out some water for Cody?"

"He'll be okay, there's a pet water dispenser in the kitchen. They've always shared it, and I'll feed him later."

Ren turned and headed into the living room, phone in hand, while I walked up the stairs. The warmth of his kiss still lingered on my skin and filled me with a sense of comfort and security. As I stepped into the bathroom, I turned on the water, letting the sound of the running bath soothe my thoughts.

Ren's voice echoed softly from downstairs, murmuring into the phone. I knew he was making sure everything would be alright, so I trusted his judgment and let my worries drift away.

Moments later, I heard his footsteps coming up the stairs. He appeared at the doorway, his eyes soft as they met mine.

"I've run the bath," I said, turning to face him fully. "But it's not for me. It's for you."

Surprise flickered across his face, followed by a look of gratitude. "For me?"

I nodded, stepping closer to him. "Yes. You've done so much today, and I thought you might enjoy a little time to relax. I want to take care of you too." I reached out, my fingers brushing the hem of his shirt. "May I?" I asked softly, looking up into his eyes. He nodded, trust and desire evident in his gaze.

With gentle hands, I peeled off his shirt and placed a kiss on his shoulder, guiding him towards the edge of the bed to remove his shoes and socks.

"You don't have to wait on me."

I smiled, feeling a rush of affection for him. "I know, I want to. Remember when you offered to sleep outside my door the night of the raccoon invasion? You take care of me already, and that's just one example. Now, it's my turn. Plus, I don't think we'll both fit. You're way too tall. I was going to *take care of you* up close and personal, but we can do that later."

"Gotcha," He chuckled, then stood, slipping out of his pants. He allowed me to lead him to the tub with a bemused smile on his face.

My gaze lingered on him, the soft light casting him in a golden glow. His broad shoulders and chiseled chest spoke of power, yet there was a gentleness in his demeanor, a tenderness that made my heart ache in the most beautiful way.

"Get in," I whispered. "I'll wash your back."

Ren sank into the bath, his eyes closing as the warm water enveloped him. I watched him for a moment, appreciating the rare sight of him relaxing in the water. He deserved this, more than anyone I knew.

"How does it feel?" I asked, my voice barely above a whisper.

He opened his eyes, a soft smile playing on his lips. "Perfect. Thank you."

I leaned down, pressing a kiss to his forehead. "You're welcome. Be right back."

Leaving him to enjoy his bath, I stepped back into the bedroom and found the caftan I'd laid out earlier. Slipping it on, I felt the silky fabric brush against my skin, a gentle reminder of the evening's peacefulness.

I returned to the bathroom, where Ren was still soaking, his eyes closed as if he could fall asleep at any moment. He opened his eyes when he heard me come in. "Ahh, there she is." He smiled as he looked me up and down. "Did you miss me, golden girl?" he murmured, his voice thick with contentment.

"Always." I knelt, grabbing the soap to wash his back, and smiling when his muscles relaxed under my touch. "You're a bit tense."

"Just worried."

"About Cody." I deduced.

"Yeah. I don't want Richard to mess this up."

"Let's think about it tomorrow. Jake has it under control. Let's try to enjoy tonight," I whispered, letting my fingers trail up and down his back and sides, then lower, between his legs where he was already hard for me.

"I'd enjoy it a lot more if you got in here with me." His voice was deep and growly, and I wanted nothing more than to climb into his lap and drive us both wild, but he had to be at least six feet five, and I was five eight. We were too tall for bathtub shenanigans, at least in this tub.

"We might flood the bathroom." I laughed lightly.

"Then I'm taking you to bed. I can't wait." He pulled the plug, then stood. I watched as water ran down his gorgeous body, over his broad wall of a chest and through the ridges of his abs, then he raised his arms to slick his hair back, and I almost started drooling.

I handed him a towel, savoring the sight of the droplets glistening on his skin. He dried himself off quickly, and we walked together to the bedroom. Ren's touch was never far away, his fingers brushing against my arm, my waist, my hip. Each caress sent ripples of warmth through me.

As he pulled me into his embrace, I couldn't help but feel a mixture of excitement and concern. Our relationship had layers and complexities that the world wasn't privy to. It was like we were in two relationships. The fake one that everyone thought was ten steps ahead of what it actually was. And the real one, where we were slowly falling in love with each other. But in this moment, everything felt simple—just us, at home, away from prying eyes.

He slid my caftan down, and as it pooled on the floor, his lips found mine, a kiss of reassurance and longing. We fell onto the bed, naked together, our bodies tangling in a mess of limbs and whispers.

With every touch, every kiss, it felt like we were stitching together the fragments of ourselves, making something whole and new. His hands mapped the contours of my body, tracing paths that felt both familiar and thrillingly uncharted. The worries of the day melted away, replaced by the intoxicating immediacy of the present. I was drunk on him, and I never wanted to lose this feeling.

We moved together with an unspoken understanding, each gesture a promise, each breath a shared secret. His lips trailed down my neck, then lower, sucking a nipple into his mouth, igniting a fire that spread through my veins. I clung to him, feeling the solid strength of his body against mine.

There was a tenderness in his eyes that was more than desire. It was a connection, a bond that went beyond mere physicality. I knew he felt the same way I did, that we were building something that could withstand anything.

He paused to sheath himself with a condom from my bedside table, then slid inside me, holding my hands above my head with our fingers intertwined as he found my lips with his, kissing me deeply as his thrusts grew harder, faster, more frantic.

"You feel so fucking good. I'll never get enough." His voice was a whispered groan in my ear.

I planted my feet on the mattress and began matching him thrust for thrust. "Don't stop, please, Ren."

Sliding a hand between us, I pressed my palm against my clit and spread my fingers apart so I could feel him as he moved inside of me, he was so hard and slick with our combined desire. It was perfect. We were beautiful together, like nothing I'd ever experienced.

"I love how you feel," he groaned. "Like I'm home for the first time in my life."

This moment was suspended in time, a perfect crystallization of everything we could be. In that instant, I wanted to believe we could find our way through whatever challenges lay ahead, as long as we had each other.

The intensity of the moment washed over us, leaving us breathless and spent as we fell apart together, breaths ragged and hearts pounding.

He rolled onto his side, his gaze locked to mine, with a soft smile on his lips. He reached out, tracing the line of my jaw with his fingertips, a gesture that was both tender and possessive. I mirrored his smile, feeling my heart surge with emotions I didn't quite know how to handle.

"I never want to forget this," I murmured, my voice barely audible.

His smile widened. "You won't because we'll have more nights like this to share. We have all the time in the world, sweetheart. No rushing, no pressure, just us." He brushed a strand of hair away from my face, his gaze softening as he leaned in to kiss me again.

"I want this," I whispered back. "With you."

"I know you do. And I do too." He rolled to his back, pulling me into his side. He held me close, sighing into my hair, then kissing the top of my head. "I want it more than anything."

"Good. Maybe we should talk about birth control. We can use condoms as long as you want to, but I have an IUD, and I got tested after Richard. I'm all clear."

He tipped his head down, his eyes smiled into mine. "I'm fine too. I just had a physical before I moved here."

We lay there, entangled, savoring the intimacy that words could never fully capture.

"I've never felt this close to anyone before," I admitted softly, my fingers tracing patterns on his chest.

"Me neither," he replied, his voice hushed as if the moment could shatter if spoken too loudly.

"There's something I need to tell you," I confessed, my voice trembling slightly. "It's important to me that you know where I stand. Um, before we go any further."

Ren's brow furrowed slightly in concern, but he continued to hold me, his embrace unwavering and warm. "What is it, sweetheart?"

I took a deep breath, summoning the courage to speak. "I don't want kids, Ren. It's nothing medical, not trauma, I just don't want them. I was worried about bringing it up, but I think I have to."

He smiled warmly, his touch reassuring and gentle. "Then we're on the same page. No deal breakers here. I don't either. We can build something just for us."

The room seemed to cocoon us in a world where time

stood still. I felt a profound sense of peace, like all the pieces of my life were finally clicking into place.

"How did we get so lucky?" I whispered.

"Maybe it's fate," he answered. "Or maybe we just have too many people in common and it was inevitable."

I burst out laughing. "God, Paige will definitely be gloating when she finds out how serious we are."

"Now, it's my turn to make a confession."

I tilted my head, curious. "What do you want to confess?"

Ren's eyes twinkled with mischief. "I used to sneak into the neighbor's yard to play with their dog when I was a kid. I wanted one so badly, but we couldn't afford it. And until now, I haven't had the time for a pet. So, when I moved into my place, I considered getting a dog, maybe two. How do you feel about that? I mean I'd like to think that someday the two of us—"

I pressed a finger to his lips. "You'd make a great dog dad. I think you should. Obviously, I'm a fan of dogs. Cats, too. The more the merrier."

His smile lit up the room. "How about domesticated raccoons? I mean, you have the space..."

"I'd hit you with a pillow for that, but I'm too comfortable to move."

"Should we put on some pajamas and let the kids in?" he joked.

"Could you be any more perfect?" I kissed his pec, then lifted on an elbow to look at him, tousled, satisfied, *mine.*

"I mean, I could try," he teased.

"No, then you'd be too good for me."

"Hey," he tipped my face up to his. "There's no such thing."

We got out of bed and into our pajamas, then fed Cody. We spent the rest of the night cuddled together.

Chapter 24
Piper

When Ren and I arrived at my grandparents' house behind the Honeybrook Inn, the weenie roast was in full swing. The bonfire crackled heartily, sending sparks dancing into the twilight sky. Chairs had been arranged around it in a semicircle. My sisters were there, and my mother, their laughter bright and infectious as they chatted animatedly by the fire's glow.

Lucy and her boyfriend Spencer were sitting on a blanket off to the side of the bonfire, engrossed in conversation with her mom, their faces occasionally illuminated by the flickering flames.

Grandma's pugs scampered about, their playful barks adding a cheerful melody to the evening. They tumbled over each other, their energy boundless, chasing their tails and each other in an adorable frenzy. Cody was at home. I decided that I'd bring him by when it was quiet to introduce him to the puppies.

Ren squeezed my hand, a smile spreading across his face as he took in the scene. "This is amazing," he murmured.

I grinned, my heart swelling with happiness. "Welcome to my childhood," I replied.

The backyard at my grandparents' place was expansive. Nestled in one corner was a small barn, its red paint weathered but still vibrant. Adjacent to the barn was a chicken coop. A fenced-in area stretched along one side of the yard, providing a safe haven for Grandma's menagerie of rescues, including Larry the Llama.

Near the house, the outdoor kitchen was a hub of activity and warmth. Built from rustic stone, it featured a large grill and a wooden table. A canopy overhead provided shade for those rare sunny Oregon days.

As Ren and I walked through the yard, I felt a wave of nostalgia wash over me. Each corner of this place held a piece of my past, and I hoped Ren loved it here as much as I did.

"Hey, sugar! My grandfather stepped out of the sliding door that led to the back of the house. "Is this your new fella? Your mama told me all about him." He stuck his hand out, and Ren took it. "Nice to meet you. I'm Joel."

"This is Ren," I introduced them.

"Nice to meet you, too." Ren smiled as they shook hands.

"Welcome to the Honeybrook. Make yourself at home. What's mine is yours." He took off, heading for the fire to sit by my grandma, who waved us over, gesturing to the chairs next to her.

"Oh, hey." My eyebrows raised in surprise when I spotted Hunter Cassidy sitting next to Paige. They'd gone all through school together from kindergarten to high school graduation. They'd always been friends. Hunter, much like Ren, was nothing but tall, dark, and handsome, as were all the Cassidy brothers, including Spencer. Their family owned an auto body and repair shop between Sweetbriar and Honeybrock Hollow.

"You know Hunter Cassidy, right, Ren?" Grandma introduced him. "Spencer's brother. He's helping Piper's grandpa restore that old Cadillac he got back when he was going through his car show phase."

"There are no ulterior motives at all, right, Grandma?" Paige playfully called her out.

"Nice to meet you," Ren said.

Hunter laughed. "You too. It's good to see you, Piper."

"You too," I answered as my grandmother winked at me.

"I do what I do, and I hardly ever think about it," she said airily.

"Things usually work out, so quit your fussing, Paige. I have a knack."

"I'm not fussing—"

Hunter choked on a laugh as he slid an arm around Paige's shoulders.

"Yeah, quit your fussing," he chimed in, nudging her gently with a playful light in his eyes.

"Where are the kids?" I asked. I was a good sister; I could tell she was getting overwhelmed by the attention.

"Down at the pond," she told me. "They're letting the goslings crawl all over them."

"I thought geese were mean?" Ren said as he took a seat next to my grandma.

"Not when they grow up like pets," I explained. "Every animal out here has Grandma and all of us to love on it. They're all pretty friendly. And when the mama goose trusts you, then you have fluffy little balls of feathers to cuddle."

Paige looked up at Hunter, a soft smile crossing her lips. "Do you remember when we used to come out here and play for hours?" Her gaze was distant as she spoke.

I wanted to hug her. It was like for the first time since her divorce she was feeling something besides pissed off.

He nodded, his arm still resting comfortably around her shoulders. "Of course. We had a lot of adventures out here. Remember that time we tried to build a raft in the pond, and it sank immediately?"

She shook her head. "How could I forget?"

"Maybe we should try again sometime?" He said, his voice warm.

Paige rolled her eyes, but her soft smile didn't waver. "Maybe, but let's not involve the kids. I don't want to be responsible for any disasters."

"The two of you were always so cute together," Grandma mused with a satisfied smile flitting across her face.

Hunter studied Paige with mock seriousness. "I don't know about me, but she's still pretty cute."

"You're adorable," Spencer shouted from his spot on the lawn where he and Lucy were currently sprawled on a blanket.

"Thanks, I feel so much better now." He chuckled.

"Well, the last thing I am is cute," Paige huffed, snapping back to reality. But I could tell it was all for show; her pink cheeks and sparkling eyes told the true story. She wanted Hunter here. They'd been circling each other ever since they were kids, but they had only ever been friends.

"Anyway," Grandpa cleared his throat. "Who is ready for weenies?"

"Well, I for one am glad two weenies will not be coming here anymore," Paige cracked as she referenced her ex and Richard. Like me, she made jokes to hide her feelings. "Even though one of them does have the perfect name for the occasion, just saying."

"God, Paige," I groaned.

"I know. I'm punning. I'm so ashamed."

"Moving on," Grandma said. "Let's not roast her too much for making bad jokes."

"Noooo," I joined the collective groan.

"I forgot the skewers, dang it." Grandpa moved to get up, but I held out a hand to stop him.

"I'll go get them," I offered. "Stay right here. Be right back," I said to Ren.

I took a deep breath as I headed towards the garage to

grab the skewers for the barbecue. The sun was setting, casting long shadows across the driveway.

I stepped inside, the cool air greeting me, and wandered over to the workbench where the skewers were usually kept. As I reached out for the drawer, I felt a presence behind me. I turned to find Richard standing there.

"Richard," I breathed out, my heart pounding. "What are you doing here?"

He stood there, a look of determination in his eyes. The dim light from the overhead bulb cast eerie shadows on his face. I could see the tension in his posture, the way his hands clenched at his sides.

"I need to talk to you," he said, his voice low and steady.

I swallowed hard, my mind racing. The memories of our last encounter flooded back, mingling with the present. I had hoped to avoid him, to keep the peace for just a little longer. At least until Jake got everything settled.

"I didn't expect to see you here," I managed to say, trying to keep my voice calm and composed. "You startled me."

Richard took a step closer, his presence overwhelming in the confined space of the garage. I felt trapped, unable to escape the confrontation I had hoped would never have to happen.

"We need to sort this out," he insisted. "We can't keep doing this."

I nodded slowly, clutching the drawer handle for

support. The skewers were forgotten now, overshadowed by the tension between us. This wasn't the time or place, but I knew there was no avoiding it by the determined look in his eyes.

"I understand," I whispered, meeting his gaze. "Let's talk." I wasn't afraid of him. He'd never hurt me before, plus with one loud yell, I'd have my entire family, and Ren, rushing into the garage to help.

"I don't appreciate the stunt at the opening, Piper. You made Dana look like a fool. And me too, for that matter. We can't go anywhere without hearing something."

"I'm so sorry." I shot back, my voice dripping with sarcasm. "Wow. And how did I look? The two of you there, together, with my dog. She called him her baby, Richard."

"She's treated him like her baby. And meanwhile you're here and you left him home. He was outside by himself, so I took him home to Dana, then came straight here—"

"Wait? You took him? He has a doggy door, which you're aware of. He can go to the garage whenever he wants. What the hell is going on? Explain. Now."

"I stopped by your house to talk this through and try to come to an understanding, about the bakery opening and the lawsuit, then I got pissed that you left Cody outside and you weren't there. I figured you'd be here. You've fucking sued me; I got the papers. I know everything, okay? What the hell, Piper?"

"Wait. Back up. Are you telling me you trespassed on my property and took Cody? How dare you?"

"You should have brought him with you."

"You know how the pugs are. They're puppies. They still have to get used to other dogs, which they would be by now if you hadn't kept Cody away from me. A big party is not the time to get them accustomed to each other. Did you dognap him from my backyard?"

"Dognap? Hardly. He's mine too. You've always had a problem with me wanting to take care of him."

"What are you talking about? No, I didn't—"

"You never let me in, Piper. You were always so closed off. So I had to turn to Dana. She can't handle working with you anymore, so I'll let you buy her out, we'll agree to that. But I'm keeping Cody. She needs him."

"Like hell you are. She doesn't give a shit about Cody. She just wants to hurt me for some reason. And you? You're talking about ten different things right now. What is the real problem, Richard?"

"She's not the one responsible for your daddy issues, Piper. I want you to leave me and Dana out of all your drama."

"Dana has nothing to do with this. You keep bringing her up as if she's the main issue. The real issue here is your complete disregard for my feelings and the way you've treated me," I retorted, my voice trembling with frustration.

Richard's face contorted with anger. "My disregard for your feelings? That's rich coming from you, Piper.

You never cared about what I was going through. You only ever thought about yourself and your precious bakery."

"How dare you! I've always been there for you, but you never let me in. You're the one who shut me out and turned to Dana. You're the one who betrayed me," I shot back, my eyes blazing with fury before narrowing on his face as I studied his reaction. "Are you trying to gaslight me? Because you suck at it."

His face reddened as his anger became palpable. "You think you know everything, Piper, but you don't. You've never tried to understand the pressure I'm under. Dana was there when I needed someone. You weren't."

I clenched my fists, trying to keep my composure. "Pressure? Stress? That doesn't excuse your behavior. If you're feeling overwhelmed, you talk it out. You don't betray the people who care about you and then expect sympathy."

"I tried to apologize to you. I accepted the blame for my part in this situation, but for some reason, you can't let it go. Dana has done nothing wrong here. This was all about me, looking for some affection. Someone who cared just a little bit about how I felt and what I needed. She was there for me when you weren't. Can you blame me for—"

Grandpa's voice interrupted our escalating argument. "Funny," he said as he came stomping around the edge of the garage door. "You're acting just like her father right now and trying to blame your failings as a man on her *daddy issues*. You're the one who lied and cheated. You're the one who betrayed her trust, and now you're trying to manipulate her into doing what you want her to do. That's all this is, Piper, and he's a weak, pathetic excuse for a man. That's what this is about. Don't try to make any sense of it because it's all a crock of shit. Like throwing spaghetti at the wall to see what will set you off so he can pick it apart and try to get at you."

"That's not it," Richard insisted. "If she had just listened to reason and forgiven Dana, none of this would have had to happen—"

"You mean, if I accepted your bullshit lies and excuses and let you walk all over me... go on, Richard. What else is my fault?"

"God. Nothing." He took a step back, his expression hardening. "I don't have to stand here and take this. Just like always, I can't talk to you. I'm leaving."

"This isn't over, Richard" I snapped. "You don't get to declare you're keeping Cody and that's it."

"I said I'm leaving."

"You can't—"

He spun back around to face me. "Why couldn't you just forgive and forget? How hard is that? Damn. I have to live in this town too." He flung his arms out in frustration before stomping off toward the Inn's parking lot.

"I'll never forgive you," I shouted to his retreating back. "But I'm going to try like hell to forgive *myself* for falling for your bullshit." I started to run after him, but Grandpa stopped me with a gentle hand on my arm.

"Let him go, sugar. No use trying to talk to him right now."

"But he has Cody," my voice trembled. I hated how weak I sounded.

"You're taking care of that, yeah? No way Jake is going to let this slide. You'll give him a call and let him tell you what to do next. Okay?"

"Okay, you're right. That makes sense."

I took a deep breath, trying to calm the storm of emotions raging inside me. Just then, I heard the faint sound of footsteps approaching from behind. I turned around to see Ren, his face a mixture of concern and determination.

"Hey," he said softly, his eyes scanning my face for any sign of distress. "We heard yelling. Are you okay?"

I nodded, grateful for his presence. "Yeah, I'm fine. I just think I need to go home and call Jake. I need to think, I—"

"Richard was here," Grandpa explained. "He went to her place and took Cody and said some shitty things."

Ren's face hardened, and then I looked beyond him to see each member of my family, plus Spencer and Hunter, standing there wearing similar expressions.

Oh shit.

"I need to go home," I whispered.

"I'll take you," Ren immediately offered.

"No, I need to go home alone. Without you."

For a moment, he looked stricken, but then he hid it. "Anything you need."

"I'm not—I mean, this isn't over, me and you. That's not what this is about. That's not what I'm saying."

"I know." *But did he?*

"Okay, let's all back off and give them some space." I smiled gratefully as Paige herded everyone out of the garage.

"This isn't about you," I tried to explain. "I mean, it kind of is. I've never seen you mad. I've never upset you, well, except for maybe right now." I met his eyes, biting my lip to keep from crying. "What if I do something wrong? Do you yell? Do you go silent? Will you go crazy and say mean things like Richard? I can't stop thinking about it." I drug my hands through my hair and spun away from him. "I swore I wouldn't do this. I promised myself I wouldn't mix up what I have with you right now with the past. I never wanted to drag you into all the things that have hurt me, but I can't stop the thoughts, Ren." I turned to face him. "I need to get rid of them, and I have to be alone to do it."

His eyes softened as he listened to me. "I get it," he said gently. "You've been hurt, and it wasn't that long ago, and it's still going on. It's inevitably going to color your perspective on what we have now."

I felt a twinge of guilt. "I'm sorry, Ren. I never wanted to make you feel like I don't trust you. I just need to get my head on straight. I need my rational mind to come back before I go nuts."

He stepped closer, pulling me into his arms. "Listen, I've done it too. I've lost a lot, and I rushed you. I was so afraid of losing you that I held on too tight. That is my issue. I understand what's happening, okay? I'm not upset with you, sweetheart. I swear."

"Do you know how amazing you are?"

He shook his head, mouth forming into a flat line of determination. "I know that I'm going to get Cody back, and you're going home with Paige. Or your mom, or maybe you should stay here. You shouldn't really be alone."

"I can take care of myself. I know I'm a mess right now, but I have this handled. Jake has already sued for the bakery, and I'm going to call him about Cody as soon as I get home—"

"I know you can take care of yourself. And I know you're good at it. But maybe you could let me take care of this because it's what *I'm* good at. In fact, I fucking love it. And I've had it with that asshole jerking you around."

"This is kind of your life's work, isn't it?" I murmured.

"Yes. It is. Exactly. And since I don't technically work for you as your attorney, I can do whatever I want this time without pissing off a judge and ending up in contempt of court. We both know that motherfucker won't turn me in."

"Okay, fine. Maybe go talk to him. It doesn't look like I could stop you if I tried. I mean, thank you, Ren. Seriously. But don't tell me you were going to do it anyway. That might make me mad and I don't want that asshole to be the cause of our first real fight. Maybe you could call Jake to go with you."

"No, he's your attorney—"

"Well, I'm not her attorney. Let's go." Hunter said as he stepped into the garage with Paige trailing behind him.

"Everyone else is at the bonfire. Waiting for you to come back." She told me.

"And you had to listen in," I accused.

"No, well. I mean, we heard some things, but I didn't mean to listen. Fine, I was worried, okay? I'm sorry. Can I drive you home? Please? The kids are staying here tonight."

"Yes," Ren answered. "You go home with Paige. I'll drop Cody off later—"

"I don't know if—"

His eyes locked on mine. He was not backing down, that much was clear. "I'll drop him off," he repeated. "Then I'll go home."

"Okay..." I whispered.

"Take her home, Paige," he ordered.

He pulled me in for a quick kiss on my forehead then he let me go and headed toward his car.

"I'm coming with you," Hunter ground out.

"Oh god." I worried. "What the hell is happening right now, Paige?"

"You finally got yourself a man worth the trouble is what's happening. Good for you."

"I want to go home."

She took my hand, squeezing it gently. "I know. We'll figure everything out from there."

She pulled her phone from her pocket. "I'll text everyone and let them know we're leaving and that you're okay."

As we walked toward her car, the night air seemed to

envelop me in darkness, filling me with more unsettling thoughts.

"Thank you. I can't think anymore."

"I got you. I have a feeling this will all be over soon."

She unlocked the car and we slipped inside. As we drove away, I couldn't shake the feeling that tonight had changed everything. I just hoped it was for the better.

Chapter 25
Ren

"Do you know where that asshole lives?" I barked at Hunter as we walked to my car.

"Yeah, and just so you know, I never liked that prick."

Hunter matched my pace, his jaw set in a grim line. He didn't say much, but I could sense his dislike simmering beneath the surface.

Hunter got into the passenger seat and slammed the door shut. The intensity of the moment weighed heavily on both of us as I started the engine.

"Where to?" I muttered, my grip tightening on the steering wheel. The streetlights cast eerie shadows, mirroring the turmoil inside me.

He gave me directions, then we were off.

"I grew up with Paige," he told me. "So I know Piper pretty well, too. She was always a sweet girl. She doesn't deserve this. I'm more than happy to back you up."

"Thanks. I'm done letting him get away with this ridiculous bullshit."

Even though Richard was a Honeybrook Hollow local, the drive felt endless, but eventually, we pulled up to the curb in front of his house.

The engine hummed softly as I cut it off, and the silence that followed was almost deafening. Hunter and I exchanged a look, the resolve in his eyes mirroring my own.

We stepped out of the car, the cool night air washing over us, heightening our senses and steeling my nerves.

The house loomed ahead; its facade bathed in the dim glow of the streetlights.

I knocked firmly, the sound echoing through the quiet night. Hunter stood beside me, waiting. I had the sense that there was more to why he was so willing to help me tonight, but I could find out later, whatever it was. The waiting seemed to stretch on forever, the anticipation gnawing at the edges of my patience.

I wanted Piper, and this asshole was the only thing standing between us. I was done with waiting, done with his shit, and done with him treating Piper as his punching bag.

Finally, the door creaked open, revealing Richard. His expression shifted from surprise to disdain as he took in our presence.

"What are you going to do?" he smarked. "Kick my ass?"

"No. I'm going to sue you. For harassment. Stalking.

Verbal abuse. Making threats. Trespassing on private property. Theft. And anything else I can think of."

Hunter shrugged. "I'll kick your ass. I never liked you."

"Call your attorney and tell him who is representing Piper," I growled. "So you'll know exactly who you're messing with."

His eyes shifted to the side.

"You already know, don't you?" I laughed. "You don't have a chance. That's why you won't leave Piper alone."

"What of it? What do I care about some stupid bakery? I'll help Dana open a new one. Big deal."

"We went to school together, asshole." Hunter jabbed a finger in Richard's chest. "Piper is practically family, and you know it. So you know what I'll do to you."

"So, it looks like you know Jake's reputation and Hunter's. But you don't know me. Piper is mine. And the only thing standing in the way of her being happy right now is you. Which means that I am now your nightmare. Aside from suing the shit out of you and reporting you to the local police for breaking into Piper's house and stealing Cody, I will do anything else I think of to make your life a living hell. And trust me when I say that unless you move to another planet, I can do it. We're taking Cody and you will not do one fucking thing about it. Do you get me?"

"Yeah, I get you."

"And when Jake gives you the papers for Piper to buy Dana out, what are you going to do?"

He didn't answer.

"What are you going to do?" I bellowed.

"Dana will sign the fucking papers, all right? Damn."

"And Cody?" I ground out, ready to shove my way inside and get him if I had to.

"He's a good dog, but I can get another one."

"You're pathetic," I bit out.

"Jesus Christ." He snarled. "This is not worth it. Dana," he shouted. "Bring Cody down here."

She showed up screeching. "What are they doing here? The damn dog is mine."

"Damn dog?" Hunter bit out. "Nice."

Richard's eyes slid shut as he shook his head side to side. "Just get Cody, please, Dana. We'll talk in a minute. I can get you another dog whenever you want."

She stomped off up the stairs, muttering to herself as she walked, returning a few seconds later with Cody following. He peeked his head out from behind her, so I called him over.

"Go on, boy," Richard told him. "Go with Ren. It's okay."

Cody trotted over to me, tail wagging, with his cute doggy grin on his face.

"What the fuck is going on, Richard?" Dana tugged on his arm, demanding an answer. "You're giving Cody back to Piper?"

"I said, give me a minute. Baby, please."

"Fine." Her eyes narrowed as she glared at him. "But bet your ass we're talking about this after they leave."

"Great," he muttered. "This ends here. Tonight. Right now. I've had enough of this shit. We're done." He grabbed Cody's leash from the coat rack near the door and hooked him up.

"As long as you stay the fuck away from Piper and sign the papers, we're done," I confirmed.

"Later, man," Hunter smirked. "Have fun with your lady tonight."

"You're an asshole, Hunter."

"You reap what you sew, dumbass. Keep that in mind." Hunter shot back.

"I'm almost disappointed I didn't get to punch him in his smug fucking face," I muttered as we got into my car.

"He's not worth it. He crumbles like a little bitch. Very unsatisfying."

My eyes shot to Hunter. "Really?"

"Oh yeah. Ask around town. Anyone who knows him has probably taken a swing at him a time or two. Which is why I was so surprised he managed to get Piper."

"What about Paige? Didn't she set them up?"

"She had no clue. Her ex had her blind for years. Richard was his friend. She probably thought it would be fun for her sister to date her husband's friend."

"Damn."

"Yeah, damn. That pretty much says it all."

"Should I drop you back at the Honeybrook?" I asked.

"Yeah, my car is there."

I pulled away from the curb. I glanced over at Hunter, who leaned back in his seat with a contemplative expression. The residual tension broke, and we laughed as Cody propped his paws on the console and licked the side of my face.

"Thanks for backing me up," I told him as I pulled into the Honeybrook's parking lot. "It's appreciated."

He smiled as he opened the car door. "Anytime. It was good to meet you."

"You too." I nodded, watching him disappear into the night.

Pulling back onto the road, I took a deep breath, trying to steady my thoughts. The drive to Loganberry Lane was quiet, save for Cody happily panting in the passenger seat.

Once I pulled into Piper's driveway, I took a moment to collect myself and prepare to go home alone after I dropped Cody off.

Paige answered the door at my knock. Bending to pet Cody after he barked his hello.

"Is she okay?" I asked.

"Yeah, we're just sorting through all the shit he left her with, you know?"

"Yeah..."

"She's not great when it comes to dealing with her feelings. Usually something big has to knock her on her ass before she starts to deal."

"That's relatable."

"Don't I know it." She laughed. "I mean, sticking our heads in the sand is a Darlington family trait."

"Can I talk to her for a minute? I'll stay on the porch, I promise."

"I'm not worried about you, Ren." Her eyes softened.

"It's why I—never mind." She turned away toward the entryway. "Piper," she yelled. "Company."

"Hey," she whispered. "You got him." Tears filled her eyes when Cody rubbed against her legs. "I can't thank you enough."

She stepped onto the porch, shooing Cody inside before closing the door behind herself. I smiled when I saw her in another caftan—purple with pink and lavender paisley swirls. God, she was beautiful.

"This was never fake for me," I blurted. "Time and time again, I tried telling myself that it wasn't real yet, or that we had an expiration date. But then I kept ending up here with you, right here on this porch, never wanting to leave."

Her eyes met mine, and for a moment, the turbulent emotions seemed to still within her. She took a deep breath, her voice steady but soft. "You know, I spent so much time convincing myself that I never wanted to fall in love again. But I was just scared of being hurt. Maybe we told ourselves it was fake because neither one of us was ready."

"Maybe," I murmured, reaching out to take her hand. "Probably." I smiled at her.

She squeezed my hand, a tentative smile forming. "I don't want to pretend anymore, Ren."

"I don't either. No more lying to ourselves about what we have."

"I still need time. I have to get him out of my head. I don't like how I feel right now. And it's not fair to drag you along while I get over all of it."

"I understand."

She released my hand and stepped closer, her eyes searching mine. "I need to figure out how to deal with all this. I don't want to keep making the same mistakes. But I promise you, it won't take long."

I nodded, feeling a mix of relief and anticipation. "Take all the time you need. I'll be right here when you're ready."

She leaned in, pressing a gentle kiss to my cheek. "Thank you for bringing Cody back to me. And I'm not talking about years, Ren. Maybe like a day or two."

I laughed. "Good. How could I ever live without my golden girl?"

"I won't make you find out. Okay? I promise."

As she turned to walk back inside, the sun cast a warm glow over her silhouette, highlighting the vibrant colors of her caftan. I watched her disappear through the doorway; my heart full yet aching with the weight of patience.

With a hopeful smile, I whispered to myself, "Just a day or two." Then I turned to go home. And wait.

Chapter 26
Piper

"Falling in love the first time is easy. Falling in love again is a leap of faith that takes a tremendous amount of courage." The softly murmured words woke me up.

I rolled over in bed to see my sister on her back, covered with my cats and staring at the ceiling with an oddly contemplative look on her face. "Paige? Did you wake up possessed by the spirit of some wise old sage? Who even are you right now?"

"Shit," she muttered, rubbing the sleep out of her eyes. "I don't freaking know. I woke up and then started thinking and couldn't stop. I have to stop doing that, honestly, it's annoying." She sat up, Nimbus settled at her side as she pulled Smog into her arms and nuzzled her face into his soft fur. "But I have to admit something to you," she whispered.

"What? That you were trying to set me and Ren up?

"

It was pretty obvious." I grinned at her. "Not your best work. Effective, but not subtle."

Paige sighed deeply, a hint of melancholy in her expression. "Actually, there's more. I wasn't just trying to set you up with Ren. I wanted you to find happiness again, Piper. After everything you've been through, you deserve it."

I felt a rush of affection for my sister; her intentions were always pure, despite her sometimes-clumsy execution. "Thank you, Paige. I appreciate it. Really."

"He's just so sweet—all stoic and kind of sad, maybe a little bit grumpy, but not in the bad way. And you were brokenhearted and reeling from Dick. I thought, why not? Right? At the very least, you'd end up with a good friend. Ren doesn't have a mean bone in his body. He'd never hurt anyone."

My eyes widened in alarm. "God, I hope he didn't hurt Richard to get Cody back."

"He didn't, don't worry. Hunter told me everything on the phone last night. He made a lot of legal threats. Hunter was the one who threatened to kick his ass, which is not surprising."

"Remember when he beat up Eli for you after prom?"

"Ugh, don't remind me." She rolled her eyes, a playful smirk tugging at the corners of her mouth. "He's still the same old Hunter—ready to fight anyone who messes with his friends."

I chuckled, recalling countless memories of Hunter's fierce loyalty. "True, he's always been like that. He was by your side your entire life. I always wondered why you didn't end up with him."

Nimbus purred loudly, demanding attention, and Paige scratched his head absentmindedly. "I guess I just never saw him as anything but a friend. It's hard to change that perspective."

I gave her a sympathetic look. "I get it. But sometimes, the best relationships start from friendship. You already know each other so well."

Paige shrugged, a mix of resignation and hope in her eyes. "Maybe. But right now, I just want to focus on getting through each day without any more drama."

"Maybe you should think about your feelings for him. I'm pretty sure he thinks about you a lot. Since your divorce, he's always around. Falling in love for the first time is easy. Falling in love again is a leap of faith that takes a tremendous amount of courage." I threw her words back at her.

"That was for you. I'm different. I can't go there with anyone. I think I'm broken—no more feelings for Paige. I just want to binge-watch random shit on TV and eat Cheetos. No more thinking, contemplation is out. I have my kids; I won't get lonely."

"If you say so."

She stuck her tongue out at me. "I do say so."

"Alright, alright, I'll stop. But if you ever change your mind, I'm sure Hunter would be there in a heartbeat. He's always been there for you, and he clearly cares about you a lot."

She sighed, taking a moment to gather herself. "I

know. I just don't want to complicate things. My life is already such a mess. Adding a relationship into the mix might just make everything worse."

"Maybe, or maybe it could help you heal," I suggested softly. "Sometimes, opening up to someone can help more than we think. Look at me. I was done with love and now—"

She shook her head, a small smile tugging at her lips. "And now, you're falling into it, aren't you?

"Yeah," I whispered. "You're just not ready."

"I'll never be ready. Are you sure you're *really* ready?"

"I wasn't. But I'm getting there, and I have you to thank for it."

"No, you have Ren to thank for it. He's wise. All I did was point you in the right direction."

"Yeah, and be there to support me through all my crap with Richard."

"Of course, I was there for you. I mean, what else are sisters for?"

I shrugged. "Rants, complaints, experiencing shared joy, nostalgia, collecting caftans, coffee porch mornings, sleepovers..."

She set Smog down and leaned into my side. "I love you."

"I love you, too."

"But seriously, though, let's change the subject before I have to get out of this warm bed and run screaming into the morning. It's getting too deep in here."

"You'll get through this, Paige. You're so strong."

"Thanks, I do everything out of spite. It's working for me."

We both laughed softly as Cody barked from the foot of the bed. I patted the space next to me, and he curled up until he had settled comfortably in my arms.

"Okay, so Violet asked me to bake Ren's birthday cake for his party this weekend. Chocolate. How's that for a subject change?"

She let out a laugh and sat up. "It's good, but I already know. She told me when she reserved the back room for the party. It's the first official reservation for Twilight Tavern. It has to go well, so I want you to go over the top. Make a showstopper. Plus, I'm adding your chocolate cake to the things I want to eat while watching TV and doing nonsense."

"I'm thinking about what to make. But over the top is the main theme, so no worries there."

She grabbed her robe and slipped into it. "Good. I want you to show off." The light in her eyes was back, and I was happy to see it. "Be a spectacle, Piper. Food as a grand gesture is highly underrated."

I laughed. "Right?"

Grand gesture...

Chapter 27
Ren

The Twilight Tavern was vibrant with music and laughter as I walked toward the back room where I was supposed to meet Violet and Jake. I could already see people dancing, their movements illuminated by the flickering candles placed strategically around the room.

I made my way through the crowd, exchanging greetings and accepting birthday wishes, and I couldn't help but wonder who the hell half the people were. I had very few friends; this was weird. Maybe I should hang out here and get to know people. I shuddered briefly, or not.

I wanted to turn around and go home. But I'd let Violet convince me to meet her and Jake here for a birthday beer. *Yeah, right.* This had to be some kind of surprise birthday party bull crap.

I made my way through the crowd, the anticipation building in my chest. My heart pounded with a mix of nervousness and excitement. I couldn't help but glance around, searching for Piper's gorgeous face. The idea of her not showing up filled me with a dread I couldn't shake. But even as my nerves threatened to get the best of me, I knew deep down that Piper would come. She had to.

Never in my life had I been so sure of anything as I was about being with her. The way she smiled, the way she made everything seem brighter and more bearable—it was all I needed. And tonight, amid the laughter and the music, I wanted nothing more than to see her walk through those doors.

The sound of the old jukebox filled the air, but all I could focus on was the hope that Piper would arrive soon.

"Ren," Paige rushed to my side to hiss in my ear. "I'm going to warn you that there is a tiny surprise party in the back room—nothing to be alarmed about. But I knew you would hate it, so I'm here, letting you know in advance. Act surprised when you get back there. Okay?"

I raised my eyebrows and tilted my head at her. "Like this?"

"God, you're bad at this."

"What, being human? I know."

Shaking her head, she hugged me. "Happy Birthday," she whispered. "There will be chocolate cake. I promise you it will be worth it."

"Yeah?"

"Yes. Be happy. Go to the back. Don't worry, they kept it real small, you'll be okay." She grinned at me.

"Ren!" Noah rushed out from the swinging doors that led to the back of the bar. "Happy Birthday, Mom said to bring you a beer the second we spot you." He handed me a frosty mug, and I took a hearty sip.

"Thanks."

"You still look grim," Paige observed. "Smile, it's your dang birthday."

"I'm feeling a bit overwhelmed," I confessed. "If I try to smile, I'll end up looking like a weirdo."

"I get you. Drink that beer and I'll bring you another. It's your birthday, time to get drunk and forget you're a year older."

The familiar warmth of the bar wrapped around me as I took another sip of beer. Paige and Noah had already disappeared back into the throng of people, leaving me alone with my thoughts. The room buzzed with laughter and chatter, the clinking of glasses and the shuffling of feet on the worn wooden floor.

I found a spot to sit, closing my eyes for a moment to try to soak in the atmosphere and shake off the lingering sadness. It was hard, though, with memories pressing in from all sides. I hadn't seen Piper since I'd dropped Cody off, and even though she wasn't really gone, and all I had to do was wait, I still missed her.

Paige returned with another beer, pulling me from my thoughts. "Here you go. Drink up, birthday boy."

I smiled, a genuine one this time, and took the beer from her. "Thanks, Paige. Is Piper coming?" I couldn't help but ask.

"Yes, she is. But you need to go to the back. Seriously, it's just Jake and Violet. I told you it's small. Almost like they know you, huh? They're waiting for you."

"Okay. In a minute."

Just as I took a sip of my beer, I saw Jake weaving his way through the crowd. His face lit up when he spotted me, and he raised his hand in a wave. "Come on, we're in the back room. Happy Birthday!"

"Thanks," I said, returning his grin. We hugged briefly, the back-slapping kind that Jake was fond of.

He pulled away, his eyes sparking with mischief. "Can't believe you're another year older. How does it feel?"

"Honestly? Just another day." I shrugged, though I knew he'd see right through me.

He chuckled. "Yeah, I get it. Come on. Violet has our table. She's waiting."

I followed him through the crowd, making my way through the clusters of people talking and laughing. I was glad to see business had picked up for Paige.

The back room was dimly lit, with a warm, intimate atmosphere. Violet spotted us and waved, patting the seat next to her.

"Hey, birthday boy!" she greeted me with a bright smile, leaning in for a hug once I'd sat down. "Happy Birthday!"

"Thanks, Vi. You know, you didn't have to do all this," I said, gesturing to the festive decorations around the room.

Streamers and balloons hung from the ceiling, and a large banner that read "Happy Birthday" stretched across one wall.

"Oh, hush, it's your special day and your first

birthday in Honeybrook Hollow, we wanted to make it memorable."

"Well, I appreciate it. And I'm really grateful you didn't yell surprise at me," I joked.

"We knew you'd hate that," she nudged my side and held her glass up for a toast and mouthed the word "surprise".

I clinked my glass to hers with a smile while trying not to scan the space for Piper.

"She'll be here any minute," Violet leaned in to whisper. "Don't you worry."

"How is she?" I asked.

"She's great," Jake answered. "She's now the official sole owner of Something Sweet—Dana signed the papers. And so far, Richard is staying out of the picture."

"Good." I nodded in relief.

"More importantly," Violet said, "she's better now. You'll see for yourself once she gets here."

Jake's phone went off with a text message alert. "Speaking of..."

He got up and headed for the employee door in the back of the room.

Moments later, I saw Jake emerge from the back door, this time with Piper by his side. She was pushing a massive cake on a wheeled tray, her face glowing with pride and excitement. Jake was helping guide the tray, his hands steadying the sides to ensure it didn't topple over.

The cake was a replica of her house.

It was white, with a bright pink door just like hers.

They stopped at the edge of the table. She flipped a little switch, and the windows lit up.

I took it in.

In shock.

In awe.

And in love with her more than I could ever hope to express in words.

Raccoons dashed across the roof, climbing down the side of the house and out the windows. Her roses bloomed brightly on the trellis, while her hummingbird feeder hung delicately from the roof line.

Tiny versions of Smog and Nimbus were perched on the porch steps while a miniature Cody sprawled in the doorway. There was even a little ball of yarn on the chair I had sat in when I first spoke to her the day I moved in.

I blinked back tears when I saw tiny models of the two of us sitting on her porch swing, she in the same caftan and ratty robe she had worn that first day, complete with green cheeks and me in my jogging clothes.

"Piper." I let out a breath. "This is amazing."

"Wait." She flipped another switch, and smoke drifted out of the chimney. "We haven't had a chance for a fire in the fireplace yet, but we will." Her eyes met mine as a tremulous smile unfurled across her beautiful face.

"I love it." *I love you.*

"Let's give them a minute," Jake said, taking Violet's hand to guide her to the arched entrance leading to the central part of the bar. "I want to dance with you, gorgeous."

I waited until they were out of earshot before speaking. My heart was full.

I pulled her close, feeling the warmth of her body against mine.

The intricate details of the miniature house she had crafted, each element so thoughtfully chosen, mirrored the love and care I wanted to pour into her.

"Piper, you have no idea how much this means to me," I whispered, my voice thick with emotion.

She smiled softly, her hand gently caressing my cheek. "I wanted to create something special for you, Ren. My house is a place where our memories will live, and it's a reminder of how far we've come and how much more we have to look forward to." Her eyes shimmered with unshed tears as she rested her forehead against my chest. "I guess I wanted to show you what you mean to me. Happy Birthday. This is where I fell in love with you, Ren. I love you."

"You telling me you love me is the best birthday present I've ever received. I love you, too."

"I thought about everything when we were apart, all that I've been through and all that I've lost. And I realized how different you are. I realized that I love you without thinking or trying. It's just there, a living, breathing part of me. Every detail matters. Every memory is part of why I'll never let you go again."

"I never want to lose you."

"You never lost me. Not really. And the fact that you gave me the space to get myself together means the world to me."

"I'm glad. I missed you, though."

"I missed you, too. And I have one more present for you." She handed me a small wrapped box with a red bow on top. "Open it."

I tore the paper off and popped the lid open. It was her knitting. A scarf? I raised my eyes to hers. "I love it."

"Yes. It is a scarf." Laughing, she took it from my hands and wrapped it around my neck, frowning as she tried to adjust it. "Well, it's sort of a scarf. It's not perfect, but it will be warm at least.

"I'll wear it every time it gets cold. It's perfect because you made it."

I looked into her eyes, the world fading away until it was just the two of us. Slowly, I leaned in, my heart pounding in my chest. Her breath mingled with mine.

Our lips met gently at first, a tender brush that sent shivers down my spine. The kiss deepened, and I wrapped her tight in my arms, pulling her closer. I wanted to meld into her, to never let her go. She tangled her fingers in my hair, and every worry, doubt, and fear melted away, leaving only the pure joy of this moment.

When we finally pulled apart, I opened my eyes to find her gazing at me with the same intensity, the same love that surged through me.

"I love you, Piper," I whispered, the words coming out as more of a reverent prayer than a declaration.

"I love you, too. Always, Ren."

Chapter 28
Piper

Months Later...

It was finally cold enough for a fire. The house was filled with the comforting scent of burning wood, and every corner of the living room felt warm and inviting.

I thought of the last few months, from the ones that took my breath away to the quiet ones. All of it had led me to this moment.

Dana and Richard had moved to her hometown, where he helped her open her own bakery. Good riddance, I mean, yay.

Something Sweet was thriving, and I was over the moon happy with it. I also acquired a new hobby—recipe testing and development. *Something Sweet,* my new cookbook, was due out next year.

I wasn't the only one with new hobbies. Ren was now good friends with Hunter, they went fishing or skiing with Jake, and sometimes Spencer or another of the Cassidy brothers would join them. Ren had settled into small-town life and loved it.

But tonight was all about being home with a warm blanket and the cozy fire blazing in the fireplace. And Ren, here to share all of it with me—this house, the cats, Cody, and now Rocket, the new puppy we had adopted together.

I pulled the blanket tighter around my shoulders, a smile playing on my lips as I watched the flames dance. Ren was in the kitchen, feeding the pets and grabbing wine and the charcuterie board I'd made earlier this evening.

He walked in with our goodies, his eyes meeting mine as he set them on the edge of the fireplace and sat next to me.

"Pour the wine?" He asked.

I turned to grab the bottle and glasses.

As I turned back around with the wine, I froze. Ren was down on one knee, holding a small, elegant ring box. My heart raced, and I felt a surge of emotion that made my breath catch. The fire cast a warm glow on his face, illuminating his sparkling eyes that were filled with love and anticipation.

He was down on a knee, but I was about to get up and jump for joy. Instead, I quickly put the glasses on the fireplace and burst out with an enthusiastic, "Yes." Followed by an "Oh crap." When I realized he hadn't even asked me yet. I slammed my eyes shut as embarrassment coursed through my body.

"God, I love you so much. Open your eyes, sweetheart."

With a deep breath, I opened my eyes. His face was etched with both hope and reassurance, making my heart soar even more.

His eyes met mine, sparkling and full of love as he slid his hand around the side of my neck, tipping my face up to his for a kiss.

"Will you marry me?" He whispered against my mouth.

My eyes brimmed with tears of pure happiness as I nodded vigorously, unable to form words.

Ren, still holding the box, let out a relieved laugh. "I guess that's a yes, then?"

"Yes, absolutely yes." I managed to find my voice, albeit shaky.

His smile grew even wider as he gently slipped the ring onto my finger. It fit perfectly, much like the way we fit into each other's lives.

I held my hand up, admiring the round brilliance of the diamond shining in the firelight.

"Beautiful, just like you," he murmured.

"I love it. I love you. I'm going to make you so happy."

"You already do."

This is how we would always love each other—honestly, without limits or fear.

Time stretched out, endless and beautiful, filled with the kind of joy that I used to believe was not meant for me.

For the rest of the evening, we sat by the fire,

wrapped in each other's embrace, dreaming about our future together. The world outside seemed to fade away as we shared our hopes and plans, the ring on my finger a constant reminder of the love that we never expected to find.

By Your Side

Are you ready for Hunter and Paige?
Here are a few of the tropes...
Small Town Romance
Single Mom
Childhood friends to lovers
He fell first
Pining Hero

About the Author

Nora Everly is a lifelong bookworm. She started reading the good stuff once she grew tall enough to sneak the romance novels off the top of her mother's bookshelf and it has been non-stop ever since.

Once upon a time she was a substitute teacher and an educational assistant. Now she's a writer and stay at home mom to two small humans and one fat cat.

Nora lives in the Pacific Northwest with her family and her overactive imagination.

Find her at noraeverly.com

9 781965 207086